Northamptonshire

DISCARDED

Libraries

A HOUSE DIVIDED

Also by Judith Cutler

The Harriet & Matthew Rowsley mysteries

THE WAGES OF SIN *
LEGACY OF DEATH *
DEATH'S LONG SHADOW *

The Lina Townend series

DRAWING THE LINE
SILVER GUILT *
RING OF GUILT *
GUILTY PLEASURES *
GUILT TRIP *
GUILT EDGED *
GUILTY AS SIN *

The Fran Harman series

LIFE SENTENCE
COLD PURSUIT
STILL WATERS
BURYING THE PAST *
DOUBLE FAULT *
GREEN AND PLEASANT LAND *

The Jodie Welsh series

DEATH IN ELYSIUM *

* *available from Severn House*

A HOUSE DIVIDED

Judith Cutler

SEVERN
HOUSE

First world edition published in Great Britain and the USA in 2022
by Severn House, an imprint of Canongate Books Ltd,
14 High Street, Edinburgh EH1 1TE.

Trade paperback edition first published in Great Britain and the USA in 2023
by Severn House, an imprint of Canongate Books Ltd.

severnhouse.com

British Library Cataloguing-in-Publication Data
A CIP catalogue record for this title is available from the British Library.

ISBN-13: 978-0-7278-5025-6 (cased)
ISBN-13: 978-1-4483-0813-2 (trade paper)
ISBN-13: 978-1-4483-0812-5 (e-book)

All Severn House titles are printed on acid-free paper.

Typeset by Palimpsest Book Production Ltd.,
Falkirk, Stirlingshire, Scotland.
Printed and bound in Great Britain by
TJ Books, Padstow, Cornwall.

For Sara Menguc, agent, mentor and dear friend

ACKNOWLEDGEMENTS

As always, I am grateful to the work of other women writers for the information on which this series has depended. Now Pamela Horn, Pamela Sandbrook, Jennifer Davies and Norah Lofts have been joined on my bookshelves by Tessa Boase. Her excellent book, *The Housekeeper's Tale* (Aurum Press), will enrage and entertain you in equal measure. Thank you all.

ONE

There is nothing more important than that ball. Forget the babies on the rug. The ball. That is the only thing in my mind. The angle. The speed. My speed. My feet must find their own way. The ball. I have it. It is safe in my hands.

And the babies play on, quite oblivious. Miss Baby FitzAllen waves at the sky. The Honourable Alexander Morton Frobisher Brewood shakes a silver and coral rattle.

By now they are probably the only ones who are not reacting. The men in the pavilion send up the sort of cheer they probably practised back at Eton or Harrow. The ladies amongst the onlookers are fainting or screaming according to their temperament. And I know that while I probably saved an aristocratic life, I have committed a most terrible faux pas.

B ea Arden peered over my shoulder. Her hands still smelling slightly of butter and flour, she reached to steady the embossed card, which I found I could not hold still enough for her to read. Or perhaps not far enough away: we both needed reading spectacles these days.

'How very grand!' she said. 'It's as grand as those that her ladyship used to prop up on the drawing room fireplace.'

'Exactly.'

'*The pleasure of the company of Mr and Mrs Matthew Rowsley . . .*' she read with relish. '*Colonel Barrington and Lady Hortensia Rowsley . . . Clunston Park . . . May 1861*'. You'll be hobnobbing on equal terms with a Lady,' she said, with a clear capital letter and the tiniest hint of a question mark at the end of the sentence.

I ignored it. 'Not just any lady: one who actually owns the marital home. Not even colonels have the sort of income to buy and maintain such a property. It was part of her marriage settlement.'

Bea turned to look me straight in the eye. 'You don't want to go, do you, Harriet? Does Matthew know?'

'I think he might suspect. He bubbles with enthusiasm at every opportunity, as if knowing he must be keen enough for two. The Colonel is one of his cousins, after all. I hardly know either him or his wife, but I am sure I will enjoy their acquaintance.'

'That's a very careful way of saying it!'

'I feel very careful. For obvious reasons, given their rank.'

'In both senses,' Bea observed.

'Quite.'

'But I know you like his cousin Mark very much, and not just because he's Matthew's favourite relative.' She smiled. 'A very handsome young man as I recall. He danced with me at your wedding. But I don't recall meeting this colonel and his good lady. Perhaps they didn't come?'

'They did. He was the one looking very smart in his mess dress . . . But neither danced. He because of his war injuries – so bad he's since resigned his commission, or whatever soldiers do when they retire – and she because her pregnancy was too advanced by then.'

'Ah. Them. Marty Baines and I were trying to work out if they were shy or snooty.' She glanced up at the clock which dominated the servants' hall, as if to remind us that we both had work to do. 'At least this weekend will give you the chance to find out and to report back. And it'll get you away from all this building work: I never knew running a few pipes through the house could take so long. Now, I must finish that pastry or it'll come out heavy as the plumbers' lead.' She patted my arm and headed back into the kitchen.

It was true that the workmen – plumbers and carpenters and plasterers – all seemed to be taking an age, and that despite all the noise and mess we seemed to be no closer to having the running water the trustees had authorized. But it was a large house, and many pipes were needed. It was also important that they were put in with the minimum damage to the old fabric: modern convenience must not damage historic walls. At least the Family wing, now a mixture of a hospital for the villagers or estate workers and a secure asylum for his lordship, now had both water and drains.

I drifted into the Room, as it was still called. Once, when I was simply the housekeeper, it had been my personal sitting room, where the senior staff would eat their evening meal away from the other servants. Although it had become my office, and less cosy, most of us still preferred to maintain the custom. But Matthew and I tried for our sanity's sake to spend at least some of our evenings in the house which came with his post as the estate's land agent. As and when guests came to the House we would return to a small suite of rooms set aside for our use when we were not actively needed elsewhere – a bed chamber, dressing room and sitting room. Soon a bathroom would be added nearby. It might seem an extravagance, but with so many unused rooms in the House the trustees had decreed that if we could not use the land agent's house to which Matthew was entitled we deserved some comfort and privacy. I thought we were likely to need both very soon. Before long there would be teams of experts on site to dig up the Roman remains found on the estate, to clean and value some of the Family's paintings, and to assess and catalogue the precious items in the library, of which, under the terms of her late ladyship's Will I was now miraculously the custodian. His lordship might still be terribly unwell, but we all hoped and prayed for a miraculous recovery, a respite at least, when Thorncroft House could return to its former glories. If not, then it must be ready for the heir whom the family lawyer, Mr Wilson, so anxiously sought.

I opened the window. Perhaps the spring air would clear my head. Why was I so daunted by the thought of this house party? It was true that my last encounter with a member of the aristocracy had not gone well, but she had been unpleasant to everyone, not just me. I was making myself a victim, not the wife of a wonderful husband, whose intelligence and love of life deserved wider companionship than that offered by our tight circle of friends. Another man might not have endured the circumscription of his life that Matthew had accepted: he would have insisted I gave up my work, ignored the duties that still constricted me, and taken me willy-nilly into the stratum of society into which he had been born. Not Matthew.

The least I could do was open my mind to the possibility of new experience – not feign excitement at the prospect, because our relationship depended absolutely on honesty – and admit that anything and everything would be at very least interesting. And tomorrow we would set out.

TWO

The groom unloaded our luggage from the trap that had taken us to the estate railway station; and the porter carried it to the platform.

'At last! We can escape from the House and all its claims on us!' I exclaimed.

'Yes, indeed,' Harriet agreed. Her smile was unnervingly polite.

It was true, of course, that we were only on our way to the home of one of my cousins. It had also to be said that Barrington was not my favourite relative – his military career, now sadly over, had taken him in a different direction from Mark and me – and it was equally true that neither of us was looking forward to it. If I was going to feel constrained, how much harder for Harriet must any weekend house party be. Yet if I praised her for her bravery she would certainly look at me askance, and perhaps might never forgive me. Socially, she might well feel awkward amongst all these leisured – indeed, idle – ladies because she was simply not one of them; her family had not had silver spoons at the ready, but a ladle of workhouse gruel if you were lucky. Indeed, unlike some of her fellow guests who could trace their roots back to the Conqueror, she had no record of any parents at all. Sometimes she claimed she was like Harriet Smith, a character in *Emma*, her least favourite Jane Austen novel, in that she was the natural daughter of somebody. But she had been loved, not by a spoilt brat of a girl but by hard-working women – housekeepers and others who had seen that she had the potential to be much more than just another tweeny. They had saved her from the predations of the employer who had deflowered her before she even knew what the word *virgin* might mean. I daily thanked God for these women, and for others who protected her, including the late Lord Croft, who had gently and chastely cherished her brain as if she were his own daughter. As a result of her amazing capacity for self-education, once she had put her housemaid days behind her, and taken over the running of the House, she had always been her own woman. She had never been 'just' my wife – however much I would be honoured if she were simply that. But I could never ask her to give up the authority she had enjoyed over the Croft household for nine years or more, with the right – indeed the duty – to speak her mind over matters pertaining not just to the household, but also to the new village being built on Lord Croft's land. When she became one of the trustees overseeing the general affairs of the House and the estate, yet more responsibilities fell on her shoulders. Yes, at least as many as fell on mine, but she dealt with everything rather better, if I were honest with myself, than I could ever have done. But now this woman, in every respect my equal, risked becoming a mere cipher in the eyes of some of Barrington's friends. Perhaps worse, she might be patronized by some as one of the poet's Angels in the House – 'that wretched Coventry Patmore', she called him, with a venom that was not at all angelic. Or there might be an even more difficult problem. Rank snobbery.

Taking her hand, I kissed it. 'Do you think Jemima's toothache is real? Or is it just an excuse not to come with us? And can you manage without her?'

'I managed without a lady's maid for years enough, my love. You may not manage your own studs, but you are becoming a dab hand with lacing and buttons.' She paused. 'Actually, I suspect that a maid will be – what was that French term you used? *De rigueur*? If it is, I am sure our host's housekeeper will provide a substitute. I would, in her place. And yes, I did believe the girl: her face was swollen and she was bracing herself for a trip to Shrewsbury and the dentist's chair. Her eyes were puffy with tears too: she had really been looking forward to the excitement of a trip away from the House.'

I turned to face her, keeping her hand in mine. 'But you are not, are you? Is there anything I can do to make it easier?'

'If I can face the loathsome Lady Hednesford I can cope with anyone,' she declared. She dropped her voice. 'However, I am a little . . . anxious . . . about one thing. What if I meet people who once visited the House? Friends of her late ladyship? I cannot but feel that that would be embarrassing – for both parties. Perhaps for you, too?' She squeezed my hand. She gave a snort of laughter, then dropped her voice so that she did little more than mouth her words. 'But even more embarrassing might be to meet someone I served with or even employed. Very efficient gossip machines, servants. Ah! The train! Now all I have to do is manoeuvre this confounded crinoline aboard! Who on earth invented this inconvenient fashion?'

I always loved watching her face when we travelled by train. If I ever took my nephew to Hamley's toy shop, his face would surely light up with wonder – but his joyful anticipation could be no greater than Harriet's. She was alert to anything she had not encountered before. She evinced excitement even at a third-rate production of Shakespeare at a fair, and her delight at the art in Florence made me see even familiar paintings in a new light. Perhaps what my cousin assured me was an excellent library at Clunston Park would compensate her for any social difficulties, and the fact that she could do no more than watch me on the cricket pitch, not play herself. How had it come to this? My dear mama had once played for her village against the ladies of another. Not a single eyebrow had been raised, she assured me. But now it seemed her sex was too gentle, too delicate, to indulge in competitive games. Bea insisted that stays and corsets were to blame, not to mention Harriet's bane, crinolines, which seemed to get wider and more cumbersome by the day. Harriet suspected that more complex reasons might be involved too. She tried to laugh away her disappointment by claiming to be too old, and that cricket was a young person's game. But ever since we had received the invitation to the cricket weekend she had been working with me to improve my bowling technique – and moreover with a bat in her hands she had despatched even my fastest balls with an ease that few men could even dream of.

Now she was enthralled by a cluster of new houses, then by a cutting for another railway line. How could she marry such delight in fresh experiences with her dogged obedience to duty?

'I believe we're arriving! Yes, the train is slowing – and look how bright and new the station is!'

Harriet, now as excited as my nephew would have been, was right. We were not just in Herefordshire but actually pulling into Clunston Halt. I handed her down, consigning the luggage to a sandy-haired lad as I looked around. Waiting right across the station entrance, to the considerable inconvenience of passengers arriving late for their train, was an elegant barouche.

'Look – Barrington has come to pick us up himself.'

Our host descended awkwardly and limped towards us. His period in the army had not been kind to him, except in terms of status. The athletic young man I admired at school, where he was a couple of years ahead of me, was prematurely bent, his once handsome face was scarred, as much with pain as with actual injury. He might have been in his sixties, not his late forties.

'Matthew! Cousin Harriet!' After a crisp salute and a stiff-shouldered bow for Harriet, Barrington shook my hand, his grip as firm as mine. Once the porter had stowed our baggage in a dog cart, driven off briskly by a young man in livery, Barrington took the reins himself – surprisingly not particularly well – giving us a commentary on the countryside through which we passed, listing all the improvements he would like to institute. 'You know about these things, don't you, Matthew? Perhaps you could give me your opinion.'

'Surely your own agent—'

'Had to leave for some reason. No suitable replacement yet. Now look at that!' He pointed with would-be casual pride as we approached the Georgian-fronted residence that was his home. Despite her ready delight in lovely buildings – and the frontage was a gem – Harriet's face became steadily less joyous; she returned my encouraging squeeze of her hand with a fierce grip.

We were greeted not on the steps but in the hallway by Lady Hortensia herself, tall, slender, pale yet composed. Was she pleased to see us? Her face had never been expressive, and her smile was polite, not joyous, belying her greeting. 'How delightful to see you. Are you well? Excellent.' She did not attempt to kiss Harriet; they exchanged the usual curtsy, hers decidedly less deep than Harriet's, of course. She responded briefly to our enquiries about her baby son, then rang for the butler.

A tall, heavy-shouldered middle-aged man, with a face cast into an expression of sour disapproval, Biddlestone silently escorted us to our bed chamber. Declaring that we had missed afternoon tea, but that he would send refreshments to our room if we wished, he withdrew. I would have liked to place an order simply to annoy him, but of course it would not have been him who was inconvenienced.

Harriet looked about her. Her silence spoke volumes.

Presumably in an older part of the house, the room was small and furnished without elegance or even comfort. Our cases – far too many, one would have thought, for a mere weekend – awaited us. In the absence of the suffering Jemima, Harriet was soon unpacking and shaking out her gowns with the competence of practice, then dealing with my shirts. Even she acknowledged that I did a decent a job with my outer garments.

'Almost as well as a valet would have done,' she assured me, kissing me before turning so that I might unhook her dress. 'Quickly: it will not do to be late for dinner.'

A tap at the door interrupted anything I might have said or done in response. Her under-the-breath comment probably matched mine, but her 'Come in' was as cheery and welcoming as anyone might wish. Creeping round the door came a child, her hair scraped back under a desperately ugly cap and her body swallowed by a faded print dress. She was perhaps ten, perhaps twelve – it was hard to tell as she was so short and thin – staggering under the weight of a huge jug of water. At last she whispered that she was Harriet's acting lady's maid. Clara. She reacted to Harriet's thanks with a look of something akin to terror.

Feeling superfluous, I withdrew to the tiny dressing room to don my evening wear – nothing informal such as smoking jackets here – listening to Harriet's encouraging comments and the poor, tight, monosyllabic replies as I wrestled with my studs.

'Isn't this beautiful!' Harriet whispered, as we were shown into the impressive saloon, which was still decorated in the original colours, with gilt sofas and chairs that appeared to have been designed and made to fit the space available. The pictures were in proportion too. What a wonderful room. Harriet's eyes opened wide in delight.

But she wasn't here as a visitor to a gallery; she was a house guest meant to mingle. She was as elegant as any of the fashionable women. Lady Croft having died only three months ago, she was still in mourning, wearing a lilac gown trimmed with grey. Some might have dismissed her as a dove amongst a flock of parakeets, but I could not admire the vivid turquoises and yellows, the startling blues and almost alarming reds that many other ladies sported. My mama lived by the maxim that simply being able to do something did not mean you should: the word *vulgar* might have reached her lips. But she would not have said it aloud. She was as much a servant of the Church as my Archdeacon father, who had entered the Church as his vocation, not because it was simply expected of him: he always joked that if you cut open her heart you would find the Beatitudes written inside it.

I tucked Harriet's arm into mine, so that I could escort her round to meet people I trusted would be old acquaintances. I saw none.

A quirk in the acoustics meant that the sounds of thirty or forty people – some house guests like us, others invited for the evening only – engaged in civilized conversation rapidly became a maelstrom of noise. Many of those present had probably spent hours on the hunting field, so they were more than used to raising their voices. Harriet would always have been an onlooker at events like this, quietly checking that all the servants were fulfilling their duties. She would never have had to try to hold a conversation with a guest – and with a stranger at that. Somehow we had become separated by the swirling skirts and I almost panicked on her behalf. But at last I located her, near one of the sofas at the edge of the room. Her head at a solicitous angle, she was talking to – or being talked to – by a tall, straight-backed older lady who was bedecked equally with jewellery and wrinkles. Her features were blurred with age, but fine bones lay underneath. I inched nearer, but was intercepted by a footman clad in a vivid blue, silver-laced livery and the sort of wig our household had abandoned before I even arrived as the estate manager. He offered more champagne. A glass only just in my hand, I was clapped fiercely on the shoulder.

'You must be Rowsley! Jameson – your vice-captain,' declared a military man, much my age, good-looking enough, I suppose, in a square-jawed blond-haired way. He thrust out a hand to grasp mine and pump it, risking the glass as I hurriedly transferred it. 'Need to talk to you!'

'Of course.' In my anxiety to support Harriet, I found myself temporarily nonplussed, needing a moment to realize that he was speaking about the next day's match. 'Do you think the weather will hold?' I asked, a safe enough question while I gathered my thoughts.

'Never known a drop of rain to fall during one of our weekends,' Jameson said, as if affronted either by my temerity in raising the issue or the possibility of a meteorological hiccup. 'Always good weather. I see no reason why this should be any different.' He looked at me accusingly. 'Not thinking of backing out at this stage, I hope?' He thrust his ginger moustache into my face as if I were one of his subalterns, breathing cigar smoke over me.

'Indeed no,' I said quietly. 'I'm really looking forward to a good game. But now, if you will excuse me—' I edged desperately back into the maelstrom of loud, tall gentlemen in search of someone, anyone I could present as a friend to my poor stranded wife. Perhaps – but now Barrington was before me.

'What's this I hear about your withdrawal from the team? A fellow can't just stand down, you know.'

'Nor have I, Cousin. I merely asked about the weather we might expect and Major Jameson jumped to the most unwarranted of conclusions.'

'Man's very busy, you know,' he said, as if that explained everything. Did something about his face suggest he did not convince himself? Or perhaps I read too much into the grimace of a smile which was all his scars would permit.

He limped away.

And then we were ushered in to dine.

There was no chance of my rescuing Harriet now. All I could do was pray that the gentlemen on either side of her might be congenial company – and could talk intelligently about something she knew about. If only I could have located Mark in the melee and pointed him in her direction. But it dawned on me that I had not even seen him. Surely he must be here? I must ask Barrington. It was too late now, however. I had to take my place between a gently lisping young lady scarcely out of the schoolroom, and a middle-aged matron who despite a silk dress and a wealth of jewellery smelt strongly of the stable. I turned first to the former, praying that further down the table some kind soul would be engaging my wife in the same gentle conversation that I embarked on now. Though with luck her interlocutor would prove more intelligent.

THREE

The dining room must have been beautiful once, if the saloon was anything to judge by, but it had recently been redecorated and refurnished. The walls bore an opulent crimson brocade, which somehow spoilt the proportions of the room, and the ornately carved furniture might have been at home in a Scottish castle but simply loomed rather menacingly here. I thanked God that her late ladyship, or more probably his late lordship, had never had the inclination so to modernize the House.

One of my dinner companions was a young man not yet twenty. He had the largest and most active Adam's apple I had ever seen, not to mention a blush so deep it looked painful. He might have been at a leading public school, but he was capable of discussing only his future in the Church. Since he was afflicted with a crippling stammer I pitied both him and his future congregations. As gently as if I were asking a new footman about his hopes and fears, I turned the conversation to what he really enjoyed doing when he wasn't studying. It transpired that he loved drawing, though from the way he bobbed his head from left to right to check he was not overheard I deduced that amongst our fellow-guests art might not be considered a gentlemanly occupation. If only I might introduce him to my dear friend Sir Francis Palmer, who had a knack of freeing people from the shackles of their expectations; he also had a colleague who was an art expert who could offer advice. But Mr Turton's future was presumably as trammelled as mine had once been. On my other side was a broad red-faced man in his fifties, a Mr Clarence Digby, who was so deaf that anything more than the most perfunctory conversation was impossible. On my side at least. He told me at some length about his time in the Indian Civil Service, simply not hearing any of the genuinely interested questions I tried to interject, but talking with some passion about fairness and justice and the Empire.

In the over-furnished drawing room, while we awaited the gentlemen, the striking elderly lady who had waylaid me before dinner summoned me to join her on a sofa that was as uncomfortable as it was ugly. It was clear from the glances of the other ladies that this was an honour, or at very least a social mismatch. As before, her conversation was carried on loudly enough for me to cringe beneath my polite and attentive smile. It was also embarrassingly informative about some of our fellow guests.

'Two lovers at least. At the same time, rumour has it! And her husband such a handsome man too, if you don't mind ginger hair. As for her—' She pointed. 'That hair might be her own, but the colour certainly isn't. Look – you can see the roots! And as for Lady Smethwick, she might give herself airs, but her husband was thrown out of Eton for buggery – so what do you make of that?'

Lady Croft at her most vehement had never been as outrageous as this. Even as I blushed, I wondered why she had chosen me as a companion. Surely she would have more fun with one of the other older ladies equally *au fait* – was that the correct phrase? – with other people's indiscretions. Yet she had seemed kind when she had accepted without question my description of myself as living quietly in the country with our host's cousin. She too was living quietly, she insisted – though clearly not in the literal sense – after a wonderful life on the Continent. 'Although I am English to the core, I married an Austrian count. Heavens, you should have seen him in those wonderful knitted trousers. Not a stitch on underneath, my dear. I fell in love at first sight – but first sight of what I will not confess. So my title is Gräfin. Gräfin Weiser. Say it after me. Say it again – Weiser.'

At last she was almost but not quite satisfied. I was happy to accede to her suggestion that I referred to her simply as 'Gräfin'.

What I had never learned – had never had to learn – was the skill of seamlessly leaving one conversation with a view to joining another, especially as being seated meant I could not simply allow myself to drift. At least the Gräfin seemed content to have a captive audience. But I was conscious that other guests were changing groups – the room swirled with colour and patterns like a shaken kaleidoscope – and that I should seek another place. If only the gentlemen would reappear: Matthew had rescued me from physical danger before, but now I faced a quite different peril – committing some dreadful but unknown solecism. If only he would come.

At last I did the obvious thing: I asked my companion for advice. 'I know there are others who would welcome the chance to converse with you Gräfin, but, as I told you, my husband and I live very quietly and I lack—'

'Acquaintance here? Of course! And what is our hostess doing to help? She should be introducing you to other guests,' she declared, surely loudly enough for Lady Hortensia to hear. 'Give me my stick, there's a good girl, and help me up. There! Now, there's Agatha. Lady FitzAllen. Agatha, my dear. How is the baby? Excellent,' she declared without waiting for an answer. 'This is Harriet Rowsley, Matthew's new wife.'

We exchanged nods and curtsies, but it was clear even to the Gräfin that Lady FitzAllen had more important fish to fry. 'Hmph! No manners, the young. Ah! There's Lady Pidgeon. With a "d". Amelia, I'd like you to meet young Mr Rowsley's wife. You know Rowsley – of course you do. Barrington's clever cousin. No, not the lawyer, the other one.'

Lady Pidgeon, a small, delicately built woman in her later years, all too clearly did not know who Matthew was, and had no apparent interest in meeting me. But she gamely and politely asked me the questions I would have asked in her situation, courteously listening to my responses. It was only when I mentioned the hope that I would see the famous gallery and library that her face lit up with a genuine smile, and suddenly, I know not how, we were talking about Mr Dickens' latest serial, *Great Expectations*. To my great pleasure, and indeed relief, the topic attracted other ladies too. Even if I did not learn their names, I could be on curtsying and smiling terms with them when next our paths crossed. But I did long for Matthew's reassuring presence.

I longed for it even more when the ladies decided that in the prolonged absence of our menfolk we must entertain ourselves. There must be music! Two of our number reacted with aplomb: it seemed that they had shared a piano several times before, and they were soon playing a Mozart duet. Another was on her feet to sing. I was ready to panic: I suspected that anyone demurring politely would be greeted with equally polite disbelief. But I had a few minutes' grace: even now a harp – a harp! – was being wheeled into the room so that one of our number might play. Fortunately she took an unconscionable time to tune the instrument to her satisfaction – did I dare suspect that she was deliberately delaying the moment when she had to put fingers to strings?

At last she started, but then she earned my prayers of gratitude by offering to accompany a friend of hers. Four or five songs later, our hostess turned to me.

'Mrs Rowsley, surely it is your turn? No, don't shake your head. I'm sure Matthew would never have married anyone who didn't share his passion for music.'

Was she indeed? I must not wince. 'Alas, he chose me because we shared a passion for poetry.'

'In that case, perhaps you would recite something? Perhaps some verses from *The Angel in the House*?'

'Mr Patmore?' I queried, playing for time myself now. I smiled. 'Surely given the company I should offer something by one of our sex.' I got to my feet. 'From *Sonnets from the Portuguese*, by Mrs Elizabeth Barrett Browning. Sonnet number forty-three . . .' There was a general intake of breath, which might have been scandalized, but I embarked on my task.

I had reached the last three lines when the door opened to admit the gentlemen, one of the first of whom was Matthew. I must not pause.

'. . . *I love thee with the breath,*
Smiles, tears, of all my life! – and, if God choose,
I shall but love thee better after death.'

FOUR

A woman screamed. I was on my feet in a second. We both were. And another scream! I was already reaching for my dressing gown when there was a third screech. And a fourth. By now we were beginning to laugh.

'Peacocks!' Harriet exclaimed. 'There were a couple on the terrace, weren't there? I wonder why they've come round here.'

'Here' of course was beneath our window. Not only was it an undistinguished room, but it was on the undistinguished side of the house, well away from the terrace on which the birds should have been disporting themselves.

'God knows why Barrington should want such noisy brutes in the first place,' I grumbled. 'I'd shoot the things tomorrow.'

'There's probably a law against it. Or perhaps it would be as bad as shooting an albatross. Oh, Matthew, that's the poem I should have recited!'

'What? *The Ancient Mariner*? All of it?'

'As much as I could remember. I think Coleridge might have been somewhat less controversial than such a full-blown love poem.'

'It was the best welcome into a room that I've ever had,' I declared, 'and this is my response.'

But it was hard to sustain even the most passionate of embraces when it was accompanied by an ongoing chorus of squawks. We collapsed in laughter. In any case, the little maid would soon come scratching at the door, and some decorum was called for.

Her eyes still warm with passion, Harriet sat down composedly. 'Tell me about your evening with the gentlemen.'

I sat too, actually very pleased to share the details of a gathering I would not have found strange five, even two, years ago when I was used to exclusively masculine social gatherings. But my life at Thorncroft House had changed my expectations of my fellow men – and now I liked the softening, indeed the humanizing, presence of the opposite sex. Not that the women of Thorncroft expected to be cosseted. Our conversations were robust and full of cut and thrust in argument – never simperingly genteel, as the latter part of this evening's chatter had become.

She nodded. 'Perhaps you were expecting Barrington to be more like Mark, and Lady Hortensia to be more like Mark's Dora?'

'Perhaps I had simply forgotten what a bore our poor host can be – and to my shame I had forgotten how bad his injuries must have been. His stoicism! Anyway, he explained why Mark isn't here. He's due to lead the defence at an important trial next week and needed to prepare for it.' I watched the shadow of disappointment cross her face.

'What a shame! But I honour him for putting preparations for his client before a weekend of pleasure.'

I put it more bluntly. 'A weekend I fancy he would already be dismissing as tedious. And you know that Dora's opinions about women like Mary Wollstonecraft would have shocked the ladies far more than anything you could say, or even recite. You did not want to come. I insisted. You were right. I'm sorry.'

'Let us accept it as . . . education. At least the evening didn't last as long as I feared it might. I hadn't realized that many of the party would need to return home while there was enough light. Come, my love: the team's plans for the cricket match – that's what you were supposed to be discussing.'

'And did. Intermittently. But there is some unease between Barrington and his deputy, Jameson.'

'Jameson? Ah, the Major, very conscious of how well he looks in his mess uniform Our villagers would dismiss him as having a bob on himself. He seems quite a charmer, though – the ladies seemed delighted to engage in conversation with him.'

'Were you?'

'I am too old for his attentions. In any case, I thought he was an ogler – of the younger women at least. But what is this unease?'

'I don't know. Just an edge between them. I hope it won't affect what Barrington will refer to as his team.'

She frowned. '*His* team? But surely he cannot play with those injuries of his.'

I replied, deadpan, 'He is planning to bat with a runner and send on a substitute when we field.'

Her eyebrows rose to dizzy heights. 'And such an arrangement appears where in the Laws of Cricket?'

'My love, you know that gentlemen can and do rewrite laws at any time to suit themselves. And in many respects the laws governing the game are notoriously lax.'

She shrugged, but asked suspiciously, 'And has Barrington adopted a flexible attitude to being dismissed? He has to be bowled three times before he quits the field, perhaps? No! Matthew, you are mocking me!'

'Not a jot!'

The tiny maid's arrival silenced us briefly. I would have been more than happy to dismiss her and take her place, but I sensed that Harriet wanted to give the child confidence and perhaps draw her out a little, so once more I withdrew to the dressing room.

'I thought she would never finish!' I exclaimed, when it was safe to return.

'So did I. I tried to be patient with her, but even the most gentle question transformed even more of her fingers into thumbs. Enough of her and her shortcomings, my love. We have other things to talk about – or perhaps not even talk about . . .'

The peacocks had the decency to remain silent throughout the night, but one gave us an early call next morning. We had the rare luxury of unhurried time together, so were content to drowse or talk or neither.

At last Harriet asked, 'Are you required to go to net-practice this morning?'

'Indeed. There's a three-line whip. But not till ten thirty. Jameson wanted eleven, Barrington ten. It took a very long time for everyone to accept a compromise.'

'Surely, within reason, the longer the practice the better.'

'You would have thought so. I have the impression that Jameson argues with me for the sheer pleasure of it, though I have no idea why. But enough of him. Mark's place will have to be taken by one of the household – the head gardener has been requisitioned.'

She looked at me quizzically. 'But you don't approve.'

'I might if the head gardener had a say in it. But it seems that he is the best batsman in the village team, so theirs will be a double loss. And they could equally well have asked the rector or curate to play – or others of their circle – instead of telling a working man what he had to do.'

'My love, your next move should not be to a greater country house but into the greatest house – the House of Commons!' Her voice was mocking, but the expression on her face was lovingly serious.

'And give up Thorncroft House? And tear you from Lord Croft's library? You see, I could not be one of those men who leaves his wife behind while he disports himself in London. Meanwhile, I have tomorrow to look forward to. For a youngish man, Jameson seems very dogmatic. I wonder,' I added stretching, 'what he will make of my new bowling technique. The one you taught me, of course.'

'For goodness' sake don't tell him that! He'll drop you from the team and send you to bowl for the village.' She turned and kissed me. 'And in your present mood that's exactly what you would like, isn't it?'

'Among other things,' I agreed.

My school and university days had taught me that there were two types of teacher: those who told you that you were wrong, and needed to do something their way, and those who were interested in what you were doing and were even prepared to learn from it. I learnt from Major Jameson that everything about my bowling was at fault, especially, it seemed, my approach to the wicket.

'They say you're an Oxford Blue,' he sneered, 'but I've never seen a run-up like that at a Varsity match.'

That was probably true. It had changed – some might say matured – since I took my degree. As a result, I was now the leading wicket-taker in our village team, with a wonderful part-nership with our wicket-keeper, who happened to be the village constable. Once I had discovered who this motley side's wicket-keeper was, and told him how I would signal each variation in my delivery, all would be well. Would the Almighty forgive me if I prayed it would not be Jameson behind the stumps? I hoped

He would, especially as Jameson was now criticizing the length of my delivery stride. Like a schoolboy, I was supposed to act on his instructions. Bubbling with fury, and totally ignoring him, I bowled faster than I ever had in my life, and with more accuracy. I actually broke one of the stumps. It was better than breaking his jaw.

Suddenly, Jameson decided I needed no more attention, and turned his guns on others he considered were not meeting his impeccable standards. There was a lot of muttering, especially when Turton, a stuttering chinless lad, one of Harriet's dinner partners, was reduced almost to tears by the man's mockery of his affliction. I should have tried to stop it all – why didn't Barrington intervene, for goodness' sake?– but my temper was on such a knife-edge I knew I might do him injury. Finally he pointed to the head gardener, the man whom Barrington had purloined from the village team. His strapping physique suggested he might bowl as well as bat.

'You. The new man,' he began. 'Harry or whatever your name is.'

'Harrison, sir.'

'Harris. Look at the way you're standing. Sloppy. Straighten your back, for God's sake. Call yourself a cricketer?'

The head gardener looked at him. Any moment he would be accused of dumb insolence.

My hands clenched to my sides, I looked around at the other players. All these brave young men desperate for a leader! How might I help? Either I floored the man, or I pretended I was acting a part from one of the plays we sometimes read aloud at home. Yes, I must be the reasonable idiot for a few minutes: 'Barrington, old man, I wonder if we might spend the last few minutes practising our fielding. Catching especially.' After all, it was a skill which won and lost matches. Though even as I suggested catching, I knew the converse was throwing, which could lead to its own problems. What if I was tempted to hurl the ball not to Jameson but at him?

There was a gratifying murmur of assent.

'Good God, man, you want us running round like a tribe of schoolboys?' His face fixed in a sneer, Jameson stormed off, Barrington eventually limping in his wake, presumably to remonstrate.

Casually I threw the ball at the nearest player, who promptly dropped it. Most players quickly understood what I meant to do. Our practice might not have been blessed by our captain and his truculent sidekick, but it lasted a very profitable half-hour. Not least because the stuttering lad who had been tormented could throw further and faster than anyone else, and because Harrison, the humiliated gardener, seemed to have glue on his fingers. By common consent he became our wicket-keeper, though it seemed he might have to borrow gloves from his village team counterpart. We had some sort of team at least. I would have continued longer, had I not recalled to my shame and chagrin that I had forgotten Harriet. She had firmly – and, as it transpired, rightly – rejected my suggestion that she might like to be present at our cricket practice and was now at the mercy of the remaining guests. So I gathered the men together. 'Gentlemen, let us simply play a good game for our own sakes. Our own and our colleagues'. And indeed for the sake of the opposition, who will sadly be lacking a very good player.' I reached over to shake Harrison's hand. He might have smiled and shaken it firmly, but I feared he still burned with anger as much as I did.

'Have you a moment?' I asked, trusting that Harriet would forgive me if she knew what I was doing. 'Because we need to learn to read each other's signals if we are to take wickets . . .'

Harriet was not on the front lawn, where a gaggle of women were cooing over the contents of the perambulators pushed by a trio of nannies. At least as much attention seemed to be paid to the perambulators themselves – these were designed to be pushed, it seemed, a considerable improvement on the system where the nanny was turned into a draught horse towing her charge. Harriet would have approved, certainly. But she never put herself in the way of children, one of the rare occasions, it seemed to me, when she betrayed her sorrow at not being able to bear one herself. At one point she had been reluctant to marry me on the grounds that I would want an heir. I wanted her, and had never once regretted my decision.

The obvious places to look were the gallery and the library. The former was deserted, but for a lugubrious maid with a long feather-duster, who appeared to detest each painting even more than its predecessor. If I wanted to stop her and tell her to look at the beauty in front of her – Gainsboroughs, a couple of Claudes, for instance – I was sure that Harriet could not have resisted. I confined myself to a mild observation about the comic figures in a Breughel, which earned a resigned bob of a curtsy, and left her to her work, heading for the library.

But it was empty.

FIVE

Matthew often spoke of his desire to take his nephew to a toyshop and to invite him to choose a gift. He imagined the joy on the child's face as he was confronted by so many delights. Which should he select? On the basis of my experience this morning, I could not imagine anything crueller. Where should I start? The gallery? Indeed, I sat in front of a Hals for several minutes, until I became aware of a housemaid desperate to dust. Should I claim my right as a guest to be as awkward as I pleased? If she was late in her schedule then let her take the consequences. But I had once been a girl like that. With a smile that clearly nonplussed her I moved away.

I was intercepted on the stairs by Lady Hortensia, with a polite but not necessarily interested question: 'Is all well, Cousin Harriet?'

'Thank you, yes, Lady Hortensia. What a lovely fine day it is.'

With barely a nod she moved on, but turned, pausing two steps above me so that she could literally look down on me.

'You should know,' she said, 'that the ladies watching the match always wear white, like the players, of course. And I think I should warn you,' she added, 'not to monopolize the Gräfin. Not good form. Quite a faux pas, indeed.' She turned and ascended too briskly for me to reply.

I could have demanded to know what she meant, insisting I might talk to whom I chose. As for the wearing of white, I knew that once Lady Croft had favoured such a fashion and I had come prepared. But if I hadn't? I suppose I could always have borrowed a maid's uniform and watched from behind the tables spread with tea for the teams.

It was probably bad form to stand there fuming. What next? It would be good to browse in the much-vaunted library.

I was greeted as I arrived by my dinner partner of the previous night, Mr Digby – and by his lighted cigar. Had anyone ever smoked in our nascent library at home, I would have ejected them. His late lordship's Will gave me the same authority in the Thorncroft library. But here I could do no more than hint that smoking put the books at very least at risk – and given that the library was at the very heart of the building a fire there would endanger everyone and everything in it. A hint should be offered in a quiet and gentle way, so as to achieve a result without the miscreant even being away of the implied rebuke. But nothing quiet and gentle would have any effect on Mr Digby. A town crier might be challenged to make the poor man hear. I had to do something – but what? The answer must be to move him outside.

'You say you've never played croquet before, ma'am? Here – let me help you with your grip on the mallet,' Mr Digby said.

For all I had judged him to be a kind and decent man, his notion of assisting involved standing behind me, pressing the bulk of his body against my back and like a villain in a novel by Richardson distorting the hoops of my crinoline – which for once I blessed for keeping more of his anatomy at bay. Somehow I must stop myself screaming. I must not stamp on his foot. I must do nothing to draw attention to myself. Because this, it seemed, was what not just servants but ladies were expected to endure from gentlemen in the name of light flirtation. Perhaps that was why so many of them fainted – either because a fierce embrace made an already tight corset even more stifling, or because falling heavily backward or forward would dislodge the unwanted leech. I had been known to feign a faint myself – but not in the open air. I must use my wits some more. After all, I was out here on a mission to save a library. I had told him I knew nothing of the house or gardens and asked what I should look out for. Of course he was going to escort me. Being too clever had got me into this mess. I must be even cleverer. To speak to him, I had to screw my head right round to make myself heard, only to be rewarded with a vile gust of tobacco-scented breath. I pointed to his ear. Surely that would indicate I wished to speak to him. At last he worked it out. I was released. I passed him a mallet. Would he show me how to hit it? He did not do it well. He blamed the brightness of the sun: he had had to squint.

An ill-advised moment of vanity assailed me. Surely I had spent enough time in my life going through metaphorical hoops to be able to get a ball through a literal one. But I knew from endless experience that men like this enjoyed flattery. A near miss was what was needed. And a request for him to demonstrate again what he had done so that I could watch him. I retreated behind a hoop to watch, apparently absorbing every word of his prattling advice. Not for the first time I agreed with Hamlet – *These tedious old fools!* Of course, a woman, like a man, may *smile and smile and be a villain.* Not that I had any villainy in my heart – just a very sincere desire to be elsewhere.

I was sure it would have been, in Lady Hortensia's words, terribly bad form to run to Matthew as he finally appeared, his face an interesting mixture of relief and guilt overlaying what looked like black fury. It mirrored my own. As a pair we could engage Mr Digby in a conversation rendered all the more meaningless by his inability to hear half of it. After ten minutes my dislike of him had evaporated, replaced by a profound pity for a man with such a handicap – hidden, but socially even more crippling than Cousin Barrington's physical injuries.

At last we were alone, walking in the warm sun. Matthew was unwontedly silent as we took a path alongside the stream that marked the edge of the estate. It was choked with reeds, but some work had evidently been done on it recently. The little humpbacked bridge was a mixture of old stone and very bright red bricks. Matthew stared at it, as if it was infuriating him. Usually he told me why he was angry; for some reason today he did not. So tucking my arm in his, I summed up my morning very briefly, omitting my encounter with Lady Hortensia and why I asked Mr Digby to demonstrate a shot. After all, I had no desire to make him angrier. In his past there had been some incident – he had never told even me quite what had happened – when he had nearly killed someone. I had seen with my own eyes the damage he could inflict on himself when enraged.

'Learning how to play croquet!' he laughed. 'So that was how you came to be with that old bore! But taking lessons from him? You?'

'Some gentlemen like to think they know everything, do they

not?' I risked asking, 'Have you had a similar experience at your practice?'

'Similar – but more! My love, you should have been a fly on the wall. But not that one,' he added, eyeing the bridge.

Soon he was laughing at what he described as a debacle. We strolled on. The day got warmer. But the bright sky was becoming slightly milky. *'When halo rings the Moon or Sun, Rain's approaching on the run,'* I remarked.

He nodded. 'I just hope we can finish the game. Though I sense some people might be relieved if we can't. I just wish I knew why. I can't imagine that you could keep away, my love, but do you think any other wives or sweethearts will bother to watch?'

'I'm sure they will at least gather on the boundary. Wearing white gowns. Yes, there are strong if unwritten rules about what constitutes the right apparel to wear. The Gräfin won't attend: she told me last night she is now too Austrian to enjoy such a strange game. What I can't understand is why she should have gone to such pains to be kind to me.' Or why Lady Hortensia should consider my behaviour bad form. If only Cousin Mark's kind wife Dora was here to confide in. 'Ah! A kingfisher!'

Luncheon was a fairly perfunctory occasion, as we needed to change into our cricket-playing or cricket-watching whites. The ladies needed cricket-watching hats, of course. Alas for the person sitting behind some of the creations. I sported – at a very jaunty angle, I must say – a pretty little straw hat that Matthew had pointed out to me in the window of our new village draper's. It would impede no one's view. If the other ladies drifted languidly to the field, I had to stop myself striding out to claim a good viewpoint. I fell into step with Lady Pidgeon, who was carrying a book.

'Many of my acquaintances seem to enjoy George Eliot's works,' she said, looking up at me. 'I must say I have never found the characters to my taste, but if I have to sit for three hours I might as well read this. *The Mill on the Floss.* Such low people she writes about!'

I had to say something, and, moreover, something that would not immediately offend one of the few people with whom I had even a remote connection. So I looked up at the sky. 'I suspect, ma'am, that you will not be sitting here for as long as you fear. Look at that line of cloud on the horizon.'

'Let us pray it arrives soon. Over there, I think.' She headed for a seat from which one could see nothing.

'Forgive me, ma'am. My husband is playing and he will expect me to watch him.' How disloyal of me. I added with a smile, 'And I will expect him to play well enough for me to want to watch.'

'Dear me. You're a little old to be a devoted newly-wed,' she said mockingly.

I took my tone from her. 'I am indeed, ma'am, no spring chicken, as the saying goes, but we have been married less than a year. And – forgive me – I do so love the game.'

'So does my husband – umpiring! After all these years watching him play now I'm supposed to watch him watching other men play.' She sighed heavily. 'But at least I have my book. Ah! I see that play is about to begin.'

'In that case, pray excuse me.' I bobbed a curtsey, taking a deckchair almost at random. I could move at the end of the over.

To my surprise she sat beside me. 'I'm sure you will know which team is which.'

'Indeed I do. The village team is fielding. Cousin Barrington's team is batting.' Sadly I was a long way from the pavilion – oh, yes, there was a tiny white painted doll's house about ninety degrees to my right – so I could not easily see who was already wearing pads, ready to bat next. But with Lady Pidgeon beside me I could not politely move closer, even though within minutes her eyes were shut, her mouth hanging open.

Cousin Barrington was apparently sticking to his self-created law that he must be dismissed three times before he departed from the crease, but already four other players had lost their wickets. Now it was poor Mr Turton's turn to bat, his Adam's apple no doubt a-bobble and his elbows and knees at all angles. All I could do was pray for him. So when would Mr Harrison be allowed to bat? And when Matthew?

Now Lady Pidgeon and I had company. Two or three young mothers, accompanied by nannies who carried blankets and an assortment of toys, camped right on the boundary rope. Had no one ever told them about fielders running hell for leather as they chased the ball? It was generally accepted that any spectators had a duty to move for them. Should I point this out? But to whom? The mothers, twirling parasols, clearly did not consider their babies to be their problem as they laughed together; the nannies, also deep in gossip, probably had no authority. Yet I got up. Whom should I approach? At least I had been introduced to Lady FitzAllen. At last she broke off her conversation with the other young mothers – who all looked like dolls from the same box – to raise an enquiring but forbidding eyebrow.

My courage did not often fail me, but it took a great deal of effort to speak. 'Your ladyship, I fear the babies and their nannies are in what Cousin Barrington would call the line of fire. They are indeed perilously close to the boundary.'

'Thank you. I will speak to Nurse about it. Johnson, Mrs – er – is worried about Miss Baby.' She resumed her conversation.

Thinking the children's safety was more important than my pride, I delivered the warning to Johnson myself.

'Oh, they'll never hit a ball this far, will they, ma'am? Anyway, this is where madam said we should be. Thanks ever so, though.'

I might as well sit down.

Lady Pidgeon awoke at this point and discovered that her novel was too tedious for words. Having helped her to her feet and watched her join another group of older ladies, I moved my position slightly closer to the pavilion, just in time to join in the smattering of applause for the latest batsman to lose his wicket. Mr Turton, flushed red right to the back of his neck, made an ignominious return having failed to score. Surely they would send Mr Harrison in now? No, Major Jameson himself, the man who was the self-appointed coach; he swatted wildly and was caught by the bowler. A gentleman I didn't know acquitted himself no better. If Cousin Barrington's side were not to be totally humiliated, then Mr Harrison and Matthew – not as good with the bat as with the ball – must achieve a miracle.

Once they were batting together, they hardly stopped running. Three runs here; five there. At one point an amazing seven when Matthew skied the ball into some brambles and it took the poor fielders a lot of effort and some blood to retrieve it. Mr Harrison batted even better. Soon the gentlemen's team had accumulated

fifty-six more runs – not enough, probably, but at least a respectable total in the overs they were allowed. The two not-out batsmen
were applauded back to the pavilion.

It was time for the sumptuous tea.

It was time for pretty girls to flirt with handsome young men.

It was time to fan oneself and complain about the increasing
sticky heat and the ominous grey and brown balloons of clouds
bunching overhead. These, however, were nothing compared to
the clouds on some of the players' faces, Matthew's particularly.
Knowing how hard it was for him to control his violent urges
– it was as if he had to retreat inside himself – I did not approach
him. He would find me if he needed me. But as I drank my tea,
since none of the ladies was troubling me with conversation, I
could simply watch. Cousin Barrington, white with an emotion
I could not determine, was arguing with the Major, whose face
was brick red. They were both pointing, the Major with a shaking
hand, at Mr Harrison, who was with apparent calm donning the
pads he would need to keep wicket. Mr Turton took him a cup
of tea, but clearly and not surprisingly, preferred to avoid a long
conversation. Mr Harrison smiled awkwardly as he took it. Seeing
him on his own again, Matthew went over and sat beside him.
Soon they were talking with some animation. I could relax.

Perhaps the umpires, one supplied by each side, could relax
too. But it seemed unlikely. The village umpire – a loyal team
member a few years ago, no doubt – looked as thunderous as
the weather. The other, Lord Pidgeon, poured something from a
silver flask into his tea, his hand shaking badly. They made no
attempt to chat, but perhaps they had nothing to discuss: apart
from regularly raising fingers to show the batsman had lost his
wicket, neither had been called on to do anything other than hold
caps and call when the over was concluded and it was time to
bowl from the other end.

Mr Turton crept up beside me. The gist of what he said was,
'It is a pity you are not playing, ma'am.'

I smiled my thanks and amusement. 'My husband tells me
that you are the best fielder in the team, Mr Turton. And probably in the other team too. Now, what do you think those two
gentlemen are arguing about?'

'The Colonel and the Major? Which weapon to deploy,' he

said, actually managing to grin. 'First b-b-b-b-owler. And who is to keep wicket.'

'It must be hard, a team having two captains. Who would you choose as wicket-keeper?'

'M-M-M-Mr Harrison. And your husband to b-b-b-bowl. Ob-b-b—' He stopped, swamped by a vicious blush.

In such circumstances I would have patted a young footman's arm – though we would never have employed one, I fear, with so crippling a speech impediment. I patted his.

He ducked his head, declaring, 'I could kill Jameson, ma'am.' Or as near as he could get to that.

This time I gripped both his hands. I spoke with quiet urgency. 'For your sake, let his rudeness, his unkindness pass. You have a better life ahead of you. I promise. Now, dry your eyes and drink some tea. Yes? Yes!'

The clouds grew almost crushingly heavy. The wind dropped. 'Do you think the match can be finished before the rain comes?'

He answered with a dubious smile and a rocking hand.

Others beside Mr Turton must loathe the Major. Even the spectators could hear him as he loudly blamed Mr Harrison for every error made by the bowlers he chose. Even in a dress like this I could have bowled better than any of them. He knew he had a brilliant bowler at his disposal in Matthew, but would not throw him the ball. The gentlemen were going to lose.

Unless . . .

Without being asked, Matthew took the ball. A snarling expostulation from the vice-captain had no effect. He ran in. The first ball was unplayable, but somehow the batsman survived. And the next and even the next. Then Matthew shrugged his shoulders slightly, in a way I recognized as a signal he'd taught our village wicket-keeper. Yes. Mr Harrison took the catch. The next ball simply toppled the wickets. The third went towards Mr Turton, who snatched it from the air and held it. A hat trick! Even the opposition applauded. Perhaps especially the opposition. Having completed his over he returned to his usual fielding position.

So why did Jameson, assuming the mantle of captain, now give the ball to the very worst bowler? The village team only needed nine runs to win. Soon they only needed three. Look at that delivery: a child could hit it. The man certainly did. He heaved the ball high and long – directly to where I had been sitting. Where the children still played and the nursemaids still chatted and the mothers—

Act. Act now.

There is nothing more important than that ball. Forget the babies on the rug. The ball. That is the only thing in my mind. The angle. The speed. My speed. My feet must find their own way. The ball.

I have it. It is safe in my hands.

And the babies play on, quite oblivious. Miss Baby FitzAllen waves at the sky. Alexander Morton Frobisher Brewood shakes a silver and coral rattle.

By now they are probably the only ones who are not reacting. The men on the field send up the sort of cheer they probably practised back at Eton or Harrow. Even the batsman slaps his bat in approval. The ladies amongst the onlookers are fainting or screaming according to their temperament. And I know that while I probably saved an aristocratic life, I have committed a most terrible faux pas.

SIX

'What in Hades does that stupid bitch think she's doing? Running on to the field of play like that!' Jameson was brick-red with fury as rain, guinea-sized drops of it, fell on his head and mine.

'The lady you refer to is my dear wife, sir!' I shoved my hands deep into my pockets. 'I would thank you to speak of her with the respect she deserves. Furthmore, I believe she may have saved that baby's life!'

The rain came more heavily; lightning only a mile or two away lit the sky. The village umpire looked enquiringly at Lord Pidgeon.

'Leave the field?' the old man squawked. 'In no circumstances. The game can and must be finished.'

'Sir – the lightning is too close,' his opposite number said. 'Look!' Getting no response, he called us all off the field. Neither Pidgeon nor Jameson would move.

The latter turned to me. 'If you can't control her, I will! She's ruined the game!'

My shirt already soaked, I stared at the face rendered ugly by his fury. It was true that the delay while everything was sorted out had let the rain arrive and thus had saved us from certain defeat, though I doubt that that was uppermost in Harriet's mind at the time. Before I could unleash all the anger I felt, Robson, the captain of the village team, stepped forward. 'That your missus, Mr Rowsley? I take my hat off to her, that I do.'

I shook the hand he had extended. 'Thank you,' I managed. 'But how sad for the match to end like that.'

Jameson hadn't finished yet. 'This is a private conversation, man! I don't recall asking you to join it.'

'At least he is talking sense,' I snarled.

'I say . . . Look here.' Cousin Barrington bustled up, almost comically unable to deal with the situation. Surely he had dealt with similar problems in his military career. 'I mean, gentlemen . . .'

Winking at me, Robson simply shook his fellow-captain's hand. 'So rain stops play and it's a tie, sir – who would have thought it?' he asked. 'Well played. But I think the umpires are right: it's time to get everyone off the field, even the dawdlers, sir – look at that!'

Fork lightning split the sky, accompanied by a clap of thunder so loud it almost drowned out the screams of the women, some of whom were heading for the shelter of the trees.

'No, that won't do, sir! Never trees in a storm. Head them off, sir!' Robson turned to me. 'Can't you get them to the house, Mr Rowsley?'

I nodded. 'I'll try. What about the villagers?'

'Already going home, most of them.' He pointed at their bedraggled figures. 'They want to get back before that bloody bridge collapses.'

'What?' But, already urging people to find safer shelter, he didn't hear me.

'Damn it man, what's the blithering idiot damned well doing now?' Jameson demanded.

'Being useful,' I snapped. 'Like everyone else.' As I spoke I saw young Turton and Harrison literally carrying a villager on to the little veranda.

By now Jameson was puce. A black eye and bloodied nose would scarcely be noticed, would they? I clenched my hand in readiness. Just there.

Breathing out, I turned my back on him, to see where I could best help. The rain draped itself in wet curtains across everything I could see. I dashed it from my eyes. Harriet? Some people were simply helpless. Others were helping them, urging them on – like my peerless Harriet, who was now quietly and efficiently compelling the young mothers and nursemaids to make haste, even at the cost of a rug or a toy. She grabbed one recalcitrant toddler by the scruff of his sailor-suited neck and the seat of his trousers to lift him into a baby carriage which she started to drag herself until a footman took over. I ran towards her across already waterlogged ground.

'Lady Pidgeon!' she gasped, seizing my hand and leading us in the direction of a tiny figure staggering under the weight of her clothing. 'Can we?'

'Look – an empty baby carriage!'

Lady Pidgeon seemed grateful to us rather than offended as we grabbed it and pushed it towards her: no, she had no reluctance to shed her dignity. In fact she was soon laughing with an almost infectious gaiety. 'As a child I always wanted to splash in puddles – and now look at me! My dears, what fun.' She let us seat her sideways on the carriage, and then, Harriet pulling and me pushing, both of us laughing with her, we got her on to the terrace steps, where we could consign her to the care of a footman strong enough to gather her up like a baby and carry her into the house.

Harriet peered through the rain, falling, if possible, even more heavily. 'Does anyone else need our help?'

'They may need help, Harriet, but not necessarily ours.'

She stared at me. I tried to moderate my grimness. 'Most of the villagers were more weather-wise than us and fled as soon as the storm broke. We have no responsibilities. We are, after all, mere guests here.' Even I did not like my words or the way I spat them out.

Under her clear gaze I dropped my eyes. I must explain – but only when I could frame an answer that would not be unbearably offensive. And also when I might work out a reason for Jameson not wishing to win the match.

But she was shouting. A child had dropped a toy under the nearest oak and was pointing and screaming. A stout maid was running to fetch it. Hardly knowing what I was doing, I dashed after her and seized her hand, dragging her back to what I hoped was the safety of the house.

A terrifying flash and crack, almost drowned by the thunder itself. The oak was no more than a smoking ruin.

In the shocked silence, still the child pointed and cried.

Stripped and swathed in towels and sheets but safe in each other's arms, we stood by the window to watch the storm, which seemed to be moving slowly away. Despite the pandemonium outside, within we could hear the chaos in the corridors. Some of our team had, probably wisely, followed the villagers' lead, risking driving through the rain to get to the safety of their own homes. But not all. Soaking wet guests were loudly demanding the services of men and women equally drenched. Of course there was no hot water. Of course there were not enough lady's maids. What did a tardy lady's maid matter when lives could have been lost?

I had yet to speak of Jameson, but first I must speak of her catch.

'Instinct. Pure and simple.' She smiled up at me. 'I suppose we could blame that for the risks we took earlier. Thank God you stopped the maid. I was so afraid you'd offer . . . My love, when lightning struck—'

We clung closer.

At last she raised her head again. 'What happened during the match, Matthew? I know something has made you . . . very angry, shall we say? Was it Cousin Barrington's strange captaincy?'

'Partly.'

'It looked as if he or the Major wanted the village side to win. But neither strikes me as an altruistic man, wanting the poor to defeat the rich,' she observed, her eyebrows in an ironic arch.

I managed a smile. 'I didn't have any expectations of the match, not after our practice. But their decisions were bizarre, weren't they? No one seemed to question them. No one remonstrated.'

'And you had to act on your own initiative. Twice.'

'You noticed?'

'Would you doubt it?'

'Not for a second.' Dear God, how I loved this woman.

'As for Major Jameson's tantrum, I couldn't hear what he said, but it was clear he did not approve of my catch.' She held my gaze. 'I couldn't hear what you said either – and by then I knew I should forget trying to eavesdrop and start being useful. He is a very strange man, isn't he? He really upset poor Mr Turton. And Mr Harrison. And plenty of others, I should imagine, on both teams. And yet he seems very popular with most of our fellow guests, the women especially.' With an impish smile I knew was covering her anxiety she added, 'Though not me. And I fancy I am not likely to be his latest flirt.'

Before I could respond, there was another terrifying roll of thunder and an unmistakable crack. The storm had circled back. Harriet choked back a scream. 'Heavens! Another tree gone! And such rain!' She tried to speak normally. 'Look. Even the paths are rivers.'

'This must be what Robson was worried about. You remember that little bridge with its cobbled repair? He hoped all the villagers could cross it before it was washed away.'

She nodded. 'And what about the other bridges, not to mention the roads and the railway cuttings through which we had travelled? We may be trapped here!' A rare note of panic cracked her voice. Of course. However much I might shudder at the prospect of mass incarceration, Harriet had far more reason.

'I fear we may. Back at Thorncroft we've had guests trapped by snow, but you and Bea were in charge there. I hope your opposite numbers here are even half as good.' I broke off. 'What's that?'

It was a note, thrust under our door. Any thoughts that dinner this evening would be a quiet, informal affair were quickly quashed. We might be gathering half an hour later than usual, but there was no hint of any lowering of sartorial standards. With a joint sigh, we changed, each helping the other when necessary. Accordingly, when Clara the timid maid appeared we could tell her we had no need of her services.

'Thank you, ma'am. Please ma'am, if you're sure I must go to the next lady.'

'Of course. Did you get very wet this afternoon, Clara?'

'Oh, no, ma'am. I was helping in the kitchen. Franny's sweet on the gardener, ma'am, so I said I'd do her stint so she could go and watch him. The *head* gardener,' she added, with reflected pride.

'That's Mr Harrison?' Harriet asked.

'Yes, ma'am. He's my second cousin,' she added with more pride.

'He played very well this afternoon,' Harriet said.

The child looked as if she might burst. 'Ma'am, is it true about you?'

The hairs on my neck crept.

'A lot of things are true. Which do you have in mind?'

'That you saved Master Alexander's life and that Major Jameson swore at you for doing it?'

I froze.

Harriet didn't. 'I just caught a ball, Clara, which might have landed anywhere. And I never heard anyone swearing. Off you go, now, like a good girl.' As the door closed, she turned to me. 'He did swear and you managed to keep your temper. I am so proud of you, Matthew. So very proud.' She kissed the unbruised knuckles.

I stuck to her side as far fewer of us than before assembled in the saloon. There was a strange reaction as we entered: all the men approached us, applauding as if we were still on the field of play, but the women were silent. Mr Turton kissed her hand, and shook mine vigorously, without the need for agonizing words. Cousin Barrington stepped forward, leading, with his champagne glass, a rousing chorus of 'She's a jolly good fellow'. If he'd known this was planned, it was hardly surprising that Jameson was absent. Though he might have framed the next question himself: 'Would your wife care to make a speech, Rowsley?'

SEVEN

There was a very awkward silence, not helped by the arrival of Major Jameson, vivid in his mess dress. Matthew filled it. 'I think you should ask her, not me.' I curtsied. I could think of a hundred things I would like to say, but none I could immediately articulate. Perhaps they would interpret my flush of annoyance as genteel modesty.

It seemed they did.

The braying voices rose again. Clearly Major Jameson was making a very vehement point, jabbing first one man then another in the chest. Matthew gripped my arm painfully hard. Then Lady Pidgeon joined us, taking my free hand.

'If I told them how kind you and your good and beautiful husband were to me they would raise the rafters all over again. I fancy you would not enjoy it, my dears. But it shall be made known. Discreetly.' She gave a firm nod. 'You are a strong woman, my dear, whatever the Major might say and do. And you are a good man, Mr Rowsley. Remember that.'

Her attention was claimed by her scowling husband before either of us could ask her what she might mean. I looked round for my patron of the previous evening, but there was no sign of her yet. But with Lady Hortensia's comments about bad form still in my memory, I did not feel able to ask where she might be.

Probably no guest but me could even have imagined the efforts it took the downstairs staff to present us with our dinner – let alone to make us presentable enough to sit down to eat it. The table had been contracted, of course, which, since it was probably laid before lunch, was no mean task. The seating must have been re-allocated, but now it seemed that one of the remaining house guests was not going to appear – Gräfin Weiser. In an undervoice Lady Hortensia was having a frantic conversation with her grim butler.

Tonight I was spared poor deaf Mr Digby, who should clearly

have been squiring Gräfin Weiser. Since his partner was in animated conversation with the gentleman the other side, he was left in solitary silence. Perhaps he preferred it. On either side of me were amiable young cricketing men, Mr Forsyth, his lanky frame topped with an open face and a mop of dark curls, and Lord Webbe, slightly shorter, with blond hair carefully smoothed down. Neither had troubled the scorer. After gently quelling their enthusiasm for my catch, and regretting it had helped cause the match to be abandoned, etiquette dictated I must talk with either one or the other. But they happily threw etiquette to the four winds.

'Did you ever see anything like it, ma'am?' asked Mr Forsyth.

Lord Webbe couldn't wait for my answer. 'Did you ever see such strange captaincy? The Major simply assumed he was in charge. Yes, it was he who was the real captain, believe me.'

'I fear you're right,' I said. 'What did the other players say?'

'A lot of words we wouldn't wish you to hear, ma'am,' Mr Forsyth said. 'The village team were making comments about closed carriages and the lunatic asylum.'

'Some of them,' Lord Webbe said. 'Some were just cockahoop. But they were angry about Harrison being recruited and then not given a chance to shine. Until he and Mr Rowsley got together, that is. Dreadful way to treat a chappie. Bet he wasn't even given a choice about playing for the house team.'

'I doubt if he was,' I agreed sadly.

'And the house umpire, Lord Pidgeon – ma'am, I do believe he was—'

I put my finger to my lips. 'Even if he can't hear you others might.'

'Lord, yes. Thank you, ma'am.' He dropped his voice to a whisper. 'He looks so fit and strong, but doesn't seem all there . . . which is why I thought . . .' He stopped, with what can only be described as a meaningful shrug.

Should I have tried to stem their champagne-fuelled indiscretions? Perhaps. But I was simply enjoying their high spirits and lack of self-importance, and always made a habit of retaining facts even if I had no obvious need for them – at home my watchword, which still caused amusement amongst the staff, was

Just in case. And it seemed that the young gentlemen were as intrigued as Matthew and I were by Major Jameson's apparent wish to lose the game. Perhaps someone could ask him. Since he was seated at the far end of the table between two non-cricketing ladies with very penetrating and decidedly adoring laughs, it seemed unlikely.

As we were served with soup, Lord Webbe and Mr Forsyth – Roddy, apparently, to his close friends, which suddenly seemed to include me – continued to talk, ignoring their other partners and chattering guilelessly to me.

'The chaps at Oxford say that the Major's wealthy though no one knows quite how he made his fortune.'

'But no one seems to mind,' Roddy continued for him. 'He mixes with all the top people, of course, but my Pa, who got on well with most people, never liked him.'

'Never *trusted* him, more like,' Webbe corrected him. 'And really, ma'am, he can be the most dreadful cad. Can't he?' He turned innocent eyes not to Roddy but to me. 'I'm so sorry that you should have to hear those hurtful words, ma'am. Not the sort of thing a gentleman should ever say of a lady. Such a bang-on catch, too!'

Perhaps it was time to turn the conversation. 'When I was young, it was considered quite acceptable for women and ladies to play. My dear mama-in-law was a noted player.'

He wasn't interested in the past. 'But that was top-notch. And people are saying that you taught your husband how to bowl: I wish you could teach me the knack he has, ma'am.'

'Ask him yourself,' I laughed. I could not stop myself asking, 'Have you gentlemen ever played with – no, I beg your pardons. He would be nearer your parents' age than yours—'

'Please, ma'am!' They had such delightful smiles, like children wanting to hear the end of a fairy story.

'Once upon a time,' I began accordingly, 'at a country house not unlike this, when I was a housemaid I met a very young man who wanted to practise his batting. I was much his age, and was happy to bowl for as many hours as he needed. We've lost touch now, as one does, but I know he won his Blue at Oxford. He played for Worcestershire before following the career his parents had chosen for him. He's now a judge.'

'I wonder,' Webbe began, his young voice ringing out across a sudden silence, 'if that might be—'

But who we might never know. The very way the butler approached Cousin Barrington suggested that something was wrong. The way Cousin Barrington paled and, after the briefest word with his wife, left the room confirmed that something was very wrong. All the confident tinkle of silver on china stuttered to a subdued clatter as eating ceased. It was replaced by a murmur – was it irritation or concern I heard in the voices, or a mixture of both? At the foot of the table Lady Hortensia sat dumb-struck; perhaps she knew as little as the rest of us. But it was her job to lead: it was what she had been trained to do since childhood.

Matthew caught my eye. Heavens, he wanted me to speak to her! I shook my head minutely: let him, as her husband's cousin, offer support. But then, despite myself, I found myself working out what I might say, and then getting to my feet. Stooping, I asked softly, 'Cousin Hortensia, is something amiss? Is one of your guests unwell?'

'*Unwell?*' she repeated, loudly enough to turn a head or two. 'One of them *unwell*? Don't you understand, Mrs Faulkner, one of them is dead!'

If only her words could have been an exit line. Instead, she burst into noisy tears. I could easily have done the same. Who had gone to the trouble of discovering my maiden name, my *working* name as housekeeper before my marriage to Matthew? And why had she chosen to reveal it now, to a room full of guests? Hurt and furious in almost equal measure, I must keep my dignity. I must stop my eyes welling with tears. And somehow I must help this woman, our poor distressed hostess. My eyes sought Lady Pidgeon's: would she take care of her? It seemed she could or would not. Matthew had to take something like charge, requesting the gentlemen to escort the ladies to the drawing room and stay with them there until he had spoken to his cousin and established the facts. Any movement was very slow.

The butler hovered.

'Mr Biddlestone,' I said, 'some brandy for her ladyship. And please summon her maid to assist her.'

'Indeed, Mrs *Faulkner*,' he said loudly.

'I beg your pardon?' I dared not say more lest I lose my temper. Disciplining him was not my role. 'Do as you are told.' Ignoring my cold fury, he looked me up and down with the pace of a glacier. 'I assume you refer to her ladyship's *dresser*?'

'I said now, Biddlestone,' I rapped out. I forced myself to open my reticule, to reach for my vinaigrette. At last – my whole body insisted on shaking – I managed to waft it under her ladyship's nose till her eyes ran.

At last the brandy appeared. I took it and, kneeling, held it to Lady Hortensia's lips. I was aware that Matthew had moved closer.

'It is curious, Biddlestone,' he said in a voice intended to carry, 'that my wife can recall your name perfectly well but that you are unable to remember hers. I know of many establishments where such a failing would result in dismissal. I am sure that you do too. You may go.' He helped me to my feet. Without waiting till the room was empty, he said, still very clearly, 'My dear wife, I am sorry I have exposed you to this petty insolence. I expected better. We would leave now, but I fear the house is enisled.'

At last able to leave Lady Hortensia with her maid – her *dresser* – we left the room together. He tightened his grip on my hand as if to quell the trembling. 'Shall we go straight to our bed chamber?'

I shook my head. 'We join the other guests and learn the news.'

'Are you sure?'

'I am your wife, Matthew, and that if nothing else should see me treated with respect. And remember, the more you run from bullies, the more they run after you.' I managed a smile, wavering, perhaps, but a smile. But suddenly I recalled the empty place at the table. 'Dear God, you cannot suppose it is the Gräfin? She was not in her place, was she? Oh, Matthew, in her way she was so kind to me.'

He kissed me. 'Are still sure you want to do this?'

'I have to learn one way or the other, do I not?'

The word rang out: 'Murdered.'

Amid the screams and swoons, I could still only repeat in horror, 'The Gräfin? Surely not!'

'Murdered in her bed chamber,' Cousin Barrington confirmed with solemn gusto.

I joined in the horrified chorus – disbelief, anger, and a desire to do something, anything, to bring her killer to justice. Yes, we wanted action – some of the men seemed to want to charge off and do – what? Instead they had to apply fans and smelling salts to their wives.

But Cousin Barrington was speaking again. 'Don't worry, ladies. You're all perfectly safe now. We've locked her killer in the cellar. She can't escape.'

'She?' I heard myself ask.

'Her maid.'

'Her maid?' Matthew echoed, disbelief dripping from his voice. 'Not Clara?'

'Yes, they caught her literally red-handed.'

Much as I wanted to mourn the dead, there was still a living child to think of. Though others might have preferred me to be silent, I asked quietly, 'Is your cellar prone to flooding?'

'It would serve her right if it was,' someone said.

'And full of rats,' added another.

'Actually, Colonel, old boy,' Lord Webbe chipped in, 'I don't think that's quite cricket, you know. No police, you know. No trial. No verdict.'

Roddy Forsyth added his voice. 'Quite right. Detain her by all means, but in a decent place. Dry and rodent-free and all that.'

Mr Turton nodded vigorously. I longed to support him, but my courage failed in the face of the ladies' vehement opposition to even temporary clemency. 'She could kill us in our beds!' was the common theme.

Matthew caught my eye, and declared, 'Clara would find it hard to kill even a fly. And Mr Forsyth has not suggested letting her roam free. If only we could send for your local Justice of the Peace.'

Cousin Barrington bridled. 'I am the Justice of the Peace! And it was I who authorized her incarceration.'

Webbe persisted. 'I believe it is wrong. Don't you, Mrs Rowsley?'

For once I was silenced. Utterly. So I nodded solemnly.

'Of course she would support a fellow-servant,' a female voice declared.

'A servant?' Webbe squeaked. 'Mrs Rowsley is a close friend of Lord Halesowen, the High Court judge! One of his most trusted advisers when they were young.'

EIGHT

The silence that greeted this announcement was gratifyingly profound. But I had an idea that Harriet was as shocked by it as the rest of the room. How would she, such a stickler for the truth even if it hurt her, respond?

'That is all beside the point here, is it not?' she said, nonetheless smiling kindly at her youthful would-be rescuer. 'Dreadful, appalling though it is that the Gräfin is dead, surely we can all agree that a child of perhaps twelve should not be locked in damp darkness. As and when – *if* and when – her guilt is proved, let her take her punishment. But we are too civilized, are we not, as part of a proud nation and a proud empire, to rush to judgement.' She looked directly at Mr Digby, speaking very clearly. Yes, she was appealing to his Indian administrative background, with its emphasis, albeit probably notional, on fair play.

While he huffed and puffed his agreement, I was praying for guidance: how might I summon my barrister Cousin Mark?

Answer came there none. Not yet, at least. So my next silent prayer was for guidance for myself and what I must do.

I turned to the butler. 'Biddlestone, shall we step outside a moment?'

He might look mutinous, but really had no option but to obey when Barrington limped out with me.

I faced him. 'Would the housekeeper have a small but dry room where Clara might be confined?'

'Mrs Simpkiss, sir?'

How dared he be so supercilious at such a time? I replied with what I hoped was palpable restraint. 'If Mrs Simpkiss is the housekeeper, yes, of course Mrs Simpkiss!' He actually stepped back a pace in the face of my anger. 'Perhaps you might have the goodness to enquire. Then let us know where it is, so that a small group of us might escort Clara there and ensure that she does not escape.' I feared that I might become even more sarcastic if I spoke longer. 'Thank you.'

Biddlestone shot a glance at his employer before bowing and setting off, albeit at a profoundly irritating snail's pace.

'Jump to it, man!' Barrington snapped.

The room was silent as we returned – clearly the aristocratic ears had strained to listen. But then a barrage of questions was fired.

Smiling at Harriet, who looked so tense that I feared she might snap, I stepped back to let Barrington take charge, which he did, with surprisingly easy authority. 'Ladies and gentlemen, before I say anything further, I would ask you to stand in silence for a moment to honour our late guest.'

There was an almost startling rustle of silk as he was obeyed.

'Thank you. May I suggest that you return to the dining room? I believe the cook has kept back our dinner. I will give you further orders – I beg your pardon, further *information* – when I can.'

Harriet and I let the exodus surge past us as I stepped forward, her hand in mine, to speak to our host. 'My dear wife and I have some experience in what you might call amateur police work, Barrington. May I suggest that we offer our services in the investigation you will no doubt wish to conduct before the floods allow us to summon the constabulary?'

'You never said you knew Augustus Halesowen,' he said to her.

She curtsied. 'Does anyone boast of their friends?' she countered. 'I could wish that Lord Webbe had not mentioned it. But this is not important now.' I felt her take a deep breath, the sort she always took when she was about to embark on an unpleasant task. She would rather run home, but she would stay and do what I – without consulting her! – had made her duty. 'Cousin, if Matthew and I are to try to discover anything, we should start now.'

'But your dinner!'

'I am sure your cook might keep us a little food for later.' As he havered, she continued, 'We ought not to waste any more time, Cousin Barrington, ought we? It behoves us to look at the scene of this terrible crime before anyone can change it.'

He stared. 'My dear Cousin Harriet! You? A lady? There may be blood.'

If only someone could have photographed her expression. Had he not declared that Clara had been caught literally red-handed? But she said nothing except, 'I think we ought, all three of us. If you feel able to, Cousin? Once you are satisfied with Clara's new cell?' she added cleverly.

'I suppose we could go and inspect that en route.'

Perhaps Harriet had not been so clever after all. Much as I wanted to run to the murder scene, to stop anyone accidentally or deliberately interfering with it, I had to fall into step with Barrington. Progress with my cousin was a slow affair. He clearly had no idea where Clara might have been housed – and why should he consider it necessary to know the below-stairs geography? Other men might, but so long as his or Lady Hortensia's orders were obeyed and their comfort maintained, he would have no need to enquire further.

The kitchens and other rooms used by the servants were reached by a long corridor with windows well above the height at which a man as tall as I could have seen out. In fact, it was almost a tunnel; it was clear from the wet flagstones that part at least was below ground level. There being no natural light, it was lit by oil-lamps. Presumably we were now in the much older part of the house. Even on a dry day it would not have been pleasant, convenient though it must have been for those serving meals, as it took the quickest route from the kitchens to the dining room. After the torrential rain, water was seeping through in many places. Buckets caught the worst drips, and rags others.

Once we emerged in the kitchen all was modern: Bea would have approved of it. The servants' hall was spacious enough, but again all the windows were set so high that though light entered, no one could look out. From the hall ran another corridor, off which opened a number of rooms – presumably the butler's and the housekeeper's, and probably the cook's as well. Where there were cooks and housekeepers, there would be still rooms and dry pantries.

We found the accused cowering in a linen cupboard near the butler's pantry. Other maids were still silently and impassively removing towels and sheets. A footman was fashioning shelves into a pallet bed. Another brought a bucket. At Harriet's suggestion, he removed it and produced a less threatening chamber pot. The best one could say was that the room was big enough and was dry. But the child was so deep in tears that she probably had no idea where she was or what indeed was happening. Where was their equivalent of Harriet to supervise and indeed to explain and reassure? I could sense Harriet controlling herself: she would want to take Clara's hands, both to comfort her and perhaps to see if there was any incriminating substance under or around her nails. I caught her eye: why not? Perhaps she baulked at the idea of hugging someone accused of killing the nearest thing she had to a friend here, but she did take those hands in one of her own, pushing back the child's hair as she did so. Whatever words she said were not meant for anyone else's ears. And she did not remark aloud on anything she might have seen.

At last we saw her provided with food – if a lump of bread may be so described – and water before she was locked in. Biddlestone took charge of the key, ready to attach it to his fob. Perhaps he did not trust that the still absent Mrs Simpkiss's heart was hard enough to keep one of her team thus incarcerated. Or, more probably given his appalling behaviour to Harriet, he simply enjoyed power.

Barrington surprised me. 'I'll take that,' he declared, holding out his hand.

I would not have been as slow in obeying him as Biddlestone was. What a strange household, when both friend and butler could so undercut the master's authority.

Barrington stared at the key as we made our way back to the main part of the house, and on up stairs that clearly challenged him. It was there that we found the white-lipped housekeeper, a tall, big-boned woman, her face quite gaunt, in the Gräfin's bed chamber. She was apparently directing a team of maids to clean it, even though a sheet-shrouded shape still lay on the bed. Perhaps I spoke more sharply than I should have done – heavens, now we might never know where she had actually been killed! Surely she had not lain tidily on the bed and waited for death? At least all the frantic activity ceased. The servants curtsied their way out, one of them picking up the wastepaper basket as she went. Almost absently I relieved her of it, mouthing to Harriet, 'Just in case.'

Barrington discovered he was still holding the linen cupboard key. 'Mrs Simpkiss,' he said gruffly. 'That little girl. See she's treated well enough, eh?' He passed her the key. 'And if that door has to be unlocked, as it may, you are the one to do it. No one else. Understand?'

She gave a bemused curtsy. 'Indeed, sir. Thank you, sir.' Did her voice quaver? Perhaps I imagined it.

I closed the door behind her with gentle firmness.

The three of us stood in silence.

'May I?' Harriet asked at last, not waiting for an answer as with gentle reverence she eased the sheet from the sharp profile. She stepped back, head bowed; we joined her in silent prayer – prayer for a woman who had been strangled to death.

She pulled the sheet back further. The Gräfin had not dressed for dinner or, of course, donned her jewels. There were bruises on the mottled arms. Someone had at least closed her eyes with bright new pennies.

Harriet delicately replaced the hand she was holding on the victim's chest and solemnly covered her again. 'She's not been dead long – her body is only just beginning to cool.' She walked to the far side of the room, to the dressing table and double wardrobe.

Barrington stared at me, open mouthed. 'How does a lady know things like this?' he demanded in a stage whisper.

'One of our closest friends is the village doctor, who treats not just villagers but also patients in the Family wing of Thorncroft House. Harriet absorbs information as a blotter absorbs ink. One of Shakespeare's heroines tells us that though she is small she is very fierce. My beloved Harriet may be small but she has one of the finest brains I have ever come across, not excluding during my university days.'

'A blue-stocking!' he gasped, truly disconcerted.

'Hardly. She's a very practical woman.' I followed her movements with my eyes. 'What is it, Harriet?

'It's something that isn't, rather than something that is. Cousin

Barrington, do guests like the Gräfin keep their jewels in your house safe?'

He stepped back as if affronted. 'Why should they? We trust our servants.'

She ignored the slight as if she had not heard it. 'I can't see her jewellery case, and she must have had one.' She looked around. 'Heavens, if only I had brought paper and a pencil: I ought to list the things we need to think about.'

He pointed at the desk in the window, and the elegant little rack containing all a letter-writer could need. Some writing paper lay ready on the blotter.

She swallowed something she was about to say. 'I could not feel at ease using hers . . .' Her voice broke.

His chivalry awakened, he hobbled to the bell, only to find the embroidered pull lying on the carpet. Had the Gräfin tried to ring for help only to have the means torn from her grasp? Something else for Harriet to write down. He did the obvious thing. Throwing open the door, he yelled down the corridor for what she needed. 'Bring candles too,' he added, for though the clouds had cleared completely – there was a vivid orange and green sunset – night was drawing in apace.

I joined her at the window while we waited. As far as the eye could see there was water, golden and innocent. I shivered. What if the village cricketers and their supporters had not crossed the bridge in time?

But here was a footman, averting his gaze from the bed, and covering his mouth with his hand as he bolted, not waiting for Harriet's thanks.

She jotted briefly. 'Cousin Barrington, on the battlefield you must have seen things that went wrong. One look and you'd assess the problem. Can you help us?'

'My dear lady, this is hardly a battle scene.'

'Indeed. But someone has been killed. Might I ask you to look round as dispassionately as you must have had to do in the army and see anything at all that is not right – that grates with you, shall we say?'

'Like the fact that the jewels have gone AWOL?'

'Exactly.'

He limped about the room, eyes purposefully narrowed. At

last he shook his head. 'Shame the maids have already been busy in here. Wonder whose idea that was. No shoes lying anywhere. Nothing like that.' He frowned. 'Is the good lady still wearing them?'

It was my turn to lift the sheet. Her feet were bare but for her stockings.

To my surprise he touched them. 'Feel damp to you?'

He probably spoke to me but Harriet responded. 'Yes. And the hem of her dress too, Cousin.'

'She said she wasn't going to the cricket so why should she get wet?'

'She took a stroll, perhaps. But where might her shoes be?'

There was, we agreed, after a thorough search, no sign of them.

Harriet said, 'One hopes it was the maids who took them away – and can locate them now. If they are found, that might help us.' Her cool demeanour suddenly collapsed. 'Cousin, who might want her dead?' It was almost a wail.

He nodded, as if realizing that a junior officer was not yet battle-hardened. 'Cousin Harriet, I believe we could discuss this in the comfort of my study. My first thought now is that I should send the servants to search for her shoes, then lock and place a guard on this room. Two men. Two more to patrol the corridors. And someone can bring us all brandy.'

Anguish choking her voice, Harriet said, 'Forgive me, Cousin Barrington, but may we delay that for a few moments? It is a warm night. The body . . .'

'Goodness me, yes. We need a stretcher party, do we not? There must be somewhere cold in this damned great pile.'

I asked quietly. 'Where do you store your white wine, Barrington?'

He blinked. 'Will the wine cellar be cold enough?'

'One hopes so. Presumably no one could reach your ice-house, wherever it is. Somehow we must be able to summon a doctor to examine her tomorrow! I suppose you don't have a guest who is a photographer? To record . . . the details?'

'Heavens! Dash it all, man – that's a bit crude, isn't it?'

'But a court might find it useful evidence,' I said, trying to sound both understanding and firm. 'Or, in the absence of a photographer, an artist.'

'Dear God, you're not expecting a lady to soil her delicate eyes with such a subject!'

'Perhaps there is a gentleman with the skills,' Harriet said dryly.

We followed in silence as the Gräfin's corpse was conveyed to the wine cellar, which Biddlestone could not resist locking with a flourish. But as before my cousin held out his hand for the key, attaching it to his own fob. 'And I want two men on guard here, and two more outside the poor lady's room. And, Biddlestone, one more thing: I want her shoes found and brought to me before anyone goes to bed. Understand?'

It was overwhelmingly apparent that the library was not the only place where cigars were smoked. The study might have been used to cure kippers, the smell of tobacco was so rank. It must have seeped into the dark, heavy furniture, the thick curtains of some miserable indeterminate colour, the blackened floorboards and once bright Persian carpet. Moreover, there were only two chairs. I might have been tempted to dismiss my cousin as a fool, but now I was changing my mind. He took in the situation quickly.

'Too hot in here,' he said gruffly. 'Stuffy. Mason!'

A footman materialized, tall and well set-up.

'Which is the coolest room? Comfortable, too, mind. And a table.'

'Might I suggest her ladyship's sewing room, sir?'

'Of course. East-facing. Excellent. Brandy there, Mason.' Chewing his index finger, he stared at Harriet, eyebrows raised.

Harriet said quietly, 'Cousin, I find I think better with Madeira. Could that be arranged? Thank you.' She smiled at him and at Mason, who bowed as we passed.

The sewing room was the sort of place I might imagine Harriet choosing, should she ever evince a desire to wield a needle for pleasure: recently painted and with delicate curtains, it was light and uncluttered. Since it still had its restrained Georgian furniture, there was more than room for the extra chair Mason brought unprompted.

The young man bowed and withdrew.

Harriet jotted until he had returned with the decanters and

glasses, which he filled and passed to us with a respectful bow. A scratch at the door had him opening it and taking a tray. Cook had provided delicate sandwiches, bite-sized cakes and a board of cheese and biscuits. Having served us, Mason backed out, closing the door quietly but not fully behind him. Equally quietly, I made sure it was shut.

Sinking an almost desperate gulp, eventually Barrington spoke. 'I just cannot understand it. How could a tiny little thing like Clarrie or whatever her name is throttle someone as tall as the Gräfin? Have the strength?' He touched a scar on his face as if it suddenly hurt. 'Cousin Harriet, I owe you an apology. I think that cellar business was an error.' He looked at her under his eyebrows. 'And that linen cupboard?'

'Is it still guarded? Well, it may help to save her from the actual killer, may it not? But, if you please, Cousin, let someone give her comfort. Not just bread and water. Some tempting food.' She touched her plate. 'And – some maids that age still have a favourite toy they still cherish. A doll, perhaps. Let her have that. Kindness. Gentleness. Then she may feel able to talk to us about what she has seen.' Harriet's eyes filled. She was remembering her own miserable childhood, wasn't she? Yet her voice was firm as she said, 'You know everyone here, Cousin. Amongst your guests and staff, who would want to kill the Gräfin? And who is tall enough to seize the poor lady's throat and strong enough to hold it till she was dead?'

Barrington gaped. 'Someone I know? Dash it, Cousin, it must have been a burglar or someone. Someone after her bally jewels. Ah! You asked me about those, didn't you?' He rang.

Mason appeared. He shook his be-wigged head in response to his employer's question. 'Why should guests need to lock stuff away, sir? It's as safe as houses here.' His face changed so quickly the effect might in other circumstances have been funny. 'Beg pardon, sir. I wasn't thinking.'

'Well, think now. First, have the poor lady's shoes been located?'

'Alas, no, sir, not in any of the public areas. But the maids and spare footmen are looking in the guests' rooms while they linger over dinner.'

'Excellent. Tell Cook to make sure they have to linger as long as possible – I don't want anyone opening their bed chamber door to find it's being ransacked.'

'Sir.' The young man bowed, ready to leave.

'Just one more thing. You're a bright enough young fellow. Tell me, apart from Cassie or whatever her name is, who could have gone into the Gräfin's room and killed her and stolen her jewels?'

'We were all at the cricket, sir. Well, most of us.'

'Clara?' Harriet asked casually, as though she hadn't told us that she was working in the kitchen.

Mason frowned. 'I don't think she could have been, ma'am. She offered to help Cook, and Mrs Dabbs isn't the sort to let anyone slack. And then it rained, and everyone who was dry had to help with everyone who was wet. Like Lady Pidgeon,' he added, with a glimpse of a smile at us.

'Of course! It was you who carried her indoors! Thank you so much.'

Harriet's smile made him blush. I added to his embarrassment by lamenting that a lad with shoulders like his was not a cricketer.

He simply stared at his feet. I was sure Harriet would notice and speak to him later about it.

Meanwhile she spoke of something else. 'Cousin Barrington has very kindly said that Clara should be offered some comfort.' She reeled off the items she had suggested before. 'Could you ask Mrs Simpkiss to see to it? Thank you.'

He nodded. 'Of course, ma'am. Thank you, ma'am, sir.' After a moment, he added, 'Sir, there is a lot of . . . talk . . . amongst the servants. About who did it. And some won't go up to the dormitories because they're afraid of being murdered in their beds.'

Barrington huffed as if to dismiss such nonsense. But he shot a look at me.

I said, 'Two things, Mason: keep your ears open all the time. If anyone – anyone, mind – says anything that *disconcerts* you, shall we say, remember it and report it to your master. Or to me or Mrs Rowsley if he is unavailable. But don't encourage gossip for its own sake. As to being murdered in their beds, I have an idea that the poor Gräfin was killed for a specific reason, and that as good loyal servants they should not be targets for her killer.'

'Do you think he's still in the building, sir?'

We all looked out of the window. The sky was clear enough now for us to see the stars, the light of which glittered on the soaked landscape. Would I have ventured out? I thought not, but then, I had no reason to try to escape. If I had, I might have been happy to risk wading through water, even though I could not have known what lay beneath – even how deep it might suddenly become.

Harriet could still surprise me. 'What would you have done, Mason? Stayed here or tried to escape?'

He pulled a face. 'There's all the fallen trees, the hahas – and no moon, of course. No one would be out and about to rescue you, would they? But no one would see you, anyway.' He rocked his hand. 'A bit of a gamble, and I wouldn't like the odds.'

NINE

I sipped my Madeira very sparingly, needing my head to stay clear – clear, when the very thought of what had happened still made me shake so hard my teeth rattled against the glass.

Almost certainly Matthew had been rash in suggesting we might investigate the Gräfin's death. I had certainly been shocked at the time. After all, we had no real authority – any I might have had had been efficiently undercut by our hostess and her butler. But now I accepted that no one else in the house, not even our host, had had any idea what might and might not be appropriate in such circumstances. At very least young Clara was no longer incarcerated in the cellar she must have thought was a dungeon.

Mason had slipped out, again leaving the door slightly ajar. I could understand his desire for illicit information – it was a habit that one or two of my own colleagues found hard to break – but surely this was not a time for rumour to do its sometimes useful job. Would Cousin Barrington be offended if I got up and shut it myself?

But Matthew was already doing it, for the second time; we exchanged a smile as he sat down. Cousin Barrington, who by now appeared thoroughly exhausted and in a great deal of pain, looked almost helplessly from one of us to the other. I sensed I dare not offer anything resembling sympathy. But a silence was growing.

'Mason was right, was he not? Venturing out tonight would be very dangerous indeed,' I observed quietly.

'By Jove, yes. I can't imagine anyone wanting to, but you never know – servants and sweethearts and such. Can't have them risking it tonight. I'll tell Biddlestone to bar all the doors. And,' he added, 'in the circumstances, if anyone wants to come in, I'll get the night staff to record their name. You never know – they might have seen something out there. Seen someone. That sort of thing.'

'What a good idea,' Matthew said. 'We can question them in the morning. It grieves me to say this, Cousin, but I must. You will have to question everyone. With no exceptions. I suggest Harriet speaks to Clara individually, since she acted briefly as Harriet's maid. But somehow you have to deal with servants and guests alike. It will be a mammoth task, and will be pleasant for none of us.'

I pulled a face. 'Since we do not know exactly what time the poor lady died, it may also be necessary for you to speak to the guests who fled in the face of the storm – as and when we can reach them. Oh, dear . . .' I straightened my shoulders. 'Oh, with luck, by that time the local constabulary will surely have taken over the investigation and we will no longer be involved in such . . . intrusive . . . work.'

Cousin Barrington gawped. 'My dear Cousin Harriet, you cannot – Matthew cannot – be suggesting that I involve myself in that! I'm their host! Their friend, in some cases.' His face was a study as he realized that as the local Justice he was now absolutely required to do far more than dispense impartial punishments. He saw a way out. 'You two – you volunteered, Matthew!'

'Sadly, however much we want to assist you, we do not have any legal authority and you may have observed at dinner that not everyone behaves to Harriet with common decency. I dread to think how they would speak unless she had your authority as a representative of the law.'

'Ah. That name business. Deliberate, you think?' He tugged his moustache, looking at me as if I might exonerate the butler.

I might. But it would be harder to forgive his wife. I tried to keep my voice neutral. 'Servants are just as sensitive to rank and breaches in the social code as members of polite society, I fear.'

'Bad business. Very bad business. I'll have a word with him, a strong word, when I give him his orders about locking up. Would you want to be present, to hear his apology?'

'I'm sure his behaviour tomorrow will speak louder than any words ground out under duress. Pray forgive me, Cousin, if I retire to our bed chamber.'

He looked first at his watch then at the elegant little clock on the mantelpiece. 'Good lord, all those people still in the dining room! At least I hope they are. How could I have forgotten? What shall I do with them?' At first clearly distressed and embarrassed, he managed to produce a smile both cunning and amused. 'Tell you what: you're tired, I'm tired. Even Mason out there is tired. Let's assume they'll all be tired too. I'll order them off to bed and tell them to lock their doors. How about that for an idea? Excellent. Now, if anyone is troublesome, tell them you are acting on my orders. And if you want permission to do anything, all you have to do is ask me. Yes, ask me first. I always told my troops they could do anything so long as it wasn't stupid and as long as they'd asked me first. Understood?'

'I hope you will find it in you to forgive me,' Matthew said the moment he closed the door behind us.

'For what? For bringing us here in the first place or involving us in an investigation for which we are entirely unsuited? Oh, I know we've helped our lovely constable and his sergeant at home, but I know every square inch of the place, and all the staff too. Not like here!' I found myself laughing. Dear me, I must not turn into a hysterical female. For everyone's sake. I found it turned into an expression of genuine, if dark, amusement.

Head in his hands, he sank on to the bed. 'I'm sorry for both!'

I sat beside him, holding out my hand, which he took and clasped as if it was a lifeline. 'I did not expect the first real snub to come from our hostess. Such a vicious one, too. And one that give licence to everyone else in the house to repeat it. That dreadful butler . . . But now we are here, and now we cannot go home, then I promise you I will find it easier to hunt for a killer than to sit awaiting the next drawling insult.' The thought put steel in my spine. 'There are in fact two matters to investigate, are there not? The poor Gräfin's death and, less important but still intriguing, why your cousin deliberately lost the match.'

'Was it Barrington or Jameson? For all that he just said about his being in charge, everyone seems to agree with my view that my cousin was captain in name only, that Jameson made all the decisions.'

'Especially the highly questionable ones. What a loathsome

man. Two in one house! I would say this to no one but you, but had he been murdered I could name six or seven suspects, myself included.'

'And me! I do not know, I really do not, how I did not break his nose or his jaw or both.'

'But you didn't. And I am so proud of you. But, my love, you will have to probe carefully but very deeply when you talk to your cousin tomorrow.'

His anguish was replaced by a cunning smile. 'Me talk to him! He is very taken with you and would surely reveal more than he would to me – especially if you feign complete ignorance of cricket.'

'As John Coachman says when he thinks I'm not listening, *That cock won't fight!* My love of the game is known – Lord Webbe has already asked me to teach him to bowl. I referred him to you, naturally.'

'Ah! Webbe. The tactful Webbe who revealed something even I did not know. More hair than wit, as the Bard would say.' He looked at me quizzically.

'If I did not know it, I would be surprised if you did,' I retorted. I could not stop a smile at the thought that the young man to whom I had spent hours bowling remembered me. Though I never imagined that now Gussie was Lord Halesowen, the High Court judge, he might consider me anything other than a helpful servant.

' "One of his most trusted advisers when they were young",' he said, kissing my hand. 'I am honoured that you are my most trusted adviser in my middle years. And will be as long as we live.' Suddenly his face changed. 'Unless young Webbe tells Lord Halesowen where you are and he turns up to claim you!'

It took me a moment to realize that he was serious. 'On a white charger, I hope! I would accept nothing less! Let us hope that his name-dropping will make tomorrow's task easier.' I got up to wash my face before the water in the ewer went cold. It could not, because there was no water. No soap, no towels and no chamber pot. Since the house had no running water and consequently no water closets, if we did not ring for a servant, we would have to trek down the puddled path to the privy at the far end of the garden. 'Matthew, are those sheets aired?'

He grimaced. 'I fancy they are the ones we used to dry ourselves earlier.'

'In that case you might be about to see me lose my temper.' I rang the bell.

There would have been something particularly satisfying in requiring Mr Biddlestone personally to make good the omissions of his now sleeping juniors. In the event, of course, he roused Mrs Simpkiss, who brought with her two weary housemaids. All were in their nightclothes, and all oozed resentment. The two youngsters received generous tips. I was tempted to let Mrs Simpkiss content herself with the sort of bow I once practised on tradesmen trying to cheat the household. Suddenly, however, I recalled – from my own experiences – that it is often poor mistresses that make servants unhappy and bitter. So as she left I followed her into the corridor.

'Goodness knows how you achieved all you did today,' I said, taking a big risk. 'Of course some things go wrong – but few people know the effort it takes to get most things right.'

She nodded. 'You're right there. I don't know how . . .' She shook her head, almost in tears. 'It was almost as if—' She stopped abruptly. 'No. I'm imagining things. It's my habit to check every room. But today . . . And of course Clara should have—' She sniffed. 'But who would . . .? I will enquire, Mrs – er—' She blushed.

'Mrs *Rowsley*,' I supplied clearly. 'Let us worry about this tomorrow, Mrs Simpkiss. Perhaps you and I might drink a cup of tea together when you have a moment to spare. I usually find some time between ten and eleven is quietest, but of course tomorrow is the Sabbath, with all the complications that brings to a household's timetable.'

She snorted. 'With compulsory church twice a day on top. And the floods! I don't know whether I'm on my head or my heels, ma'am, and that's God's truth.'

'And here am I keeping you from your bed. Good night and God bless you.'

We exchanged a smile, perhaps wary on her part, before I returned to our room, closing the door softly behind me. I found myself stepping straight into Matthew's arms.

'You did well there, my love. It sounded as if you won her over.'

'I'm not sure. One smile does not an ally make.'

Despite his apparent confidence, Matthew was already seated at the dressing table when I awoke next morning. Although the peacock had been mercifully silent – perhaps the rain had rendered his grand tail unusable – neither of us had slept well, but I had clearly done better than he. Swathing myself in my dressing-gown – who knew what time our hot water might arrive – I threw open the curtains, to reveal a still partly water-logged landscape. The sun shone encouragingly – but at home the Thorncroft gardeners would have sucked their teeth claiming it was too bright too early, and that those tiny puffs on the horizon might grow into storm clouds. I had a suspicion that the quiet of the still silent house might similarly metamorphose. Moving away from the window I looked over Matthew's shoulder. Like me, he liked to try to marshal his thoughts using headed notes, augmented by a set of asterisks and arrows.

'Where do I start?' he demanded.

'Is that a real question or a rhetorical one?' I kissed the top of his head. 'If you really don't know where to start, I'd have Cousin Barrington roused early so we can have what he might call a council of war. He's spent his life organizing people. He wants to be in charge so let him really be in charge of the hows and whens, even if we have to supply the whys. He alone has the authority to confine his guests and servants – we really do have none at all here, even if he gives us permission to do something. Let me see – it's six-thirty. The staff are on duty already. Let us ring for our hot water and send a message to him.'

TEN

'This is something like!' Barrington declared, rubbing his hands with apparent pleasure as he took his place in the sun-filled sewing room, the clock I could see that Harriet admired telling us it was seven minutes past seven. 'It's good to have people working with me who understand the importance of time. Now, I've already placed an embargo on all staff comings and goings.'

'What about food coming in, sir? Your cook will be expecting deliveries of milk and eggs from your home farm if the floods have dropped enough. Though I am sure Mrs Simpkiss will have stores to last for several days. That is the usual practice in great houses.'

He looked bemused. 'Ah. A good point, Cousin Harriet. All the same I need to keep the commissariat happy, don't I? But not have people thinking they can escape that way. Church? If we can't go to church, then I'll send for the rector to come and do his padre stuff here.' He paused. 'Assuming he can get through, of course. Tell you what, I'll get that gardener chappie to organize a recce. Bright young man.'

I inhaled sharply. We both knew that Mr Harrison was disaffected, to say the least, and that he would resent being given a task he'd think was more suited to a pack of stable lads. 'I'll undertake the task of briefing him, shall I?' I jotted it down before Barrington could argue.

'I have made the acquaintance of Mrs Simpkiss,' Harriet said. 'I know she and her team will be frantically busy now, but I will suggest she keeps everyone behind after servants' breakfast, when I can speak to them, if you think I dare leave it till then?'

'Hmm. The maids are already about their work, of course. What if anyone tries to smuggle anything incriminatory out with the waste?' I asked. I answered myself: 'Human waste and slop buckets apart, you might despatch an immediate order that the waste baskets must be left unemptied?'

'Good thinking. I'll get a note to Mrs Simpkins immediately.'
I dared not catch Harriet's eye.

Barrington jotted and rang.

Mason appeared as swiftly as if he had had been at his post all night, depositing three black armbands on the table before leaving with equal speed.

Hitherto Cousin Barrington had been all happy bustle. Now, however, he had a nasty fact to face. 'It's not just servants we need to worry about, is it? All these visitors, Matthew. Guests. I'm going to have to break it to them that they're confined to barracks all day, you know. They're not going to like it.'

'The weather may assist us here; clouds are building already. And of course there is the giant moat surrounding us.'

There was a gentle tap at the door. 'Cook was wondering, sir, if you might care for a pot of coffee and some drop scones. She didn't think her ladyship would like the smell of kippers in here, sir.' Mason did not risk a smile.

'Quite right too. And we can always join the others later.' My cousin's face fell. 'Her ladyship prefers guests to drop in for breakfast as and when they please, and I could really do with speaking to them en masse, the earlier the better.'

'If you wished, sir, the other footmen and I could visit each room and ask them to gather together at – shall I say nine?' It was an eye-wateringly early time for a Sunday. Did I detect a smidgin of enjoyable revenge? 'I will warn Cook to have everything ready for then.'

'Good man. Nine it is. And you might drop a hint that we don't want people to come dawdling in late. A strong hint.' He nodded home the point. As Mason withdrew, however, it was as if he lost his focus. 'What do I do then? *We*,' he corrected himself quickly.

'I fancy that if the police were here, they would question everyone and take statements from them. But that will take time.' I paused. 'Your guests are going to have plenty of that to spare, of course. Might you ask them to write down an account of everything they did yesterday, up to and including the news of the Gräfin's death? Not just what they did, but where they were and who they met – people they nodded at in passing, as well as those they had a conversation with. It would be very helpful if your wife could provide a list of your guests' names and rooms, so we know if we've missed anyone.'

'What about getting them to make a timetable too? Easier for us to read,' Barrington said. 'Because all they say will have to be double-checked, won't it? Cross-referenced.' He smiled. 'Good job we've got three good pairs of eyes.' He paused while Mason served our early breakfast, which included far more than griddle cakes, and left, nodding at me as the young man left, added, 'As I said, I didn't like the way Biddlestone behaved to you last night, m'dear. And I like bringing on a decent young man. At least I hope he is. What if he's our killer? Dear God, anyone in the building might be. Or someone out there!' He pointed wildly to the window, his arm shaking.

Harriet, at his side with a cup of coffee, asked with a calm that was almost bathetic, 'Do you take sugar, Cousin?'

It took long moments for whatever he relived to disappear and let him return to polite normality. Then he was gesturing us to sit down and reaching for a pencil and pad. 'Always a bad time before the first skirmishes in a battle,' he said, still breathing hard.

We ignored the tremor that made writing almost impossible for him. We tried to make eating the drop scones a matter of rumination, as if we were too busy thinking to say anything aloud. Perhaps we were. When he was ready to write, we were both ready with questions, which we asked at the same time.

Cousin Barrington nodded at Harriet. 'Ladies first.'

'Jewellery apart, can you think of any other reason why someone would kill the Gräfin? A personal motive? Or someone who would actually profit from her death, which seems . . . All I know about her, Cousin, is that she was kind to me, a complete stranger who knew no one else to talk to.'

'Really?' There was no mistaking his astonishment. 'She could be a cantankerous old biddy. Actually,' he added, dropping his voice, 'her tongue sometimes ran away with her. Not ladylike at all.'

'In that case, may I put an awkward question?' she pursued. 'Why was she a house guest? And in particular for a cricket weekend when she did not like the game?'

'Malice! That's what my wife thinks.' He tried too late to wind back the indiscretion. 'Thing is, we invited her for last weekend, when there were a lot of card-players like her, but she never left. Just stayed where she was. But she's my wife's god-mama, you know. Can't be offending her, can we?'

'Card player?'

'Whist – she's extraordinarily good. Was. Didn't suffer fools gladly, though – you soon knew if you'd played the wrong card. People feared her tongue, I can tell you.'

'Do your guests ever play for money? Or just for pleasure?'

'Wasn't much pleasure if you didn't follow her lead! Money? Pennies only, I assure you. At least that was the rule.' He frowned. 'Dear God, shouldn't be speaking ill of the dead, should I? I wonder why she liked you – no, please, don't take that the wrong way. But she had been known to reduce young ladies to tears. Between ourselves, young men too. Come, Cousin: you said she was kind to you, but what impression did you get of her over all?'

If she had been a man, she might have tugged her moustache while she considered.

'Do you know, I wonder if she was being kind to me simply to be unkind to others? She gave me a detailed commentary on several lives, in a voice that was meant to carry. She might even have been – how can I put this – making my life worse by drawing attention to me. But I did not think either of these things at the time. I just felt grateful to have someone talking to me.' From her tiny gasp she realized – too late – that she had just made, by implication, a decided criticism of his wife.

He shot a look at her under his scarred brows. Though he opened his mouth to speak, he shut it firmly again. Reaching for another drop scone, he asked, 'I suppose she didn't suggest that you might play cards with her?'

'No. She kindly introduced me to another guest, Lady Pidgeon.'

'Interesting choice.' He stared at her but said no more.

'It transpired that we share a love of books.'

'And you and Mason said something about carrying her?'

'Matthew and I found ourselves involved in some of the rescue work.'

'And nearly made damned fools of yourselves when that lightning struck. Lady Pidgeon, now . . . did you know her husband stood as one of the umpires?'

'Is he an old friend?' I asked, almost absently.

'Bit of an old duffer, now, truth to tell, isn't he? It's a good job he didn't have to give any leg-before-wicket decisions – I think he was asleep on his feet, most of the time. All that brandy – no longer sound in the head, poor devil. But he does love to be involved. Don't know about next year, mind – as you saw, the other umpire had to remind him to call "over" and so on. Sad, very sad. But sometimes – no, he's not always the gentle doddering old soul people see.'

I nodded. 'He was very angry when the village umpire abandoned the game.'

There was an awkward silence.

'How did you recruit your team?' Harriet asked, stepping in to break it.

'Mostly neighbours. Some of Hortensia's old friends volunteered their husbands, you might say.'

'And the youngsters? Young Lord Webbe, for instance – he's quite a different generation from some of the other players.'

'Got to involve the young sooner or later: got to keep the tradition going. Important for country life. That's why I keep going, damn it. Tradition. He's my godson: I knew his father. Broke his neck on the hunting field. Young Forsyth's another godson. I'm not sure why that young man with the stammer is here – something to do with the rector, I fancy. Or another godson. Can't keep up with them all. Turpin or something. He's going into the Church, you know. Ah! I suppose I could get him to lead the service tonight. No. Perhaps not. Useless batsman too.'

'You wouldn't have the team-sheet about you?' I asked. 'So we can check we've missed no one.'

'In my study. Remind me.'

'Barrington, can you tell me anything about Mr Jameson? I beg your pardon – *Major* Jameson.'

'What about him?'

'It's just that I really know nothing about him.' Barrington did not respond to my smile. I ploughed on. 'He and I got off on the wrong foot, didn't we? I still don't know how I offended him.'

'Well, you certainly annoyed him when you took over the practice session. An officer expects subalterns to obey orders, you know.' He spoke fine words but looked decidedly shifty.

I could not let the subject go. 'And he was very . . . outspoken
. . .' I stopped. I was being pusillanimous when Harriet had been
brave. 'Let me be clearer. He was actually very rude indeed,
when Harriet took that catch. Extremely offensive.'

'That's just his way. Like me. As I said, used to giving orders,
used to having them obeyed.' By now he was clearly very uncomfortable. 'I'll have a quiet word, shall I?'

As if to head off trouble, Harriet smiled her housekeeper's
professional smile. 'This coffee is almost cold. Shall I ring for
more, Cousin Barrington?'

'Pretty well finished here, I'd have thought,' he blustered.

'So we are. Though I suppose we could use the time to start
constructing a timetable, a big one, so we can plot everyone's
movements.'

'You'll need big sheets of paper . . . Very big,' he added doubtfully. He rang.

Mason's face was a study. 'Very big sheets, sir?'

Cousin Barrington looked at me. I looked at Harriet.

'You may need glue,' she said. 'Unless any of the rooms has
been hung with wallpaper recently? Ceiling paper would be ideal
– something plain.'

'I will see what I can do, ma'am,' he said, backing out.

'One moment,' I added. 'We will need something to attach it
to, something we can prop up. Not a door, with panels. Something
flat.'

'Like a teacher's blackboard and easel, sir?'

'Exactly that, please, Mason,' Harriet said, with her most
winning grin.

ELEVEN

Clearly I would have to talk to Cousin Barrington about the Major in a very roundabout way. Feigning ignorance of the game would not work after my catch, and the voluble admiration of the kind young men. So I must come at the cricket problem obliquely, and when we were alone. And I would speak to other people – the servants since I could not imagine cross-questioning any of the guests. Not with any success, at least. I would only be exposing myself to further insults, would I not?

What had changed in me? I could once tolerate the most humiliating behaviour from house guests I was serving. Of course, I understood it was part of my job to be diplomatic, to be selectively deaf, to toady if necessary. But lately I had learned what it was to be treated as a human being, capable of feeling and thinking, and I did not want to be returned to my box.

One person I would not mind speaking to was young Mason: I was interested in his response to Matthew's observation about his bowler's shoulders. For a sunny and obliging young man, he had seethed with barely suppressed resentment. Presumably that would be nothing compared to Biddlestone's fury at the presence of one of the lower orders like me who was giving herself airs – this was the worst condemnation possible. Was it giving oneself airs to help investigate a murder? Quite probably. And it was not just Biddlestone but all the servants I had to confront at servants' breakfast in five minutes' time. Should I give myself more airs by requiring one of the footmen to escort me down to the kitchen? Or should I simply materialize? Whichever I chose would cause great frustration at a time when every last man and woman had urgent duties to perform.

In the end, Cousin Barrington solved the problem for me, by summoning a footman who had been scurrying past on some errand. As soon as he had completed his task, he was to return to take orders from me. The young man's bow left me in no doubt of his disdain; I might as well add fuel to his smouldering anger by asking in front of his employer if I might go to the servants' hall by way of Clara's cupboard.

'Of course, my dear. What an excellent idea! Green, go and get the key from Mrs Simpkins. Then come straight back here. And you take your orders from Mrs Rowsley, remember.'

I could not hope that that would ease the situation, but once he had returned with the key I set off in Green's wake. His back was rigid with anger or disapproval, or possibly both.

'Mr Green!' I stopped in my tracks

He had to stop. 'Ma'am?'

'How are you all this morning? Yesterday must have been chaotic for you, with the extra guests, and then the Gräfin's terrible death.'

His nod was grudging, but he retraced his steps. 'Very hard, ma'am. Thank you for asking, ma'am.'

'I ask because, as I said to Mrs Simpkiss last night, as a housekeeper myself I am probably the only guest in this house who can imagine the difficulties afflicting you all. At one point, as you may know, I was one of the very few people who doubted Clara's guilt. And now I seem to be one of three people determined to find out who really committed the vile murder. I shall need the help, not the resentment, of everyone downstairs. Everyone. I shall respect all of you, but I need you to respect me. Do you understand?'

He had the grace to look shamefaced.

'Excellent. Shall we start again? Good morning, Mr Green.'

'Good morning, Mrs Rowsley.' The poor boy's face was scarlet, with an angry rash where his antediluvian wig met his forehead. 'If you please, ma'am, my name isn't Green. That's my cousin's name. He left to go to Coalbrookdale. Good money, they said, but – oh, ma'am, he's been maimed for life and like to be stuck in the workhouse till he dies. So I've got to stick it out here.' Perhaps he might prefer to stick out life as a servant elsewhere, but the poaching of other people's staff was not widely approved of.

'I'm sorry to hear that. But,' I asked with a gentle smile, 'you have a name of your own. Mr . . .?'

'Billington, ma'am. So people confused the name with Mr Biddlestone.'

'I see.' I did indeed. 'What would you like me to call you?'

'The staff call me Billy, ma'am.'

'And you're happy with that? Well, Billy, let us go and see how Clara is, shall we?'

The child was far from well, and not speaking to anyone, let alone a stranger like me. She had been sick, and no one had yet emptied her chamber pot. I gathered it up myself. But carry it to the privy I would not, so I left it outside the make-do cell, where two pot-boys played guard. 'You'll see this is dealt with, Billy? And that she has a clean one? And fresh water? Breakfast? Imagine she's your little sister and treat her accordingly. But now please lead me through the rest of this rabbit warren to Mrs Simpkiss.'

Mrs Dabbs, the cook, greeted me with as much enthusiasm as if I had entered the servants' hall carrying Clara's slops. Mrs Simpkiss was inclined to be more conciliatory, perhaps, especially when I returned the key to her safe-keeping.

'The truth is, Mrs Rowsley, that we are very short-handed. Both Cook here and I have made repeated pleas to her ladyship for more staff, but . . . but to no avail, shall I say. Yet we have more and more visitors.'

'And most of them don't bring their own servants like they used to,' Mrs Dabbs put in. 'Mrs Simpkiss is so hard stretched and now – well, one more short.'

'I would have thought,' I said carefully, 'that I might suggest to Colonel Rowsley, in his capacity as Justice, that Clara should be set free without a blemish on her character. Even if he does not completely agree, there must be really useful jobs she can do under supervision, though that might be more in your area, Mrs Dabbs, than in the house itself. That still leaves you one short, of course, Mrs Simpkiss. And I know what that's like, believe me. If only I could think of something to help.'

'Unless you're prepared to put on a print dress and a cap and sweep a room or two, I can't think of anything. But here are the staff, ma'am. Do you want to speak to them before or after they've eaten?'

I glanced at the great clock on the wall. 'I have so much to do for the Colonel that I'd rather speak first, if you please. Though you may find it harder,' I added with a rueful smile, 'to enforce the rule of silence afterwards. Would you mind if little Clara took her usual place? I can't imagine she'll touch a morsel while she's locked in that cupboard.'

'Just what I was saying. A sin and a shame to lock her up.'

I scratched my earlobe. 'Something has been puzzling me. They say she was caught red-handed. But no one says who caught her. Who went into the Gräfin's room?'

The women stared. 'All we know is that there was a great hoo-hah and she was dragged down to the cellar and locked in. Who were the footmen doing the dragging?' Mrs Dabbs asked.

'That's what I'd like to know. Big brutes. And who told them to, more to the point?'

Nodding, I smiled at her. Exactly the questions I wanted asked.

'That's Mr Biddlestone's area, of course,' Mrs Simpkiss said. 'Question his young men I dare not.' She looked me straight in the eye. 'He's a bad man to make an enemy of.'

I nodded. 'I am all too aware of that.' They exchanged a glance. 'But I don't have to work alongside him. I can go home and work alongside an altogether more amiable butler. So while he may be rude to me, I will be the one to ask.' At last we shared a comradely smile. 'In fact, while everyone assembles here in the hall, I will go and beard him in his den.'

Mrs Dabbs' eyes widened as she looked over my shoulder. 'He's just coming in here now, ma'am.'

He was indeed. And had the advantage of me. 'I did not expect to see you here, Mrs er – Rowsley – though perhaps I should have done. Your proper milieu, after all,' he added with a French pronunciation worse than my own.

'Hardly, Mr Biddlestone: like Mrs Simpkiss I have a Room. Which is where this private conversation might take place, if Mrs Simpkiss permits? It is her domain, after all.'

'Here is good enough for whatever you might have to say.' There was a faint but insulting emphasis on the pronoun.

'Indeed.' I raised my voice very slightly. 'Good morning, Mr Biddlestone. Might we have a word in private?'

He went white with anger. 'I told you. I will speak to you here.'

'Very well. Though I am sure that Colonel Rowsley would

prefer all our enquiries to be confidential. Who were the footmen that brought Clara down to the cellar last night, and who summoned them? And, furthermore, who had her locked in the cellar?'

'I will check the roster to ascertain, and report my findings to the *Colonel.*'

My far from amiable smile showed my anger. 'Excellent. With answers to all of my questions, of course – in the next ten minutes, please. Cousin Barrington is extremely busy and depends on everyone's prompt cooperation. Including yours, Mr Biddlestone.'

The three of us watched as he turned on his heel and left the hall. I closed the door behind him.

'Even you didn't come straight out and challenge him,' Mrs Dabbs observed sadly. 'So what chance do we have?'

Mrs Simpkiss shook her head. 'You're wrong, Annie. She told him good and proper only he chose to ignore it. You had more backbone than most of us, ma'am, and never raised your voice, either.'

'I wanted to, believe me! But I felt I had pushed as far as I dared and truly getting the information quickly is more important than scoring over a sad and sour old man.'

Mrs Simpkiss nodded. 'Like the Colonel says, pick your battles if you want to win the war. It seems that everyone is here: would you care to speak to them now? I will bring young Clara in. If she's well enough.'

'I'll wait till then. Mrs Dabbs, you are working wonders – that breakfast you sent to the sewing room . . .'

We talked shop until Mrs Simpkiss returned with Clara. Her tearstains had been washed away, though her face was still wan and puffy, and her hair had been brushed. Mrs Simpkiss had found her a fresh dress and pinafore, and seated her with the other girls – why were there so few women on the staff? – to eat her breakfast. She could hardly keep herself from reaching for her spoon while I spoke. I meant in any case to use the fewest words I could – that they would need to account for their move-ments and also for those of the guests. This wasn't spying or snitching: it was to pinpoint the real killer. They could talk to me or, if they preferred, to either Mrs Dabbs or Mrs Simpkiss, who would pass their message on. I ended with the simple grace we used at home on the Sabbath. They might not be able to talk, but at least they could eat. Clara fell on the porridge as if it was manna. Smiling, I curtsied my thanks to the two women, and turned to leave.

Billy leapt to his feet and held the door open for me, then, to my surprise, he fell into step with me.

'Don't want you getting lost in this warren, ma'am, do we, especially with a murderer on the loose.' Was he trying to comfort or alarm me? I hoped and prayed it was the former. He continued, matter-of-factly, 'It's got to be a man, hasn't it? A tall lady, the Gräfin. And it's not as though she'd lie down and say, "Kill me," is it?'

'Is that what most people think? And do they think it was a guest or one of your colleagues?'

'I reckon most of us would have been too busy!'

'It doesn't take very long to kill someone.'

'It depends how you kill them, I suppose.'

Was he feigning ignorance or had no one told the servants? I could not believe that. Perhaps, however, he was simply making conversation. 'I suppose it does. And how much you wanted them to suffer.'

He shrugged. 'Or if you just wanted a quick get-away.'

'True. Who do you and your colleagues think killed her? Between ourselves, for the time being at least.'

'Some folk are saying it must be old Lord Pidgeon. Sometimes . . . well, we wonder if he's right in the head. Dead moody he is. Sorry, wrong word, that. One day he can be civil, at least. Next the maids don't like being on their own with him: although he's frail in the head, he's got more strength in his body than you imagine, see – and once or twice we've noticed bruises on Lady Pidgeon's face.'

'Good heavens! Are you saying he—?'

'I'm saying nothing, ma'am. Not my place.'

'Have any other names been mentioned?'

Sighing, he looked around. 'Some of the maids – well, some of us footmen too, to be honest – don't like the Major very much. Most of the time butter wouldn't melt. Then suddenly he's using language a navvy would blush at. It's like a dog: won't pick on anyone with power, but once it senses a victim . . .' He hesitated.

'Let me get this straight. We love the Colonel, because in his way he does his best for us. In his way. But it's almost – no, I hardly like to say it.'

'It's almost as though the Major . . . It's almost as if the junior of the two officers is giving orders to the senior?' I suggested.

'You said it, not me. Well, if you watched the match, you'd see, wouldn't you?'

'Do you think he meant to lose it?'

'That's what people are saying. Why would a man like that, keen on his honour as a military man, want to do that, that's what I want to know.'

'One last question. If I asked you why a military man of honour would do such a thing, what word would you come up with?'

He stared. 'Money. But I never said that, ma'am.' He looked genuinely scared.

'Of course you didn't. Billy, we'd best get on: they'll be looking for you.'

He bowed. We walked in silence.

'This way, ma'am.' He opened a door I did not immediately recognize.

I felt a sudden frisson of fear. He was not a tried and tested Thorncroft man. He had other loyalties. Had I been naive, perhaps even foolish, to trust him so implicitly? I braced myself.

'A short cut, ma'am. Her ladyship's sewing room is just here on the right.'

I hoped he did not see the relief in my smile of thanks.

As he bowed himself away, on impulse I spoke again. 'You mentioned dogs a moment ago, Billy. There isn't a single dog in the house, is there? Why is that?'

He snorted. But the sound of approaching footsteps silenced him and this time he retreated without ceremony

It seemed that Mason had been unable to run a blackboard to earth, but at least the table had been extended and baize and then thick card had been laid on it. This made a good base for the rolls of ceiling paper that Mason had managed to find. Matthew and Cousin Barrington had already set to work, marking up the paper as a giant timetable. I walked round the table to peer at it.

Matthew pointed. 'See, Harriet: we have one column for locations and another for people in that location. So at 11.30, say, you would be in the garden with Mr Digby and then me.' He straightened his back and sighed. 'Ideally all this could be cross-referenced, but I have no idea how. Sadly, Barrington's librarian has left for another post, so there is no one here with the expertise we need.'

Barrington muttered something about his wife: I hoped Matthew had caught the gist at least, for I did not. Cross-referencing? How on earth did you do that?

The clock chimed the three-quarters. Cousin Barrington jumped almost comically. 'Damn me, I thought it was time to go and confront the ravening hordes. Before-battle nerves. I always get them.'

'What sort of reaction are you expecting?'

His shrug was surprisingly expressive. To my amazement it was followed by an unnervingly accurate impression of the huffs and haws of protest I'd expect from the men here. I joined in mimicking the chirruping of their ladies. For a moment we were more than allies: we might have been friends.

'Are you expecting trouble from anyone in particular?' Matthew asked, pulling a face as he patted a surely cold coffee pot.

His cousin shook his head. 'My wife won't like it – it would be hard provisioning a place this size when you can't bring in supplies, wouldn't it?' It was a rhetorical question, surely, not another snide reference to my profession. It also revealed something I suspected: he hadn't told Lady Hortensia yet. 'And one or two of the older men will resent any curbs on their freedom. I suppose some of the youngsters will think it's a lark. Dear God, it's raining again!'

'Do you think any of the young men at university might have skills we could use?' I asked. 'Doing this cross-referencing, whatever that means?'

'It's just a way of checking one fact, one assertion, against another,' Matthew said. 'So if Mr A says he was in the garden with Mrs B, we can simply look up Mrs B.'

'Ah! Like Bea Arden at home. She lists all her recipes with possible accompaniments. Look up a vegetable dish, perhaps, and you get a reference back to the chicken that it suits. Very clever.' I laughed. 'You could always ask Mrs Dabbs, if you need help.'

Cousin Barrington stared. 'Mrs Dabbs is . . .?'

'Your wonderful cook,' I said, managing not to scream. 'Though I cannot imagine anyone in this whole house could be as busy as she must be today. What about the men? The Major must have experience in organizing things,' I added, hoping it sounded an innocent suggestion.

'He probably delegates to a willing subaltern,' Matthew said quickly, registering, I am sure, that his cousin had gone white. 'Everyone delegates, my love, do they not?'

Except us. And perhaps this was one task we should keep to a tight-knit group.

I sat down. 'Cousin Barrington, might I ask you something? What was the Gräfin's background? I know she was a clever card-player, could be both kind and malicious, and I know she outstayed her welcome. I was told that I should not spend so much time with her, but in the sense that I was monopolizing her, that others would welcome a chance to further their acquaintance with her.'

'Who said that?' he asked swiftly.

'I can't remember now,' I lied. I suspect he knew I was lying. 'But remember, there are unspoken rules for polite society, just as there are for servants. And I cannot pretend I know them, so I am grateful when someone puts me right with a gentle hint.'

He grunted. 'Well, she was a very well-connected lady. Old family. As I said, my wife's god-mama. And then she ups and marries this foreign count. No one quite knows why. If he'd been a handsome Frenchman, the ladies say they might have understood. But I've never met a dashing Austrian, have you? No, well, but you know what I mean. He'd got a title, but it was a foreign one. You never know about those. No children. Anyway, she disappears from polite society here for years, doing whatever ladies do in Vienna to amuse themselves. Then her husband dies – she never did say anything at all about his death – and she turns up back here.'

'Does she have her own house?'

'Rents one in a decent part of London. Not the very best, actually. But decent. More than just respectable.'

'Did you like her?' I risked.

He looked so furtive I almost laughed out loud. Then he put his face back into more military lines. 'It's not a matter of liking or not liking, cousin. It's a matter of duty. Someone might be a cantankerous old bat or a thuggish bully but *noblesse oblige* and all that. Matthew – you were raised to it.'

'And Harriet was trained in it, as I have told you, Barrington. She could abandon her post tomorrow – but she sticks to it through good times and bad. Things are bad at Thorncroft now, which makes her all more determined to stay. When the lawyers have finally run the heir to ground, we hope our lives will at last become easier.' He smiled at me. 'Italy calls, does it not?'

'Oh yes! One day. But, as in the matter we're discussing now, sometimes events must take precedence over one's wishes. Sometimes I am too frank, Cousin, but it may be easier for an outsider like me to ask questions, even offensive ones. If the Gräfin was the cantankerous old bat, let me ask a question that you may find offensive, and I apologize if you do: is Major Jameson the thuggish bully? Everything I have seen of him fits those words.'

The clock saved him, its silvery tones striking the hour. It was time for breakfast.

TWELVE

Whatever his feelings, Barrington would not express them in front of the servants. I sensed, however, that Harriet had gone a little too far. He had a long memory, and while he might forgive a born lady for being cantankerous, he might not excuse a woman he still clearly thought of as a social inferior for being so blunt. On the other hand, he might relish a bit of bravery from the ranks. I did not know him well enough to guess. I did think, however, that he was sufficiently pragmatic not to want to rid himself of one third of his enquiry team – two thirds, because I would certainly step back if he was disrespectful to my wife.

Smiling down at her, I tucked her arm into mine, and we set off together. Who would we have to sit next to? I was glad to see young Webbe pull back a seat for her and be thoughtfully attentive. Poor young Turton sat the other side. Meanwhile I was claimed by Lady Pidgeon, who had managed to conjure from somewhere a complete outfit of deepest black. The other guests and all the servants had to be content with black armbands, hurriedly handed out by Mason to those still lacking them. What did the faces about me reveal? Lady Pidgeon's suggested a deep weariness I had not noticed before. On others, there was a lot of puzzlement, and definitely irritation – perhaps the early hour accounted for some of that. There was also some of the huffing Barrington had so accurately predicted, though the women were more subdued than Harriet had expected.

Looking about him to see that all his guests were there, Barrington took his place at the top of the table and touched a water-jug with a spoon. The silence he requested came raggedly: his guests were too busy speculating aloud to their neighbours on what he might say to listen to what he actually did.

At last he coughed his way into their awareness. 'You are all sensible people,' he said. 'You know that a dreadful crime has been committed and that the murderer must be found. To that end—'

'So why is she no longer locked up?' a woman's voice demanded. 'Why is she eating and drinking with the other servants?'

There was a rumble of agreement – no, less than a rumble than a dawn chorus, since most of the assent seemed to be female.

'My enquiries so far show that the maid in question could not have committed the crime. In fact, I haven't quite got to the bottom of how she came to be imprisoned in the first place. A bad business, very bad.' The tone of his voice, his posture, reminded us of his successful military career. No one was going to argue with a commanding officer like this. 'I repeat, the real murderer must be found, and since the police are unlikely to be able to reach here for some time I have deputed two people to help me. I ask for, no, I demand, your total cooperation. They may ask questions you do not like, but they have my personal authority to do so. Is that clear?' There was a subtle pause between the three words of his question. 'You will speed matters up by writing a complete statement of all your activities yesterday – times, places, people you talked to. Even people you saw but did not speak to. Each bed chamber will be provided with stationery and writing equipment.'

This time there was a rumble. Male voices were demanding a chance to ride or shoot some damned pigeons.

Barrington responded with a snort of laughter. 'My dear chaps, in this weather? And in these floods? No, duty calls. Many of us have been officers; every one of us is a gentleman. And I put you on your honour to stay in the house and write your statements.'

'Who is going to read them?' asked a young lady I couldn't see. 'There may be . . .' She tailed off.

'There may be matters we prefer to keep private. We don't want prying eyes going over what we write,' someone finished for her.

There were a couple of girlish giggles.

Then came a more adult voice. 'A servant poking her nose—'

To my astonishment, Lady Pidgeon laid her hand on my wrist, raising her index finger in warning. 'Let me address that inanity, if I may. If you allude, Caroline, to Mrs Rowsley in such terms, then let me tell you do yourself, not her, a disservice. She is a woman of considerable intelligence and absolute discretion. Mr Rowsley, our host's cousin, is a professional man, with huge responsibilities for other people's property. It was the Rowsleys who risked their lives in yesterday's storm to see me safe. Have you heard a word of that from them? Did they tell you how ridiculous I must have looked? Of course not. They are not cheap gossips. Give respect where respect is due.'

Even as I murmured my thanks, I heard resentful whispers, catching the information that she was one of those wanting votes for women – as if that in any way detracted from her opinions.

Webbe, of course, had to chip in: 'I for one cannot imagine any friend of Lord Halesowen being anything other than the soul of discretion. I am sincerely glad too that Clara has been released and trust that the experience has not harmed her.'

'My dear fellow, she's just a servant! Too.'

But the cheap comment got no support. Barrington simply stood as tall as he could and stared the idiot down. 'Now, breakfast is about to be served. At the end of the meal, I expect you to disperse and carry out your ord— my requests. To the letter. Turton, you're the nearest thing we have to a padre on the premises. I'd like a word with you in the sewing room – that's my temporary HQ – as soon as you have eaten.'

As soon as the other guests started to leave the breakfast table, Harriet got up too. Judging she might want a few moments of reflection, I waited five minutes longer before returning to the sewing room, where she was already installed. Calm and composed she might appear, but she was pale to the lips. Had she eaten? I doubted it, and she had probably eschewed coffee lest anyone hear her cup rattle against the saucer. Her lowered eyes and bowed head almost suggested she might be praying. I took my place beside her, but said nothing.

At last she spoke. But her words came as a complete surprise. 'I'm so very glad we all treated John Timpson as an equal.'

Timpson had been a clerk in the Thorncroft household, but had a past that none of us cared to refer to – apart from the members of the servants' hall, who resented his presence and played cruel tricks on him. Why was she thinking of him? The painful reason dawned on me: because, of course, the news about her status and the release of Clara might well have come from the other side of the green baize door.

I took her hand. 'You did. You led the way. And he has a very good job now, one he couldn't have dreamt of without his experience with us. Now, you didn't eat any breakfast, did you? Would you prefer tea or coffee? Look: we have a plate of breakfast scones and – yes – raspberry jam? Yes, Mason – I should imagine it was he? – has augmented our supplies.'

She managed a smile. 'Bless him, he gave me the most unauthorized wink as he brought them. What a good butler he'll make one day. Do you remember how resentful he appeared when you asked if he played cricket? Did you ever find out why?'

I snapped my fingers. 'I had completely forgotten. Should we bother? We have enough things to worry about without discussing a young man's thwarted ambitions.' But Mason had showed he might be our ally. On no other grounds than that he was a human being in a house where servants were not happy, I must ask. We heard voices. 'You're right. Here are Barrington and Turton. Shall I slip out and thank him for the jam? Unless you would prefer to?'

'I'll stay,' she said quietly. 'Mr Turton might be less self-conscious in front of me. Possibly.'

To my shame, I was not sorry to be spared the agony of his stammer, poor devil.

Mason seemed surprised to be thanked, and even more surprised when I drew him slightly away from the sewing-room door where he had been hovering.

'The other day – was it only yesterday? – I assumed that you would be one of the cricket team. I think I touched a nerve – offended you. Am I right?'

He flushed as far as the tips of his ears. 'It's not my place to be offended or not, Mr Rowsley, sir.'

I smiled. 'It might not be your place to have a tantrum and smash the china, but you are allowed feelings, Mason. A straight answer, if you please. Were you disappointed not to be playing yesterday?'

'Between ourselves? In that case, sir, I was hopping mad. Especially when you saw the mess most of the house team were making of it – with a couple of notable exceptions, sir.' He bowed at me with a decided grin.

'Have you any idea why you were not picked?'

'Ask the Major, sir. Not me. I bowl nearly as fast as you, sir. I'd have . . . never mind.' He bunched his hands into fists. 'And something else – snatching the village's best batsman and not making use of him? What was the Colonel thinking of? Or, more like, the Major.' He mimed spitting.

I patted his shoulder. 'Thank you for your honesty – you have my word I will not breathe a word of what you said to anyone except my wife, who,' I added with a smile, 'sent me out here to thank you for her breakfast. You use your eyes and your brain, young man, don't you?'

He nodded cautiously, as if bracing himself for another – even more awkward – question. He was spared. Our hostess swept along the corridor. Mason and I bowed as one.

'Thank you, Mason,' I said. He took the hint.

Lady Hortensia – I had not yet been invited to stop using her title – did not appear pleased to see me, so I asked neutrally, 'How is young Baby Arthur this morning? I understand some children are afraid of storms,' I added vapidly, in the face of her continued silence.

She smiled glacially. 'He behaved as one would hope the son of a distinguished soldier would behave.'

I could think of no immediate response to that, for to remark that a child not yet six months old was unlikely to be aware of his heritage would clearly be inappropriate. All I could manage was a feeble, 'Excellent.' I sincerely wished I had never embarked on the topic of children. It would give her an opening, if she wanted one, to comment on what she would perceive as Harriet's unconventional behaviour at the end of the match. 'And how are the ladies coping? I hardly had time to speak to anyone at breakfast.'

'In a ladylike way, I should hope.'

I did not like her smile, or the stress on the adjective. Heavens, was it she herself who had spread the information about Harriet? Not trusting myself to ask, I offered a neutral bow. I had to say something, so it might as well have an element of truth about it. 'Would you excuse me? I am running an errand for Barrington.' I regretted my choice of words at once. It demeaned me. Nonetheless, I set off for the servants' corridors, where I hoped to borrow some suitable outdoor clothes and obtain precise directions to Harrison's cottage.

The answer to the question I was supposed to ask – did Harrison think that communication with the outside world in general and the rector in particular would be possible today – was tacitly answered by the stable lad who provided me with both a horse and waders. When he greeted me outside his cottage, mercifully on a slight hill, Harrison himself didn't offer another view, but he seemed almost touched to see me, reaching up to shake my hand. It was easier to talk as equals if I dismounted, however, so soon I was leaning on the gate beside him, watching the ripples on a flooded dip in the field I had crossed.

We exchanged a few platitudes about the weather and the floods – we agreed that he was lucky his cottage had survived untouched – before I felt able to ask, 'What happened at that match yesterday?'

He turned to look me straight in the eye. 'A lot of jiggery-pokery, that's what. And,' he continued, 'a lot of money at the bottom of it all, if you ask me.'

'I do ask you, and I'm interested to hear everything you want to say.'

'Sometimes I talk better if I listen first,' he said firmly.

'Very well. First I assumed that the removal of the best batsman – you! – from the village team was to make sure Colonel Rowsley's team would stand a better chance of success. It would have tied in with that strange notion that he had to be dismissed three times before he was out.'

'Don't you worry your head about that, sir. That's what we all agreed when he came back so badly injured, poor bugger. He's a decent man at heart. No, I had the same idea as you: the house team would be able to win more easily if I had to bat for them. Which is why I was so bloody cross. But then when you and I were put right down the batting order, I was more puzzled than cross. Why was the Colonel's team trying so hard to lose the match?'

'Because someone was betting on the outcome,' I replied, suddenly sure that he was right.

He nodded, adding, with a slow smile. 'Now you just have to find who.'

THIRTEEN

Lady Hortensia peered at the chart her husband and I were preparing. Pointedly she asked, 'Husband, is that a task for a gentleman?'

'It's the task for a secretary, if we had one,' he said, the edge to his voice making me apply myself to the chart even more diligently. 'But we haven't, of course. Or a librarian.'

'And you allow people to smoke amidst all those precious books!' I shouted – in my head. Carefully I underlined several headings.

'And you know perfectly well the reason why!' If only she would spell out the explanation, as people did when they had quarrels. Or perhaps only unladylike people. 'And work like this is not fitting for the Sabbath. Which reminds me – how do you propose to convey everyone to church?'

'I think we have to accept that we cannot get to the village this morning.'

'Perhaps. But we should not miss evensong as well!'

'I hope we may find a way. Matthew is asking the gardener chappie to reconnoitre even as we speak. But it looks to me as if the Lord might have to manage without us today – unless Mr Turton can oblige. Ah, here he is! Come on in!' He sounded genuinely welcoming, or perhaps just relieved.

Our hosts said all that was proper in greeting before her ladyship swept out. In his fashion, Mr Turton replied – and then, realizing I was there, he strode to the table and kissed my hand. He quickly grasped what I was doing and joined in with a will. Head down, he said, 'Good to help.'

Cousin Barrington pounced on the verb. 'Actually, we were wondering if you could help us this evening, Turton. We may not be able to get to the village church for evensong, and I thought you might take it for us here – in the ballroom, perhaps.'

Mr Turton went so pale I feared he might faint.

'Damn – I rushed my fence there, didn't I? Thing is, if you're going to be a clergyman, you might want some practice.'

'I fear – as you say – I am not yet trained. Not qualified. Would be presumptuous of me.'

'Nonsense! Good experience under fire.'

'No. No, pray, Colonel, I am sorry, but I ask you to accept my decision.'

Cousin Barrington was surely making matters worse by trying to finish each sentence, each word, for him.

'But you might help us in here?' I suggested, keen to end what was clearly torture. 'When we have people's accounts of their day coming in, it would be so very useful to have someone cross-reference them.'

He beamed. 'Better finish mine first.' He bolted.

Cousin Barrington rolled his eyes. 'Silly idea, I suppose. I can't make out one word in three for all his stutters and stumbles. Poor bastard. I beg your pardon! But why should he want to go into the Church?'

'Do you really think he does? Or is it his parents' wish, not his. What are your hopes for young Arthur, Cousin?'

Surely he did not wince? At last he sighed. Gazing at me appraisingly, he said quietly, 'I should wish he would follow in my footsteps. But upon my soul, I can't. Supposed to be stiff upper lip and all that, isn't it? But I'd do anything to stop him.' He dropped his gaze. 'But that's between you and me.'

'Of course.' I nodded and underlined a few more headings while I worked out what so say next. 'Were you expecting anyone to object to outlining his or her activities?'

He snorted. 'The old lady would have done without doubt. And of course there's always . . .'

'Always?' I prompted.

'No, that's not cricket, is it? Let's give everyone the benefit of the doubt.'

'I don't know if you can afford to.'

'And what, madam, do you mean by that?'

Flinching from his sudden anger, I said mildly, 'Only that the clock is ticking. That soon the waters will subside and people will leave even if they do not have permission. And also – Cousin, they say that if you kill one person it is easier to kill a second.'

He stared. He rang the bell. Mason appeared. 'Isn't Biddlestone around?' he asked.

Mason looked embarrassed. 'I believe he is otherwise engaged, sir. That's why I am here.' Why did he not make a more opaque excuse for his senior colleague? I would not have expected our colleagues at home to have, in their parlance, *dropped someone in it*.

Cousin Barrington's poor scarred eyebrows staggered up his forehead. '*Otherwise engaged*? Very well, you've done well so far. Carry on as you are. Next assignment. Every guest needs to hand over their statement within the half hour: tell them that. And you and your colleagues will be at hand to collect them when everyone gathers for morning coffee.' His voice changed. 'Look here – you're clever at this sort of thing: can you devise some sort of private place for depositing them?' He gestured vaguely.

Mason nodded. 'Perhaps the hall post-box, sir? I could move it to the breakfast room where coffee will be served, the luncheon table in the dining room already being laid.'

'Good thinking. Everyone to be present – understood?'

'Understood, sir.' Mason bowed himself out.

Personally I thought the schedule a little tight, but I could scarcely protest, instead picking up the nearest pencil and writing down my own timetable in terse, information-packed sentences. Who, when, where. I added another W: witnesses.

'Will you care to join us for coffee in the breakfast room, Harriet?' Barrington asked, an anxious edge to his voice.

'Thank you, Cousin – but I think not. I think I should go and talk to young Clara, don't you?' A smiled established we both thought that would be better all round. 'Perhaps Mason would guide me through that labyrinth.'

It seemed that Mason, like Biddlestone, had other duties, but I was happy to have Billy's company again. We talked about his family – he was the middle of seven children – and how his eldest sister was courting the village curate, but his mother didn't approve because she could have the blacksmith and the curate was as poor as a church mouse.

At last I felt I could ask for information I really wanted to know. 'Earlier I was asking you about dogs, Billy. Largely because most country houses like this have them everywhere, and a dratted nuisance they can be, too, for us servants.' I pulled a face. 'But there's not a single one here. Why is that? At home,' I continued, 'we couldn't have dogs or cats because they make her ladyship ill.'

'Lady Hortensia dislikes them, ma'am.' He clearly wished to say nothing more. We continued in silence.

Clara was busy in counting pots of jam for Mrs Simpkiss, who jotted the totals as she went. I simply joined in, talking idly to my opposite number about the shortage of plums the previous year and admiring the colour of her strawberry conserve. To my delight, with a meaningful nod, Mrs Simpkiss simply slipped out, leaving me with her pencil and list to continue: my voice could simply replace hers in Clara's ears. It took the child time to register the change, which nearly involved the sacrifice of a jar of rhubarb and ginger jam – but she caught it in time.

'Mrs Simpkiss would have killed me if I'd dropped – oh, ma'am!' Her eyes flooded.

'It's all right. It's safe and sound, isn't it? A bit runny, maybe?'

'Oh, that's how her ladyship prefers her jam. The Colonel prefers his nice and stiff.'

'Do they argue about it?' Did I feel disloyal?

'Sometimes. And Mrs Dabbs has to send up pale toast and dark toast.'

'How did the Gräfin like her toast?'

'Never touched it, ma'am. Mrs Dabbs had to make her some special Foreign Bread. Nothing else would do. Black cherry jam or apricot jam. Nothing else. And special coffee too. Never tea, ever. Rotted your insides, she said it did.'

The smell of fresh-baked biscuits insinuated itself into the room. 'Heavens, something smells good!' I declared.

'Biscuits. I could ask Cook if I might bring you one,' she said.

'Yes please. I would love – two!' I said, hoping I sounded daring rather than demanding.

So gently, as we shared a plate of biscuits which came with a glass of milk and a pot of coffee, I learned about her time in the

workhouse and how she had met her brother who was likely to
go for a soldier. And she did so hope he wouldn't end up like
the poor Colonel. The Gräfin had talked about duelling scars,
and even though men were supposed to be proud of them they
spoiled nice faces too. She had talked about dancing in Vienna
and rides in landaus and – 'and something she wouldn't talk
about, because I was only a little girl, really.'

'Ooh, that sounds mysterious. Something you knew about or
something you didn't?'

'Something like cashino? Where there were strange wheels?'

'I wonder what they might be . . . Do have the last biscuit.'

'I daren't, ma'am – Mrs Dabbs says I mustn't spoil my appetite
for servants' dinner because she's done a lovely roast.'

'You could put it in your pocket for later. Clara: you know I
don't mean you or any of the other servants any harm, don't
you? It's not so very long ago that I was doing exactly your job
at just the same age as you. Sometimes guests, once even the
gentleman of the house, did things that frightened and hurt me.'
However many years had passed, the memory sometimes had
the power to bring tears. I swallowed hard. 'You were treated
horribly last night, being put in that dark cupboard. Do you know
why they did that?' I took her hand, still sticky from the biscuits.

'They said I'd killed the Gräfin.'

'Who did?'

'One of the gentlemen guests, ma'am. I think. I'd just gone
into her room to make up her fire and fasten her necklaces and
such and there she was lying down in her bed and I couldn't
wake her and I screamed. And suddenly he and other men – servants, footmen, I mean – were in the room shouting, and they
dragged me out. And next I knew I was in the cellar –' the little
hand clutched mine – 'and then I was in the linen cupboard and
I don't know how anything happened, ma'am!' She sobbed into
my shoulder as I held her.

At last I asked gently, 'When you went into her room, did you
see anyone in the corridor?'

Biting her lip, she shook her head.

'And do you know which gentleman it was who came when
you screamed? Maybe not his name, but if he was big or small
or had a moustache or a beard?'

She shook her head.

I would not argue. Had anyone asked me to describe the man who raped me, a man I saw every day, I could not have done so, not until the shock and terror had subsided. Now I could still see him in my nightmares, right down to a small round scar on his cheek. And I could still smell him.

'You've done very well, Clara, to recall what you have done. If you think of anything else, no matter how little or silly it might be, promise me that you'll ask Mrs Simpkiss to send for me – in fact, I'll ask her myself, just to make sure she agrees. Now, go and wash your face so you'll be ready for that lovely roast dinner.'

Before I plunged back into the subterranean world I really did not like, I saw Mrs Simpkiss herself returning to the Room. She responded to my gentle knock with an immediate invitation to enter, rising in apparent shock and smoothing her apron when she saw who her guest was.

'Oh, do sit down, Mrs Simpkiss! Please! Heavens, we're both housekeepers together, aren't we?' I said. 'And we're both worried about little Clara too. Counting jam jars was a brilliant idea,' I added, sitting opposite her as she reluctantly returned to her chair.

'I want to keep her where I can see her,' she said frankly. 'And I guess you know why.'

I nodded. 'We both think she saw the killer, don't we? And could be in great danger.'

'If anyone lays so much as a finger on her,' she said with sudden cold fury, 'I will kill him. And that's God's truth.'

FOURTEEN

On his feet, Turton had folded his lanky body over the table, filling in the giant chart as if his life depended on it. No one had remarked aloud that Harriet had been gone a long time, but Barrington looked at the clock with something like resentment on his face, as if Harriet had abandoned her post. I looked at it for another reason: I was anxious about her. More anxious as each moment passed.

But here she was, smiling as I reached out a hand to take hers. We did not need to speak: I knew from the expression on her face that she had news she did not want to share with anyone else. She did not apologize to anyone, but simply joined Turton, reading statements and underlining, as he had done, anything that drew her eye. The chart-filling gathered pace.

As the clock ticked towards luncheon, Barrington made one more attempt to make Turton change his mind. How could the household and guests manage without some sort of collective worship?

Quickly suppressed mischief gleamed in Harriet's eyes. Her face was entirely serious when she said, 'In some households I have known, the master of the house would read the service to everyone. In others, the butler would read it to the servants, leaving the master to address the family and their guests.'

Perhaps Barrington didn't hear, intentionally or not, but Turton certainly did. Harriet had made a friend for life.

'Barrington,' I asked, 'how would you like us to react when your guests question us at luncheon, as they assuredly will?'

He blinked, as if I had asked him to discuss Darwin's latest theory. 'Question us? By Jove, so they might! Do you think we should eat in the breakfast room? Harriet?'

'I might have to excuse myself altogether,' she said in that slow way she had when she was hatching a plan that would worry me. 'If I am the only one not in attendance, that might look strange . . . people might draw the wrong conclusions. So

– assuming you approve of my idea – I would indeed prefer our little cabal to eat apart from the others. That way my absence will go unremarked.'

'Absence? What are you planning?' I asked, torn between amusement and panic.

'I am going to clean the guests' bed chambers,' she said sweetly. 'I have arranged to borrow a maid's uniform and cap—'

'A maid! My dear Cousin!' Barrington veritably exuded horror at the very notion. 'In one of those dreadful dresses and hideous caps!'

She did not grace his crass comment about his own servants' uniform with a reply, simply inclining her head.

'Would you be alone?' I asked her urgently.

'To tell the truth I would like a footman or two within call.'

'Two – lest one of them . . .'

'I trust no one – but I wonder if the killer was not a servant but a guest here.'

Barrington sat down fast enough to hurt his back. 'I cannot believe . . . What in heaven's name gave you that idea?'

She touched her lips, looking meaningfully at the door. 'And I would be much happier if none of this conversation were repeated. I believe it would put someone's life at risk.'

Barrington surprised me. 'You're tall enough, Matthew. All that livery. The white wigs – God knows why we haven't dispensed with them. You will be one of the footmen. Who else?'

Nonplussed, I scratched as if a wig were already irritating my scalp. 'How could I find livery without anyone knowing?'

By now with an almost amused smile on her face, Harriet looked me up and down. 'Mason? Or, if he's too busy with his usual duties, Billy. And perhaps you, Mr Turton, could lurk? Could you be sketching some of the sculptures in the corridors?'

He nodded with great passion, but looked enquiringly at my cousin.

I nodded. 'This would mean that you, Barrington, would have to maintain the fiction that all four of us are busy here. No, don't tell anyone yourself. And – dare I say this? – I think you should lock yourself in. Or would that look too particular?'

He smiled, making the scars pull and twist. 'I shall snarl at the footman on duty that I have one of my heads, and that you are taking the air. No one disturbs me when I have one of my heads.'

But something did – immediately. A knock on the door announced Mason, his face grey. 'Might I have a word, sir?'

'Better be serious if you're interrupting – by Jove, it is serious, isn't it?'

Mason nodded. 'Sir . . . sir, it's—'

'Spit it out, man!'

'Harrison has just come running up to the house. Says he's found a body.'

Barrington paled. Could he even speak?

'Whose, Mason?' I asked.

'Don't know yet. Harrison says he wouldn't touch it. Now he wants to know what he should do.'

'Tell him to leave it where it is. In fact, tell him to stay where he is so he can take the Colonel and me. Yes, Turton, what is it?'

'I could come? Bring my sketch pad?'

'Really? Why?'

'So the police, when they get here, can see exactly what we found.'

'Brilliant idea, Turton. If you're sure you're up to it? And if my cousin agrees?'

'Sound idea. Sound idea. But it may not be pretty, mind. Harriet—'

'Would you prefer it, Cousin Barrington, if I postponed my plans and broke the news to her ladyship? But her alone, if you please, and I will ask her to keep mum. It will be hard for her – she will have to maintain appearances during luncheon without you to support her.'

'I'm sure she will manage perfectly well without me.'

Oh, dear. I exchanged a swift glance with Harriet.

'And I will ask Mrs Simpkiss and the other servants to say nothing. You've told no one, Mr Mason?'

'I came straight here, ma'am. But you know what below-stairs is like – the tiniest bit of gossip spreads like wildfire.'

She nodded with grim amusement. 'I do indeed! There'll be half a dozen corpses before you can say knife. I'll come down with you now. I'll speak to Lady Hortensia immediately after that, Cousin.'

By now, Mason was scarlet. 'Ma'am, I'm very sorry ma'am. I had no right – I meant not offence.'

'And no offence taken. You simply spoke the truth. But we waste time.' She led the way from the room.

Harrison greeted me with obvious relief: 'I was just seeing if we could find a way through to the village, Mr Rowsley – and then I saw him.' He had already organized two pairs of waders and spirited from nowhere another pair for Turton.

We set off as quickly as Barrington could cover the uneven ground. At last he waved us on. 'Time is of the essence! Go ahead. Bloody hip!'

Harrison hesitated. 'He won't be going nowhere, sir. And you're the gaffer—'

The effort Barrington made to become once more a leader of men was painfully obvious as he tried in vain to straighten his shoulders. I would have offered him my arm, but that would have been to humiliate him.

I think Harrison saw and understood. 'Mighty treacherous after the flood, sir. You need to watch your step, Mr Rowsley,' he added after I'd feigned a slip. 'More haste, less speed, as they say.'

Mason had said that anyone trying to flee from the house might slip in hidden obstructions and drown. It looked as if the man in the water had done just that. Where he had fallen was a tangle of roots still half covered with toffee-coloured water. As we removed our hats and stood in silence it occurred to me that that explanation might just be too pat.

I gestured to the others to stay back. 'We can't save his life now, can we? So let us all use our eyes. Is there anything suspicious – even unusual – that catches our eye?'

'Your prints are clear enough, Harrison.' Barrington pointed. 'You can even see where you stopped walking and started running towards the body. And you certainly ran back.' A shift in the light as a cloud scudded from the face of the sun brought a sharp ejaculation. 'By Jove! Bend down a little. Over there. More footmarks. One man by the look of it.'

Turton nodded.

'Good man. Can you sketch them? And maybe . . .?' He eyed the corpse.

Turton was already at work. Heavens, he had talent. We hardly had to wait two minutes before he had given a good impression of what we could see: a big man, with dark hair, who was wearing a frock coat and boots. Not a wet-weather outfit, not a walking over wet terrain outfit. More of an indoor servant's outfit – no, surely not.

'Where were you when you saw him?' Barrington asked Harrison, who pointed in the direction we had come, where the grass had clearly been disturbed by our feet.

'I could just see his legs, sir – damn and blast!' He turned to the bushes and vomited.

Staying where he was, Turton occupied himself with sketching the corpse in situ. He pointed to a detail he had registered: a big bruise on the back of the victim's neck. No need to speak.

Barrington had already unscrewed the cap of his hip-flask when, still ashen, the gardener re-joined us. 'Here. You need this.'

Harrison took a sip.

'Deep breaths. Another swig. That's the ticket. If someone lends me their arm, I'll look. Seen enough dead bodies in my time.' He turned to me.

I was ready to oblige. But I stopped short and pointed. There was only one set of footprints. 'How can a man have walked here on his own and managed to hit his own head so hard that he fell and died?

Barrington turned to me agape.

'Look. You can see all the mess we've made in the mud. You can see where Harrison stopped in his tracks. But I can see neither tracks approaching nor tracks leaving the corpse.'

'Act of God?' Turton offered, his dark humour all the more shocking for the clarity with which he delivered it.

Barrington was far from amused. Eyes narrowed he peered at the stream. 'Waders,' he said. 'Like ours. Someone sees the man. Doesn't like him. Picks up a rock – plenty of them to choose from – and creeps up behind and thumps him.'

It sounded a very plausible theory.

Harrison, like a schoolboy, raised his hand. 'But why should anyone stand still and wait to be hit? You don't turn your back on a stranger.'

I nodded. 'Perhaps if we can recognize the victim it might clarify the issue – though I must say I think the notion of waders or boots is very sound, Barrington.'

'Hmph. Very well. Very well, Matthew – into battle!'

We picked our way gingerly through the mud. Yes, I might not have noticed at first, but Turton was right about the bruise. As to what caused it, Barrington could have been right about that, too. Had it been a vicious enough blow to stun him so that he fell and the water did the rest?

If Barrington was to stay upright, I had to turn the body. It was hard work: the clothes were heavy with water, the body offering nothing but resistance. One last heave.

'My God!' Barrington gasped. 'What the hell is he doing here?'

I had not liked Biddlestone, but the water had not been kind to him.

Barrington turned. 'Harrison. After yesterday I know you can run like a deer. Can you leg it back to the house and get a hand cart and some strong men? Good man! Turton, are you sure? Drawing him?'

The young man nodded. 'Why fear a corpse? His soul has already left,' he said, plying his pencil with a will. If only the poor devil's tongue could be as free as his hand.

As for Barrington's question, none of us had come up with an answer – and the only reasons I could think of put the butler in a very suspicious light.

Less than an hour later, with Biddlestone's body now stowed near to the Gräfin's in the cellar, Barrington had joined what he called his corpse detail in the servants' hall and was ordering coffee and brandy for them all. 'Well done, Harrison. Excellent work. Now we need you to do one more thing. Move heaven and earth to get to the village. Pick your own team to go with you. Plenty of tall strong men around to choose from. Get the village constable here at all costs!' From one of the men there was a muffled snort, hastily turned into a cough. 'And Dr

Highworth too,' Barrington continued smoothly, as if he had not heard and did not endorse the obvious doubts about the constable's ability to deal with the situation. 'Take them to the spot first. Then they come here. Now, I wonder if Cook can find any food for you stretcher-bearers. Harrison – we'll keep some back for you and your men. Turton, Rowsley – sit yourselves down too.'

Which was how I came to see a woman in a print dress and a very ugly cap wink at me from the doorway.

FIFTEEN

No matter how much I told myself and my partners in what was I hoped not really a crime that there was no risk, I knew that were I to be found out there would be a scandal that might cost them their posts. From her response to my request for a list of the occupants of each room, Mrs Simpkiss knew too. 'Only her ladyship, no one else, she says, is supposed . . . I don't know why, considering we're in and out of the rooms all the time.' Then she smiled. 'But there's nothing to stop you making your own list, is there? As you go into each room I could tell you whose it is and you could write it down.'

'Of course I could. But whether I should . . . whether I should involve you in this at all . . .'

'What would you do if this was going on where you work and you thought I could be useful?' She held my gaze. 'Well, then. And I shall be doing what I'm sure you do with your young maids – teaching them what to do. If Clara learns something and tells us something, then that'll be a boon.'

'You're sure Clara should be with us?'

'With *me*, Mrs Rowsley. Where I can keep an eye on her. We'll be in earshot, never fear. But not with you. In the room opposite or next door. Working. And when you see the state some folk leave their rooms in you won't argue.'

'I know all too well, don't I?'

Mason insisted on accompanying us. He had provided himself already with an excellent excuse for giving any guest leaving luncheon early a reason why he or she must not enter the room I was in: one of the staff, he would say, was dealing with rodents. I had used that excuse myself once to keep guests under control, as it were. But I had not been such a stickler for detail as he was; he had actually located mouse droppings and scattered some about the corridors. A butler in waiting? Surely he deserved a

better chance on a wider stage! And he was young enough
to take any chance life offered.

I started impartially enough in rooms where I expected to
find nothing – guests whose names I still could not attach
to faces, an indictment if ever one needed one of our hostess.
Twice over – had I not asked Cousin Barrington for a list of
the rooms' occupants? And why should she tell Mrs Simpkiss
not to reveal it? So impartially, but not calmly. All those years
as a maid, and I was as nervous as a newcomer! It took me a
huge effort to be calm, even as I applied myself to my task.
Between the squabs and down the back of sofas, I found a
haul of coins: imagine, losing a guinea, even a half-guinea,
and not noticing. Or if you noticed, not caring enough to search
for it. There were also a pretty little ring, some shirt studs and
a very compromising love letter. As I finished in each room,
Clara and Mrs Simpkiss went in and gave it an official tidy
just in case I had left things as I would at Thorncroft, not as
they were left here.

Then I came to the Kirklees' chamber – the parents of one of
the babies on the rug yesterday. As far as I knew we had never
exchanged a word since I had been here – not so much as a
thank you for my catch. Part of me, the part of which I was not
proud, would have liked to find something highly incriminating
there. They were a messy pair – shoes, clothes, even jewellery
left lying around. But there nothing interesting at all. My hands
had sweated and my breath come short all for no reason.

Then to the next room and then the next. The ones I hated
checking most were those of the young men. It felt like a
betrayal. Thank God there was nothing. Then I came to the one
I feared doing most: Major Jameson's. I knew he was a bully.
I knew he had a foul temper. But if I thought about either I
would not be able to do my job. So as methodically as if
I were a young chambermaid afraid of my master, I went through
every crevice of his room. To my chagrin, apart from a note
stuffed deep into the sofa, I found nothing immediately incriminating – unless a strong-box might suggest he had something
of value to protect, even conceal. I even went through his bin,
which had some shreds of paper screwed into a ball. A letter? I
had no time to read it. It went with everything else in the apron

pockets. But I made myself give both the inside and the outside of the bin a good rub, as a well-trained maid would. There. I was glad to leave.

How dared I go through the Pidgeons' rooms – he slept in the dressing room? I hated every moment, especially when I saw the Bible beside his bed, and *The Mill on the Floss*, a bookmark in place, beside hers. Though many times in my life I had cleaned rooms for people who had been kind and generous to me, people I liked, this was different. Morally different. I must turn my heart to ice as I checked their bin. More shreds of paper, and nothing else. They went into a different pocket.

One more room, another anonymous one. Heavens, how did anyone find anything in this chaos? I picked up and folded like any good tweenie – until I recalled that Mrs Simpkiss and Clara were waiting to do precisely that. Except that . . . did I see the letters IOU scrawled on that sheet of paper? Fifty guineas was a sum indeed, almost certainly more than Mrs Simpkiss would earn in a year. If only I could decipher the signature. But I was not wearing my chatelaine. So my reading glasses were in the Room with my clothes and nothing would make those letters clearer.

Perhaps Mrs Simpkiss, ready to take over from me, would have better luck.

One last room. The Gräfin's. The scene of a dreadful crime. And it was my duty to scour this for anything that could assist the police. I could work with the clearest of consciences and great purpose. And at last I found something of real interest between the bed-head and the mattress. A key. And since there was no jewel or strong-box in the room that it might fit, I fell on it as if it was a prize.

There was no reason now for Mrs Simpkiss to keep watch, so, hoping and praying it would not upset the child too much, I asked her and Clara to join me. Mrs Simpkiss did what I had baulked at doing: she went through the pockets of all the dead woman's clothes.

'Did you do this in other rooms too?' I asked, quite embarrassed by her bravery.

'Of course. All the guests' pockets. But we must talk in the Room, not here, Mrs Rowsley. The sooner Clara is downstairs the better.' She turned to the girl. 'Be a good girl and tell Mrs

Rowsley exactly what you saw when you came in. Slow as you like. What did I say? Nice deep breaths.'

The child made a huge effort. She pointed to things that had been tidied up into the wrong place, mentioned the Gräfin's preferences – lavender soap only – and showed which clothes she liked folded and which hung up. And then she turned her attention to the dressing room, and it was as if she were a candle held to the fire. Slowly but inexorably she fell to her knees in a ball of terror. 'He came out of there! The man.'

Her tears became hysterical and increasingly loud.

Mrs Simpkiss said tersely, 'Get Mason.'

I obeyed. In an instant the young man had scooped her up and was carrying her down the service stairs.

Over her shoulder, Mrs Simpkiss said, with an authority I'd never seen before, 'Give me some time to calm her down.'

'Of course. When would you suggest?'

She pulled a face. 'The way things are, it might have to be this evening. By the way, Mrs Rowsley, you do realize you're still wearing our uniform, don't you? Best come with us down the back stairs.' She set off.

I followed her down to the Room hoping I could change my clothes before I met anyone who might recognize me, disguise or not. Inevitably, of course, I ran into a person who would know me anywhere.

Matthew excused himself from a group of men in the servants' hall and slipped out to join me. 'You've not been – please tell me you've not been prowling round without me there!' he said, far too loudly. 'Without protection! Harriet, after all our careful plans!'

I touched my finger to his lips, dropping my own voice as I replied, 'No risk at all. First of all I waited till all the guests were at lunch and would be for some time. I believe they are still on the dessert course. And then I had expert support. Mason, Mrs Simpkiss and, most important, young Clara! But first – whom did you find?'

He almost mouthed the name: 'Biddlestone!'

'Good God,' I breathed. 'The keystone of the whole household! When is Cousin Barrington to break the news?'

'He's hoping Harrison can get through to the village and find the constable, though I gather he's not universally admired. Although Barrington might not want to make an announcement now, I can't see the purpose of waiting, especially as the men who brought back his body are bound to talk. Everyone in the hall must have their ears flapping for information that we might let drop accidentally. Ah! He seems to have decided to speak now.' As Barrington's voice rose we edged further from the room. 'How did Lady Hortensia deal with the news?'

'Without emotion. She might just as well have asked aloud, "What is a body more or less?" I'm not sure whether her insouciance was admirable or outrageous. It may crack a little when she discovers that she lacks a butler, of course.' I think my tone shocked him. 'I'm sorry – such humour is out of place, is it not? But I have to deal with . . . things . . . somehow. My love, I think Barrington is looking for you. Ah, he's coming over.'

'This could be interesting. Shall we tell him who you are or let him find out?'

'The latter.'

Apart from a minimal nod he ignored me as I gave a deep curtsy, head lowered.

'Matthew, we need another council of war, don't we? Have you any idea where that clever little wife of yours might be? Hortensia says they've spoken, but that was before luncheon. And I'm worried she went ahead with that hare-brained scheme of hers. No, not hare-brained. Far too bright for a hare. But very risky. What if she's been caught in the act?'

'I promise you she's all right, sir,' I declared, maid-servant Harriet, with another demure bob.

'So where the devil is she?'

Yet another curtsy.

Barrington rocked on his feet. 'Good God! Dear lady, I never realized!'

'Good. That was the intention. But I should dress properly before I appear at your council of war. I must collect my own clothes first . . . Oh, Mason, thank you so much!'

With a solemn bow and a huge wink he presented me with a rush basket discreetly covered with a towel. With another bow, he withdrew.

'In the sewing room in fifteen minutes, Cousin Barrington?

Ten if you can come and undo these wretchedly inaccessible buttons, Matthew!'

'It may,' he said grimly, as we climbed the stairs together, 'take a little longer than that. Harriet, Harriet, why did you take such a risk? No Turton? No – damn it, no me!'

'I promise you, the risk was very small. I consulted Mrs Simpkiss – hence the uniform – and every time I searched a room she was in the one next door, ostensibly cleaning. In fact she too was searching. She suggested that we ask Mason to keep an eye on the corridor, ready to intercept any visitors returning to their room – he would ask them to wait until some vermin had been dealt with. Mrs Dabbs played her part too: she promised to send up the courses at longer intervals than usual.'

'Where did you start?' Now, in the safety of our bed chamber, he sounded perhaps more interested than furious.

'In rooms of people to whom I'd not been introduced. Much easier.'

'And there was no sign of the occupants themselves?'

'None. They were at luncheon, remember. Oh, Matthew, I didn't like invading the rooms of the boys, but by far the worst was the Major's. To be honest, I was afraid – and not just of him, but of your reaction if he'd discovered me and hurt me.' I took his hands and kissed them. 'It was in his room I found this love-letter. It was crammed down the back of the sofa.'

He turned it over and over.

Dearest A

9.30.

Your adoring G

'There's nothing to suggest it might have been to the Major, of course,' he said. 'Did you find anything else?'

'Some torn-up paper in his bin. It's all here.' I emptied my pocket, popping the contents into an envelope from the stationery rack on the desk. 'These were his. I could not bring it with me but whoever occupied the room next to the Gräfin's had on his washstand an IOU for fifty guineas.'

'Fifty guineas owed here? My God! Who signed it?'

With a scowl I explained. 'But with luck Mrs Simpkiss will have deciphered it. And I also have some scraps of paper from the Pidgeons' room.' They went into another envelope. 'But the most significant find was in the Gräf—'

There was a tap at the door. I stowed the key in the nearest thing to hand – my reticule – before Matthew opened the door to a maid. 'Sir, ma'am: the Colonel asks me to tell you that refreshments are served in the sewing room.'

I had rarely changed so quickly in my life.

Mason appeared with plates of sandwiches and other delicacies to sustain us: I was impressed that Mrs Dabbs had managed to produce them when she might need to prepare a quite different menu for the guests' afternoon tea. And on a Sunday too, when she might reasonably have expected time off to herself.

After several sandwiches and a glass of wine, Barrington seemed relaxed, so I took a risk. 'Cousin, with all the times and locations on our chart, we lack one thing,' I lied, since I had of course made my own. 'The guests' rooms. I am sure Lady Hortensia must have a list somewhere. Do you think we might borrow it? I could copy and return it within minutes?'

'Don't see why not? But you never know – she might have left all the arrangement to Simpkins.' Nodding, Barrington slipped out.

'Why not ask Mrs Simpkiss herself?'

'Because she's much busier than Lady Hortensia!'

Without our host the atmosphere was considerably lighter. When Mason came to ascertain, as he put it, that all was well, he found us laughing. At first the young man managed to maintain his professional decorum and not ask a single question, though his head must have been fizzing with queries, not least with those concerning his own future. At very least he must hope he would become the acting butler, and perhaps in time get a permanent promotion. Meanwhile, I now thanked him very publicly for his part in our little plot.

Visibly relaxing, he bowed as if he regularly lurked in corridors to protect a fake maid searching guests' luggage and cupboards. 'If I may say so, ma'am, you would make a very good burglar. No one could tell that anyone had even entered their room except to clean and tidy it.'

'I should hope not! After all, I started my training when I was Clara's age – or younger. She was very brave, was she not?'

'I was proud of her, ma'am. Do you think she will recall anything more about yesterday evening?'

'Should we hope she does? It might help us find the murderer. But it might not do her any good to think about . . . her experiences. I know she is the most junior of all the indoor staff, but I am sure you will all take extra care of her.'

He grinned. 'No one will be locking her up in any cellar on my watch, ma'am.' He flushed scarlet. 'I mean—'

Matthew dived in to rescue him. 'Who put her there last night?' he asked.

Was this a question too far? It was clearly pertinent enough to make the young man look over his shoulder, as if to make sure his employer was not within earshot. 'It wasn't actually the Colonel's doing,' he said. 'It was Mr Biddlestone who dragged her downstairs and locked her in. But he isn't – beg pardon – he wasn't the sort of man to act without orders. Very keen on obeying orders, he was, as well as giving them.'

'So do you have any idea who gave this one?'

'The man young Clara says she saw, I should think.' He looked from Matthew to Jeremy Turton. 'She was doing really well remembering what had changed or not changed in each room until she got to the Gräfin's, and then she said something about a man in the dressing room . . . Poor Clara! We got her out, quick as we could. Go back in she would not, no matter how much I told her that both rooms were empty.'

Matthew nodded. 'We've still no idea who this man was?'

'No. And my money's on him as the killer. Yours too, ma'am, I should imagine.' He slipped back into butler-mode. 'Will that be all, sir? Ma'am? Thank you.' He bowed, holding the door open for Cousin Barrington, who sank too quickly into a chair and winced in pain.

'Cousin Harriet – I want to hear all about your escapade.'

I had rather he had produced the guest list, but I simply laughed. 'Believe me, Cousin, it was far from that. We knew that all your guests were safely at luncheon. All we did was arm ourselves with feather dusters and cloths and give their rooms a good clean – perhaps behind and within things that are not part of a servant's daily duties, but were beautifully clean nonetheless.'

'God bless my soul! That's very efficient.' He paused while

Mason entered, with two bottles of wine, one red, one white, and of course the appropriate glasses. 'Did you get involved in this charade, Mason?'

'I had the honour of patrolling the corridors outside the bed chambers – I believe Mrs Rowsley's watchwords are *Just in case.* As it was, the only major task I undertook was to carry poor Clara down the back stairs when going into the Gräfin's room reduced her to tears. Quite hysterical I'd say she was at one point. A cup of Mrs Dabbs' finest cocoa seemed to soothe her, I am happy to say.' He ensured our glasses were full, passed round the refreshments, and prepared to withdraw. As he did so, the door was flung open in his face.

Lady Hortensia. Should I stay seated with the rest of the team or curtsy my way out? I forced myself not to rise: after all, I was a guest, was I not? An equal. But if she did not consider me one, it was hard for me to behave as one.

In fact, it seemed that it was her policy to ignore me – and Matthew and Mason for good measure. Her nod to Jeremy was at best perfunctory.

'My husband and I require a word in private,' she announced.

Was it about the list I had asked for? If so, this did not look like the best moment for him to ask her anything.

'Let us adjourn to your private sitting room, then, my love.'

'There was a maid in there. On the Sabbath.'

'Dear me. We must speak to Mrs Simpson about it.'

Clearly this response was inadequate: she stared implacably about her. At last he straightened. 'My love, we are trying . . . this murder is taxing our brains. Look what young Mr Turton and Cousin Harriet have achieved.' He gestured at the table. 'Now, I am sure the servant must have finished in your sitting room. Mason, could you have some of her ladyship's special tea sent up for us straightaway?' Tucking her hand under his arm, he escorted her from the room, Mason in their wake.

I stood, as did the others.

Matthew rubbed his back. 'I think we all deserve a break – perhaps a little fresh air. Harriet, Turton, would you care to join me in a turn about the terrace?'

I nodded, but Jeremy clearly thought the idea repellent. He cast a longing look at the table. Yes, thin youngsters needed their food and he in particular would hate the light chat that would be expected if anyone else was out there. In our turn, we would welcome some time together. But perhaps, after all the trouble to which Mrs Dabbs had put herself, we should eat first.

At last, all of us having done justice to what we had been offered, I smiled. 'Don't work too hard, Jeremy.'

He shook his head. 'No. Coming. Bringing a sketch book. Best put on a show.'

Matthew saw us out, locking up as he left, and pocketing the key.

'So you searched Hortensia's sitting room too?' Matthew asked in disbelief the moment we shut our bed chamber door.

We had returned to don the smart outdoor apparel necessary here for even the most casual airing.

'Not I. I confined myself to the guests' rooms. But,' I added, 'the fact that someone else was in there almost makes me regret I wasn't. If Cousin Barrington failed to penetrate my disguise, I cannot believe that she would have done. And I do wonder which servant it was. I must ask Mrs Simpkiss. Matthew, imagine – they seem unable to remember the names of their own servants. That is hardly the recipe for a happy household.'

'I recognize a change of subject when I hear it.'

'Very well – let us go back to this morning.' I produced the key from my reticule. 'What could this open?'

'A very large door.' He looked at me anxiously. 'I should have asked earlier: how did you get past the footmen guarding her room?'

'I believe they were needed to serve luncheon,' I said primly.

Matthew did not often swear, but several oaths passed his lips. 'So someone directly disobeyed Barrington's orders? The men themselves or the person who required their presence elsewhere?'

'I do not think that it is a very happy marriage,' I said. 'Do you?'

'I'm afraid not.' He passed the key from hand to hand. 'Should we try to return it? Let the village constable find it – when he eventually gets here?'

'Hard for me to get in if the footmen are no longer serving

strawberry meringue. Yes, strawberries – they won't be ready in the Thorncroft succession houses for another week at least. But – assuming I can – I would like to copy it first. At home I could make a wax impression. Here I might have to confine myself with tracing it as accurately as I can. I don't even want Jeremy to know about it, or I would ask him. What are you doing?'

'Sharpening a pencil, my love. The least I can do after all you have achieved.'

I looked at him. 'You are not as used to corpses as Cousin Barrington. How do you feel after your sad expedition?'

'Chastened, if you want the most accurate response. A man in his prime, struck down quite literally – yes, there's a duck egg of a bruise at the base of his head – and drowning in three inches of water. It's very . . . sobering. The strange thing is there are only his tracks to the water. I'm sure we didn't walk over anyone else's. I hope not, at least. So how did his killer get there and how did he get away? Barrington's theory is that he approached and left through the stream itself.'

'Or she. Throttling even a woman needs a certain brute strength; hitting someone probably quite a lot, but not so much. As for getting there without leaving a trace I can't even guess. I'd need to see where it all happened, perhaps. Which is not on the terrace, where we are supposed to be taking the air.'

'The key first.'

He held both paper and key firmly as I followed the complicated line of the business end of the key. 'We'd need a locksmith to identify this properly unless we try every door in the house. Or?' He looked at me quizzically.

'It couldn't be a safe key, could it? It looks a bit like ours at the House. Which makes the question of who left it there even more interesting. Meanwhile, if I can't return it, I must make sure no one else can find it. Those envelopes will fit in my reticule, but the key spoils the shape and someone might notice.' I pondered. 'I never thought I'd ever say this, but thank goodness for this corset. No. Too uncomfortable. I'll have to hang it from the crinoline cage.'

'Do you have to do it immediately?' he murmured.

I found I did not.

SIXTEEN

At last, we were ready to go downstairs. I would have lingered even longer, but Harriet's intermittently inconvenient conscience was troubling her.

'Oh, how tempting . . . But poor Mr Turton is down there on his own, and no doubt wondering if he must force himself into light conversation or if people will nod kindly and drift away.'

I silently cursed Turton.

'If only someone could help the poor boy. One of his late lordship's friends practised a strange ritual called hypnotism; he employed it when one of my fellow servants needed a tooth drawn. He seemed to put her to sleep, and she later claimed she felt no pain at all. Could afflictions like a stammer or hysteria be similarly treated?'

'Who can tell? But if anyone might mention the idea, it is you, isn't it my love?'

To my shame, I was relieved when I saw Mr Turton busy with his pencil, apparently too absorbed to want any conversation. Perhaps he was pleased to be left in peace.

Lady Pidgeon had ventured out too, installing her husband on a bench and leaving him there while she made her surprisingly regal progress. She had been watching Jeremy work, but now turned towards us, making her silver-handled walking cane more of a fashion accessory than merely a simple means of helping her move, necessary though that might have been.

She grimaced as she came to a halt, holding out her hand for me to kiss. 'Yes, my dears: yesterday may have been a great adventure but it was not kind to my rheumatism. But it was even less kind to poor Gräfin Weiser, was it not? The *on-dit* is that you dear souls are forgoing all the pleasures of a country house weekend to discover who did it. Tell me, was her throat truly slit from ear to ear? And was her maid soaked through in her blood? The notion is sending a splendid frisson through us all.'

However disconcerted I might be by her levity – she was referring, after all, to the death of an old acquaintance – I laughed as I replied, 'Your ladyship will understand that until the constable gives us permission we cannot tell you any details. I think, however, the rumour of all that gore vastly exaggerates, and even distorts the truth.'

'But what about the rumour that the murderous maid is free to wander round wherever she chooses?' She did not ask this question lightly. There was an undertone of the other guests' anger.

'I suspect that your ladyship has already met the terrible fiend – unless you brought your own maid, she might even have brushed your hair. Little Clara?' I smiled encouragingly.

'That child? Even shorter than I am? That is half a rumour scotched.' She nodded with apparent but not complete satisfaction. 'But she has her liberty?'

'She is doing useful work under close supervision,' Harriet said firmly. 'The staff here are working so hard I am almost expecting an invitation to don an apron and pick up a duster.'

She narrowed her eyes. 'You're a brave woman. But don't expect admiration from all quarters. Or even courtesy. Now, another rumour concerns a servant. Is it true the butler has committed suicide?'

'That's something I've not heard,' I said truthfully. 'When the truth becomes public knowledge I'm sure you will be among the first to hear, your ladyship.'

Harriet asked, 'Your ladyship, why on earth should anyone want to harm the Gräfin? She was kindness itself to me.'

'Perhaps not to everyone.'

'People she played at cards, perhaps?' Harriet ventured.

'Ah, you know about that.' Lady Pidgeon was clearly not pleased. 'Who told you?'

Harriet side-stepped the question. 'It is common knowledge that she enjoyed her whist. But in what way was she unkind to her opponents? Did they perhaps play for money?'

She earned an extremely hard look. 'I see I am wanted, my dears. Please excuse me.'

Harriet curtsied deeply as the old lady swept past, her face stony.

Had anyone been trying to attract her attention? Someone behind me? I might ask Harriet later. As it was I simply smiled and bowed.

I straightened to find Harriet's young cricketer friends beaming at us.

Lord Webbe took Harriet's hand to raise her from her curtsy. 'Roddy and I were wondering if you might have time to teach us that bowling action, ma'am.'

She laughed. 'And outrage the whole household! Your lordship—'

'Charles, ma'am, please.'

'Charles – if you are sure? – I tell you I am in bad enough odour as it is. Spending the Sabbath trying to work out who killed the Gräfin is bad enough, but to be enjoying myself! That would cut me off from polite society for ever.'

I stepped forward to shake hands. 'We can do better than that, gentlemen. Come and stay with us during the long vacation: it would be a pleasure to work with you both.'

Harriet's face declared she was even more delighted than they were – and definitely more surprised. 'It would indeed. Please say yes.'

'Yes, twice over. It would be an honour! But,' young Roddy added dolefully, 'if I am to get into the first eleven, I need to improve now. What time do you depart tomorrow?'

'We may not be able to leave,' I pointed out. 'Actually, we might all need to stay here until the police say we may go. I'm sure you have heard the rumours: there are two bodies now.'

'But everyone says the man in the river – that death's head of a butler – topped himself because of what he'd done to the old lady.'

I raised an eyebrow. 'Does that sound logical to you?'

Webbe shook his head doubtfully.

'Why should a butler kill a countess in the first place? Do people just kill at random?'

'Only if they're maniacs, I suppose – and I doubt if a maniac would be overwhelmed with guilt. So,' he began, 'I suppose one would look for who would want to kill her and why?'

Roddy nodded sagely. '*Cui bono?* you might ask. Who here could possibly benefit from an old lady's death?'

'Exactly. You know your fellow guests better than we do: do you have a theory? And,' Harriet added, with a smile but very quietly, 'if you do we would love to hear it – but perhaps not in so public as spot as this.'

The boys' grins matched. 'What better opportunity for us to talk to you than while you both coach us at bowling?'

'What indeed? But Matthew must be your teacher, not me.' Harriet looked up at me. 'Yes?'

'But surely—!' Webbe began.

'This is the Sabbath, and the house is in mourning,' she said gently.

'Even so—'

'You gentlemen are less subject to . . . social convention,' she said.

Their faces switched from comic to tragic masks. Forsyth summed up her sentiment succinctly: 'You mean a man can get away with a lot more than a woman.'

Webbe nodded, adding with a quite moving sincerity at odds with his irrepressible mop of hair, 'You are right, ma'am. And when I am able I will do all in my power to redress the balance. I promise you. And I promise my sisters and my nieces.'

Forsyth had managed to find a dry patch of ground, an isthmus of green amidst the area still glinting with surface water. The threatened rain held off, and the sun was strong enough to make steam rise from the shallowest puddles. Soon Barrington's guests would be getting restive – and why not? In their situation, I would be desperate to leave the place and return to the safety of my own home. I would want to keep Harriet safe from the killer at all costs. So why was I leaving her on her own? Surely I should abandon these boys to their play and stand by her side. But I could imagine her response. After all, I was more or less acting on her orders. I turned my attention to Forsyth, who was tossing a ball from one hand to another. Then Webbe reached us, with not one but two notebooks.

'It's jolly good of you to teach us, sir,' he said, as his friend paced out the distance we needed.

'Even though you'd rather have learned from the original

expert. She's right, you know: it would not have been at all the thing for her to be seen enjoying herself.'

Forsyth nodded. 'Why are the ladies so beastly to her?'

'Because we men aren't?' Webbe suggested. 'And because she uses her brain and they don't have to. But I can't understand why Biddlestone was so rude in public. And how he got away with it. If Swain, our butler, ever mistook a guest's name, even accidentally, he'd be in the soup.'

'But not dead,' I pointed out. 'Biddlestone was murdered, gentlemen, and though Harriet might have disliked what he did – and to her credit she let him know it – on the evidence I saw she did not kill him. Her brain's as good as any man's, but not her strength.'

'So who would want him dead? Who would profit?'

Forsyth responded with more questions: 'Is it revenge for his killing the Gräfin or did Biddlestone try to blackmail the killer?'

'What good points,' I said, making a mental note of my own. 'Might he indeed be the murderer, now killed in his turn? Or, as you suggest, did he try his hand at blackmail? Now, lest we are being watched, just remind me of your run-up.' It was very good, fluid and even, until the stride before he actually bowled the ball. Then he bent his back in a way that made accuracy very hard.

'I'm trying to copy yours,' he said shyly. 'Don't quite manage it though.' Then he put his head to one side. 'Why did Major Jameson criticize you so rudely?'

'Why did he want to lose the match?' I countered, hoping I could trust them.

'Exactly what we've been asking,' Forsyth said. 'Deliberately throwing it away. Only a bounder would try to do that. I told you my pater doesn't like him.'

'Did your father ever explain why? Or even give a hint?'

He shook his head. 'But I know why I don't like him: he's all charm and politeness when he wants to be – and a lot of the ladies here have a soft spot for him, especially Lady Hortensia, I'd say. But he can be an out and out bully. Look at how he humiliated young Turton. In public. I wouldn't have blamed Turton for taking a swing at him, would you?'

'In fact,' his friend continued, 'if someone had murdered

Jameson, not the others, I wouldn't have been surprised, not one bit. Hey, I wonder if that's why he's lying low: I've hardly seen him since the match – apart from when he came down when we were all cheering Mrs Rowsley, of course.' His face froze. 'Rowsley, should we be here at all? Really? Shouldn't we be protecting her?'

Forsyth nodded eagerly. 'We can say it was just too wet to practise. Which it is, really.'

'Thank you. I'd feel much happier to know she's safe. Just one more try,' I suggested. 'And a couple of balls from you, Webbe. Then we can talk about technique as we walk back . . .'

The two lads responded eagerly to my suggestions, Forsyth even drawing a little diagram to which they could both refer – it seemed they were in and out of their college rooms like brothers. Now they bickered fraternally on what they should do next. Webbe rightly dismissed his friend's suggestion that they cling to Harriet like limpets, but then came up with an idea that seemed quite plausible, if not attractive from their point of view: they should hunt down Jameson and ask him to coach them.

'That way we can keep him out of everyone's hair and maybe work out what his thinking was during the game.'

I said, 'You told Harriet, Webbe, that your father neither liked nor trusted the man. I think you should ask yourself what he would have said to this idea – yes, and your father, too, Forsyth.'

'But there'd be two of us. Can't be safer than that, surely.'

'If – and this is a big if, and I am not making any accusations – if he is Biddlestone's killer he must be a very strong man. I do not want anyone, particularly any of Harriet's friends, to take any risks. My advice would be to— No, I can't advise you, because I really think I should be talking to him, if only I could think of some plausible reason to speak to a man I find entirely loathsome who presumably has the same feelings about me. My heart tells me your limpet idea is best. Harriet would love your company. But she is also very strong-minded and may try to get rid of you while she talks to other guests. You would have to be tact personified.'

Forsyth shook his head. 'If it's too much of a risk for two of us, it's too much of a risk for you on your own, sir. I'd say you'd need the Colonel at very least beside you.'

'No. Poor devil could hardly fight off a fly these days,' Webbe said, shaking his head sadly. 'But I think we should talk to Jameson. Your pater and he are acquaintances, after all. We'll hunt him out, sir, just to talk about cricket, of course, and we'll report back to you.'

SEVENTEEN

From the library windows I could watch the interplay of the promenading guests without having to engage with them. Moreover I was with friends: the books lining the shelves. Despite the lingering noxious smoke of Mr Digby's cigars, the underlying smell of old leather and paper was very comforting. It took me back to my younger days, when the late Lord Croft had treated me as he'd have treated his own child, gently educating and enlightening me. I came to love books as much as he did, whether it was an infinitely precious Book of Hours or a brand-new novel.

Instead of watching people, I found myself browsing, losing sense of time and place.

'What the devil!'

I almost dropped the book I held, a first edition of *Tom Jones*.

'What the hell are you doing here?'

The second question gave me time to catch my breath. I could not have managed a slighter curtsy. 'Good afternoon, Major Jameson.' Dare I go further and ask him the same question? On the whole I thought not. I knew he was capable of verbal violence and suspected he might have no trouble in striking me – or worse. Furthermore, of course, since I had come here for solitude, no one knew where I was.

'Well? I believe I asked you a question.'

How much of the luncheon wine had he consumed?

'I should imagine we both came for the same reason, sir. To read.' I held up the Fielding.

'They say you're sniffing round everywhere. You! You damned interfering bitch!'

I had briefly forgotten about the catch. 'I am merely here to read, sir.' But I carefully closed and replaced the book. I had known people deliberately harm things others cherished. It would not happen to this if I could help it. I moved sideways to place myself behind the lovely buhl desk.

'Aping your betters. Insulting your fellow guests. Ruining the cricket match! You – you trollop!' He was working himself up into the sort of tantrum that afflicted the present Lord Croft and which resulted in his being eventually confined to the Thorncroft House family wing.

I did not want to speak in case my voice shook. But I must. 'I am sorry that my presence so offends you. Pray allow me to leave you in peace.' I dropped a slightly more appeasing curtsy, hating myself for having to do it.

He stepped closer to the desk, cutting off my escape route.

Would calm or apparent panic give him more excuse to attack me? And how could I respond? Before me were a paper-knife and an inkwell. If I grabbed either, he was strong enough to wrest it from me and use it against me. And he had another weapon at his disposal.

No. He would not rape me. I would not endure that again. And God had given me a skill I could use. I picked up the beautiful, solid inkwell. I said, very clearly, 'It would be such a shame if I had to throw this through a window, would it not? And I have to tell you, sir, I am as good at throwing as I am at catching. As my dear friend Lord Halesowen would no doubt be delighted to confirm. Good day to you, sir.'

'You will regret this. I swear you will regret this.'

'Good afternoon, Major Jameson,' came a voice.

'Good afternoon, Lady Pidgeon,' I said, raising my voice in case she could not see me at this end of the room. Trusting she had forgiven me for what she had clearly regarded as an impertinent line of questioning, I said brightly, 'You will never guess what I have found! I was just showing Major Jameson a first edition of *Tom Jones*.' I pointed to the shelf, leaving her to draw her own conclusions.

She did. She knew I was in trouble. 'Were you indeed? I would love to see it.' She bustled closer. She might be small and frail, but she was powerful enough to silence the Major. 'You do love your books, do you not, my dear. Major Jameson, can you believe that Mrs Rowsley actually enjoys *The Mill on the Floss*?' Her eyes narrowed. 'Dear me, you did not come in here to smoke, Major?'

'Indeed . . . indeed . . . I . . .' He stuttered like a village lad caught scrumping apples. He recovered enough to kiss her hand with some panache, earning, despite everything, an indulgent smile.

'Well, someone has certainly done precisely that,' she declared. 'I will have a word with Hortensia. Heavens, one careless spark could cause a conflagration with terrible consequences. Do we know who is responsible, dear Major? Mrs Rowsley, do you?'

'Indeed, no, your ladyship.'

'Ah, Mrs Rowsley, it is clear that you do. And you are too kind-hearted to identify the miscreant. I am ashamed of you!' She patted my hand. 'I joke, my dear. My intuition is that Mr Digby is the one at fault. Let us go and beard him together. By the way,' she continued, taking my arm and leaning quite heavily on me, despite her cane, 'I hear that the village constable is on his way.'

I managed a grim smile. 'Let us just hope that his name isn't Dogberry.'

Jameson stepped back, but not quite enough. I had to lift my skirt so it would not brush him.

We progressed slowly outside. 'What a fortunate coincidence, my dear.'

'Indeed, your ladyship, I believe you probably saved my life.'

She shook her head. 'You exaggerate, my dear. I heard enough of the encounter to be convinced that you could have saved your own – even if you would have left the most beautiful room in the house spattered with ink and some lovely old glass shattered. How strangely the Major was behaving – I have always found him to be a most charming gentleman. You know, he's quite popular amongst our fellow guests – the poor, dear Gräfin might have told you such tales . . . But I am not as naughty as she was and will keep my lips sealed.' We reached the terrace, where she quickly located her husband. 'Ah! Pidgeon! There you are.'

His body might have been, but his eyes were glazed and vacant. Was he drunk, or suffering that most unkind of old people's diseases, where the mind can no longer match the outward appearance?

She spoke to him as if he was a child. 'Your hip-flask if you please, Pidgeon! Your hip-flask. Thank you.'

Her husband made a space for her on his bench, producing the desired item. Though he looked at me with inexplicable venom he unscrewed it, punctiliously wiping the rim with a linen handkerchief still showing the ironing folds, and passed it silently to his wife. 'Drink,' she told me.

Despite hating spirits, I drank. And it tasted like nectar. What should I do with the flask now? I almost laughed: I had never swigged from one before and did not know the etiquette, if there was any. Lord Pidgeon solved the problem by seizing it from my grasp and wiping it with his handkerchief.

'You're that woman—'

'No, my dear, you're mistaking her for someone else.'

I think she added that I was much shorter, but at this point my two young friends joined me with whoops of delight. They relived every moment of their brief coaching session with Matthew; their innocent joy brought me back to something approaching myself. But even as I laughed with them, I wondered how much I dared tell Matthew. But tell him something I must, to put him at very least on his guard. Meanwhile, Roddy was charming girlish giggles from my saviour and Charles was attempting to discuss cricket with her husband. Might I excuse myself to speak to Matthew? But he was nowhere to be seen. I was ready to panic when Mason materialized.

'The Colonel's compliments, ma'am, and would you care to join him and the gentlemen in the sewing room? Might I accompany you there?'

Apparently the parish constable had arrived at four-fifteen exactly. At first glance Constable Davies was a man of little presence and less chin, on which he had a fierce pimple likely, I was sure, to become a painful boil if he did not stop his fingers constantly exploring it. It was all too easy to see why he was held in derision by the footmen, each, after all, picked for height and manly beauty and an ability to speak clearly in the Queen's English. Davies might be as tall as them but stood as if he needed his stiff uniform – he was sporting one of the new tunics – to hold him up; he had a decided Welsh accent, rushing his sentences as if embarrassed by them. Our own village constable was a Welsh-speaker and could use his bilingualism to good effect if necessary, so I reserved judgement on this man – and then was almost shocked into laughter when he announced he had his birds on the case.

'Carrier pigeons, see. Soon as I hear there are two dead people, I know I might need help. So I get a message to my cousin Geraint in Hereford – a sergeant he is, we're all very proud of him – and he gets a message back saying Colonel Rowsley here should telegraph Scotland Yard. That's if you think it's necessary, sir,' he added with a blush. 'Meanwhile, he'll be on the first train that can get through. The Wye's risen, see – but not as bad as here.'

'The flooding is general, then?' Matthew asked.

'Not what I'd call general. More here and there. Worse here because of that damned bridge, begging your pardon for my language, ma'am. Jerry-built, I think the term is now. Sorry, Colonel, but it's best to speak truth to power, as the gospel tells us – and whoever built that robbed you something shocking. And now it's no use to man or beast – and it's a good step to cross that stream without it.'

Barrington flushed, but nodded graciously enough.

'Now, Colonel, I walked up – long way round, remember – with the parson. I know he prefers to be called a priest, and Father too, Father Howells, that is, but that seems a bit odd in an ordinary parish church, doesn't it? Now Mr Harrison told him you needed someone to read today's service, and he, being High, like, wants to pray over the corpses too.'

Matthew looked up.

The constable looked at him shrewdly but continued without pausing, 'But I thought – no disrespect to the cloth, mind – if I looked at them first it might be best, mightn't it? And took any loose belongings into what you might call protective custody? So Father Howells is in the servants' hall getting outside a pot of tea and plate of cakes. Perhaps –?' He looked round expectantly. 'The fewer that know what I'm up to the happier I shall be.'

For answer, Matthew stood. 'I'll take him along, shall I, Barrington?' He was off, without waiting for an answer. Could Barrington even have given one? His face was bleached with pain.

'Cousin, should I ring for more tea?' I asked gently.

'Might have something a little stronger. Thank you, my dear. Good of Matthew to take that constable off. Wonder why he doesn't want any prayers till he's looked at him. Remind you of a rabbit, does he?' Amazingly he put his hands to his head to make a pair of ears. 'Interesting he's sent for his cousin. Carrier pigeon, God bless my soul. Whatever next?'

'Is Father Howells acquainted with the Gräfin and Biddlestone?' I asked, as idly as I could. 'Oh, well done, Mr Turton!'

Blushing, Jeremy held up a deft sketch: the constable indeed looked like a rabbit. Cousin Barrington roared with laughter, his face crinkled in the first signs of happiness or even amusement I had seen since we had arrived.

Then his eyes narrowed. 'I've seen worse artists than you make a decent living,' he said, jabbing with his index finger. 'I know you're meant to take Holy Orders, but you have a talent, young man, a real talent – and you know what it says in the Bible about burying talents.'

Mason knocked and entered with a tray of decanters. 'Your favourite, Colonel?' he asked almost tenderly, clearly taking in his employer's now grey skin.

'If you please. Just a mere splash of water. Thank you. Harriet? Turton? No? Well, leave it in case they change their minds. Good man.'

Mason adjusted the cushion a little in the most comfortable chair. 'I will ensure that there is plenty of hot water, sir.' He bowed himself out.

Hot water? Whatever its purpose the news drew a grateful smile.

Barrington soon started to snore, so I gently removed the whisky glass from his hand. He had not answered my question, of course – but I was sure Matthew would elicit all the information he could. As for the information I had acquired, I thought I should wait until I could tell not just our little team but also the constable. What else could I do? Wishing to find something, anything, that would incriminate Jameson, I applied myself once more to completing the huge chart. This entailed re-reading the original statements to see if there were any discrepancies, a task with which Jeremy was quick to help. There were plenty, but none truly incriminating. It was a shame: I wanted something useful to offer the spotty pigeon-fancier. I did wish that every time I thought of his bird my mind's eye did not see Lady Pidgeon in flight. I wonder what her poor feeble-minded old husband did all the time apart from carry such useful brandy: curiously we had no statement from him. I made a note – not that I saw him as capable of either killing, but because I disliked having an omission in our system. And yes, there was that furious look he had given me earlier: what on earth could I have done to merit that? Then I recalled what Billy had said about him. I must bear his words in mind.

I took a deep breath: 'Jeremy, you know all these people far better than I do – their class, their type, at least. I can observe from the outside. But you see from the inside. Help yourself to a glass of whatever you drink and help me!'

With a wry smile, he poured two glasses of water, handing me one. He pointed to his mouth. 'This makes me an outsider too. I don't have easy charm like Webbe and Forsyth. People avoid me. But you're right. I'm one of the tribe. So my answers may be as slow and painful as this one, but ask away.'

Dare I risk it? 'You drew that wonderful rabbit. Draw yourself as you imagine others see you.'

Scratching his head, he grimaced, but applied himself.

I took the caricature he offered me and drew him to the mirror. 'You see a literally tongue-tied idiot dragging your knuckles like one of Mr Darwin's monkeys. I see a tall and handsome young man, with good bones and clear skin and eyes to melt any young lady's heart. And, as Cousin Barrington says, you are such a talented artist. Do not dare bury that talent.' I smiled. 'Enough of my sermon. Now, help me with your observations. And talk to me about the person no one seems to want to mention: Major Jameson.'

The boy opened his mouth to speak – but Mason opened the door to announce the return of Constable Davies, who stood back to let Matthew precede him. Our host woke with a start.

'Constable, this is the young man whose work I mentioned. Turton, do you have with you those drawings of where we found Biddlestone? I think he'd find them very useful.'

There was a tiny pause while Jeremy, blushing to the ears, concealed his two comic sketches before, with something of a flourish, producing what Matthew wanted.

Davies' eyes opened to what I judge would be their furthest extent. 'Amazing. As good as a photograph, if I may say so.'

The four men gathered round the table. Had Matthew forgotten something? He made a space for me with a shamefaced grin.

'Ma'am – this is not fit for a lady's eyes!' Davies gasped.

'Are you sure? Heavens! Look at that bruise! So Biddlestone's assailant stunned him so he fell? Or did it actually kill him? I'm sorry – I'm sure the gentlemen have already asked you.'

'I'll give you the answer I gave them: I wouldn't care to speculate. I'll ask the doctor to look when he arrives, ma'am. At a childbed he is, and, he says, bringing the living into the world trumps speculating about the dead. And I couldn't find it in me to argue, ma'am. Er – I hardly like to ask, ma'am, but have you seen the . . . the actual bodies?'

'Only the Gräfin's. I have a strong stomach, Mr Davies, but no desire to challenge it! It was not so much Biddlestone's body that interested me,' I said, touching the sketch, 'as how it got to the river before it got into the river.'

'We're sure he walked. And Colonel Rowsley's theory that the assailant came at him through the water is the most likely.' He mimed walking and hitting. 'So we're looking for someone strong. And ruthless.'

'My wife and young Turton have transcribed all the inform-ation we could obtain from the guests,' Matthew said, 'so we should know their whereabouts—'

'Ostensibly,' Jeremy managed, creeping through the rest of what he had to say. 'They don't all match up. But none of them breathes a hint of a motive.'

Davies' attention might have flagged under the pressure of his embarrassment at Jeremy's disability, but the final word lit up his face as if someone had set a lamp behind it. 'Exactly! Often a man or even a woman might have a motive for killing one person, but for killing two! Two very different people. Very different. So we might have a lot of people with a lot of motives. We get some gossip down in the village, of course, about a lot of things – and Mr Biddlestone doesn't come well out of some of it. Colonel: you were his employer. How did you find him?'

Cousin Barrington inched from the table and sat very carefully, wincing as he did so. 'Between these four walls, Davies, I didn't like him. But he has – had – worked for my wife's family here for years. It – it wasn't my job to dismiss trusted retainers, shall we say.'

'And this – this foreign lady?'

'Gräfin Weiser? English as they come, actually. Just married a foreigner. Lived abroad for years. My wife's godmother. You should talk to her ladyship about her, not me.'

'With due respect, sir, I need to talk to everyone about both the victims. And since I have several of you here, this seems a good place to start.' He polished his pimple. 'I am more than happy to speak to you in private – or to hear what you have to say right now.'

Someone had to break the silence.

'Constable, I am happy for everyone to hear what I say. I had every reason to dislike Mr Biddlestone, as downstairs gossip will confirm. And upstairs too,' I added ruefully. 'By profession I am a housekeeper, and my presence here with my husband, Colonel Rowley's cousin, was a source of irritation and amusement to many. Both the guests and the staff. Mr Biddlestone and others thought it diverting to refer to me by my maiden name.' Try as I might, I could not keep down my blush, or stop my anger and pain infusing my voice. And I could not recount the afternoon's incident in front of them all. Not yet.

He looked me straight in the eye. 'Did you kill him, ma'am?'

Disconcerted for a moment, I shook my head. 'Physically, if he'd been sitting or bending down, I could probably have hit him hard enough to stun him. Maybe kill him? I don't know. But he was a tall man, like you. If you care to stand you will see my problem. There. Without a stool I wouldn't have a chance. Furthermore, Cousin Barrington believes that whoever killed him left no tracks because he walked along the stream bed.'

'He or she,' the constable pointed out.

'Have you ever walked with a wet crinoline? Especially through water?'

'You could have had accomplices.'

'I could. But who? Matthew or Mr Turton? I give you my word that I neither killed him nor incited others to. As for the Gräfin, I think I liked her more than some other guests did, perhaps because I never joined her at a card table.' Yes, that was a nice plump cat to drop among the pigeons – however you might spell them. It earned a sharp intake of breath from Barrington.

'Are you alleging that she cheated?'

'How could I? I told you, I only ever conversed with her. She was kind to me, in her way.' I took a deep breath. 'But I was warned against playing cards with her. Others will be able to tell you far more, perhaps.'

Those rabbit eyes gave me a very shrewd look. And then looked straight at Barrington. 'Well, sir?'

Barrington went puce – but choked back anything he meant to say as a tap on the door had Mason announcing Father Howells.

'We'll talk in my study, padre,' Barrington said. 'Davies, you can use this room as your HQ, but mind your tone, eh? And Cousin Harriet, you might need to reflect on yours, too. And those,' he flung over his shoulder as he left, 'are orders.'

EIGHTEEN

Before I could speak, Davies said quietly, 'You are clearly a brave woman, Mrs Rowsley. Now, I was wondering if I might ask you to do something even braver.'

'My supply of courage is rather low,' she said with a wry smile. 'Remember, Constable Davies, that we did not know when – indeed if! – you would be able to get through. So I need to confess something to you. Perhaps foolishly I dressed as a maid and searched the guests' rooms while the men were dealing with the body. I'm sorry, Jeremy, that included yours, which, thank God, didn't seem to contain any missing jewels. Please forgive me.'

Though the boy looked troubled, he stepped over to her and kissed her hand.

'Did any room have any interesting contents?' Davies asked.

'I found some things that may or may not be of importance. I must ask you gentlemen to step from the room so that I can produce one of them.'

I did not follow the others immediately, but took her in my arms. 'He says some of the roads are clear. No one would blame you if we were to leave now. You should not have to endure . . . even Barrington . . . That was unforgivable, and I shall tell him so.'

'When he is in less pain I'm sure he will apologize. Could you untie the key? I find my hands are shaking.'

So were mine. But at last I could lay it on the table. And pour her a tot of what smelled like excellent single malt whisky.

'Good heavens, it's like drinking mud and hay! No, grass. No . . . In any case, I think I need a clear mind. Matthew, after what I did how can I join the others for supper? And for entertainment afterwards?'

'You did right. Heavens, you would have genuinely cleaned their rooms with not a qualm had Mrs Simpkiss asked for help.

There is no need for a moment's shame. Is there? And do you seriously believe that a single one of those people would not actively betray even a friend to exonerate him or herself? No. Now we must show Davies this and your pieces of paper and then, while he considers them, I suspect we should go to Father Howells' service,' I said, without enthusiasm.

She straightened her shoulders, but her voice was tranquil enough as she remarked, 'It might be good to think of God, not man, for a few minutes. Best call the others back, I suppose.'

Davies returned without Turton, who, he said as we sat round the table, did not feel that more people than were absolutely essential should be looking at other people's property. 'And I can't say I disagree,' Davies said.

Harriet flushed at the implied criticism.

'We all understand his reservations, including you, of course, my dear,' I said. 'But if my wife has been brave enough to retrieve this material, then the least we can do is look at it and see what we can make of it.'

'And then destroy it if it is irrelevant,' she said quickly as she passed him an envelope.

The young man shook his head. 'We won't know if it is relevant or not until we have somehow uncovered the murderer or murderers.' Suddenly he smiled. 'Ma'am, you obviously had something very particular about your person. Might I see it?'

'There.' She put the key in his hands. 'It's the thing that troubles me least, since I found it in the Gräfin's bed chamber. We've no idea what it might unlock,' she added, as he continued to weigh it in one hand then the other. 'It seems a little large even for the jewellery box that is missing – but since I have never seen the box I might well be wrong.'

He nodded. 'This is certainly evidence. Later I would like you to show me where you found it.'

She nodded with clear reluctance.

'And the other things you found, ma'am? Shall we look?' Tipping the crumpled shreds of paper on to the desk, he straightened out each one, laying it face up with tedious meticulousness. Harriet pointedly averted her gaze. I did the same as he rearranged them as if they were part of a jigsaw puzzle.

'For now, I must also treat this as evidence,' he said solemnly.

'I know you would rather not know the contents, but when I have discovered more I may have to ask you to give your opinion. Or maybe my cousin will. Or the Scotland Yard men from London.' He shrugged. 'For now, though, everything will return to the police house with me and be locked in the safe there. Now, what next, ma'am?' He spoke with more authority.

So did she. 'You will hear – have perhaps heard already since I can't believe it hasn't been the subject of a lot of village gossip – that Major Jameson behaved very strangely yesterday. You may even have seen? Surely you went to the match?'

'I was shooting a dog that was worrying Farmer Cross's sheep, ma'am. And then, to be honest, I had forty winks. The twins are teething, mostly at night. Very well. Major Jameson. What did you find of his that troubles you?'

She pointed to a folded note. 'I wish I knew whose initials they are. Here you are, Constable. The Major also has a sizeable strong-box in his room, which I did not attempt to open. I have to say, there may be other items from other rooms. My – accomplice – on the staff here had no qualms about going through people's pockets. We planned to look at what she found this evening, but I would be more than happy to hand over the task to you.'

'That would be . . .?' He looked almost apprehensive.

'Mrs Simpkiss. Like me, she has been trained from childhood to be honest and discreet. Actually, she may flatly deny everything in case she thinks she is putting me at risk.'

'Suppose you write her a note by way of explanation, ma'am.'

'Of course. Then, if you will excuse me, I should attend evensong, no matter how short it has to be.'

I had never held Harriet's hand during a service before, but I did this evening. Otherwise I think she might have stormed out. The family sat. The guests sat. The servants stood. Perhaps I misjudged her: she might just have gone to stand at the back.

The servants adjourned.

The guests sat through a mercifully short, almost perfunctory sermon, and then galloped off to change for their pre-dinner drinks.

*   *   *

The moment our bed chamber door was shut, she took my hands. 'There is something I must tell you. Must. Something potentially very unpleasant. So I suggest we sit down together for a moment before we change. No. We need to sit, my love.'

I obeyed, making sure I could see her face.

'This afternoon, I wanted – wanted to escape from all the carping and the criticism, yes, real or imagined. And I thought that the library might offer sanctuary. I had books aplenty. I had quiet. And if I wanted I could watch the people parading on the terrace – much as one might watch the animals in a zoological garden,' she added, with a valiant attempt at irony.

'But something disturbed your idyll,' I prompted.

'Yes. The Major disturbed my idyll, with a few well-chosen words and a . . . a menacing presence that reminded me of when . . . of when . . .'

Of when she was raped as a child. I gathered her to me and waited for the racking breaths to quieten. At last I could feel her shoulders straighten.

'I really feared a physical, if not a sexual, assault,' she said, her delivery now as clipped as if she were on the witness stand. 'There was a paper-knife on that lovely desk, but I was afraid that if I used it he would turn it on me. There was also an inkwell. A big heavy one.'

'Wouldn't that have been just as risky?'

Suddenly her face was impish. 'Not if I'd thrown it out of the window, which is what I threatened to do. And then Lady Pidgeon appeared, and in the politest and firmest way threw him out. And insisted her poor husband gave me some of his brandy. And I've been waiting all this time to find a time to tell you without making it look . . . particular. And to give us both time to calm down.'

I could not argue. In fact I could not speak. In silence I clasped the most treasured gift life had given me, one that might have been taken without my knowing.

'I wonder,' she asked at last, in an approximation of her usual tone, 'if anyone has thought to offer that interesting constable some refreshment.'

'I'm sure Mason would,' I said, breaking off to take the hot water from the footman knocking at the door. 'Are you sure you want to dress? To go down to face all those . . . those chimpanzees?'

'I am not looking forward to the evening, I admit. But we owe it to Cousin Barrington, do we not, to put on what he would probably call a decent show.' She spoke with very little conviction.

'My love, it will be an ordeal in every respect, but I suggest that while we cannot escape dinner, we can avoid the after-dinner entertainment.'

'Good. Because as you know I have already made a tentative arrangement to sit with Mrs Simpkiss after dinner. But you . . .?' She turned to face me anxiously.

'If you are happy to miss the singing and recitations – or would you prefer to recite the whole of *Don Juan*? – I could look through Barrington's accounts. I'm intrigued about the work done on the bridge, and how it ever got paid for. Not to mention how much.'

'Will he consent?'

'I hope so. I very much hope so. Because I might just ask Constable Davies to suggest it – on the grounds that he was, in Davies' words, robbed.'

'Checking accounts on the Sabbath? Hortensia won't approve of that!' But she was laughing, not genuinely shocked. Then she frowned. 'What a strange woman she is. All this insistence on observing the Lord's Day, but as far as I can see not an ounce of charity in her whole body. Her coldness . . . No, I don't want to drift into self-pity again.'

'I don't see an ounce of self-pity. You make a valid point. Why all this show of religion? It seems rank hypocrisy to me, if you will pardon the pun. You know, I really can't see why a fundamentally decent man like Barrington should look at her twice.'

'Her lineage, her blood, Matthew!'

'Which is blue twice over, once with her lineage, and once with cold. And while Barrington's family is good enough – though I suppose I might be biased! – an earl as a grandfather does not put you to the top of the marriage mart, especially if you are as badly injured as Barrington was. Heavens, the arrival of young Arthur must have been a miracle.'

'Hence her piety, perhaps. She got the son she was praying for.'

'Possibly. Or, there again, possibly not. Anyway, with luck,

Hortensia will never know that I broke the Sabbath looking into the estate finances, assuming I can get hold of the ledgers, of course. Officially you and I are – I don't know – indisposed.' I clicked my fingers. 'I will have a migraine and you will be sponging my forehead with vinegar. Would that be acceptable?'

'Provided Cousin Barrington knows. Either you or Mr Davies ought to tell him. While you ponder that, I suspect we really must go down. Perhaps we should talk loudly so that they can stop gossiping about us before we enter.'

For all Lady Pidgeon motioned her to join her on a sofa as we drank sherry and Forsyth managed to take a place at her side for dinner, I feared that Harriet might succumb to a genuine migraine, the atmosphere was so tense. She was even cross-questioned over the first course about the jet necklace, her simple and truthful explanation about how she came to possess such a wonderful piece all too clearly disbelieved by her simpering but spiteful interlocutor. Fortunately the large presence of Mr Digby, whose monologue overrode everything this young lady tried to say, spared her a great deal. Meanwhile I was grasping my forehead and tried to look bemused, much as my cousin used to do when he was about to be afflicted with the strange lights and prostrating headaches that made a misery of much of his younger years.

When the ladies rose, I could do no more than stagger to my feet. Harriet was by my side in an instant. We left – slowly but inexorably – together. I insisted on accompanying her to the Room, but then slipped back to spend the rest of the evening in the sewing room, hoping to find that Davies had obtained the relevant accounts. He had. I picked up a pen, ready to make notes.

The constable occupied one end of the table, picking his way through scraps of paper, presumably ones that Mrs Simpkiss had removed from pockets. There was a companionable silence, but for the scratching of heads and pens.

While we both eased our backs, he asked, as if we were in the middle of a conversation, 'And how do you propose to slip back to your bed chamber unseen? You don't want to be caught out in a lie, man.'

'I shall take the subterranean route, and, with luck collecting Harriet on the way, go up the servants' stairs, not the main ones.'

'I might accompany you underground at least. Do a little looking round on my own account, like. And your wife's advice might be useful. Why do these people do it, Mr Rowsley?' He jabbed at the collated statements. 'Without naming names, do they not grasp the difference between the truth and the whole truth? I suppose they will when they address the Coroner at the inquests into the two deaths. And maybe other courts too,' he added dryly.

'I hope so.' I dropped my pencil. 'Dear me, none of this makes sense.'

'What's the problem, Mr Rowsley? What can't you make out?' Davies asked, already on his feet.

'Who is responsible for what. Has my cousin assumed full responsibility for all the decisions? Or does he take advice and if so from whom? Come, Davies, you're a village man. You must have a fair idea who does what and why. And,' I added with a grin, 'what people think of the arrangements.'

'Are we talking just about the bridge? Or about the family's finances in general?' His eyes narrowed. 'Or was this accounts stuff all a load of flannel and you just came here to pick my brains?'

It was best to be honest. 'I truly wanted to see if the figures would tell me anything. Which they don't. So now I'd like to talk about everything you can tell me. Officially or not.'

For a moment I thought I had offended him. But his laugh reassured me. 'As a sort of price for all the information your wife and the poor gentleman with the stammer have obtained and organized? No, I'm not serious. And if sharing information with you makes my job easier, so be it. Tell me, did your cousin recruit the stammering man for any special reason?'

'Actually, he volunteered. I think Harriet might even have said extra clerical help would be useful.'

'Hmm.' He lowered his voice. 'This is not the best place to talk about the family affairs, is it? Perhaps the late butler's room might be better. Tell me, has anyone but me looked at it yet? Well, come on then. Lead the way through these mysterious tunnels. By the way, did I tell you I'm having both the corpses moved tomorrow, weather permitting?'

'I believe everyone will be relieved to hear it.'

'But they won't hear it. Not from me, and not, I hope, from you. I'm still in hopes that someone will make some attempt to rob or otherwise interfere with the corpses. If they do they may get a bit more than they expected. My brother-in-law's not a shepherd for nothing, Mr Rowsley.' He gave an extravagant wink.

For a moment my mind was a complete blank, but light slowly dawned. 'You mean he's given you some of his reddle, so that—'

'Any miscreant will be literally caught red-handed!' He roared with laughter, but narrowed his eyes. 'What do you need to tell me, Mr Rowsley?'

'Something that happened to my wife, that almost left someone black-handed. Me. Black with bruises.' Sitting down again, I explained. 'So you will understand if I ask you something you may not wish to tell me: is Major Jameson one of those whose statement is not the whole truth?'

Davies frowned, an expression to which his face was not suited. 'He's not the only one, sadly. And being extremely offensive to a not quite defenceless woman and trying to lose a cricket match – sadly they don't quite add up to murder. Motive and means, Mr Rowsley. I suppose you'll tell me he's a strong man, and as ruthless as Satan. But I don't see an opportunity in his timetable and I don't see a motive. Yet.'

'If he wants to lose a match, and goes to a great deal of trouble to do so, money might well be a motive, surely. That's not just my view, either.' My confidence in his ability was ebbing briskly, as briskly as my temper was rising. 'Perhaps when you interview him, you will see why I suspect him.'

'I must admit you're not the only one. And you're not the only one to think he wanted to lose the match – for a bet, most say. As your wife imagined, it's the talk of the village. It's something I'll be asking him about, never fear. Him and any other men involved, staff or guest.'

'Don't exclude the women, my wife particularly. She was watching the entire match. And,' I added slowly, not sure I was doing the right thing, 'if you want to talk to my wife about her dreadful experience in the library, be aware that this was not the first time she has been . . . No, that is not my story to tell. Let us agree to disagree at this point, Constable.' I offered him my hand. 'Shall I lead us into the underworld?

'So long as you can lead us out again!'

In the gloomy corridor, he produced a key, squinting at it in the light of a feeble oil lamp. 'I found this on Biddlestone's person, and thought I might as well use it. Hmm. At least the lock is well-oiled.' Stepping inside, he lit all the candles he could find – four in total. 'A bit grim, isn't it?'

At Thorncroft, Samuel, our much-loved butler, had spent his working life living in a room like this: dark, furnished with other people's leavings, desperately in need of some whitewash and new wallpaper. This was even worse. Damp stained the outer wall. Even the rag rug before the fireplace was worn through. There were no pictures, no books, nothing to suggest that a living individual had spent years of his life here.

Davies shook his head. 'My home isn't much,' he said quietly, as if he might disturb some residual shade of the dead man, 'but at least I make it my own. My wife does, truth to tell. Bronwen. A couple of embroidered texts here, the Bible beside the bed: you'd get more sense of his life. Or not,' he added grimly. 'He doesn't have much of a name as a God-fearing man. Efficient, yes, and more of a house steward than just a butler these days, I'd guess. Land steward too. But the other servants would be able to tell you more. They were scared to death of him when he was alive, I can tell you.'

'And someone was more than scared,' I mused. 'Davies, if you don't mind, I really do recommend we ask my wife to see this. She may see something that mere males like us have missed.'

'I thought she was going to talk to Mrs Simpkiss? And who knows, she might get to worm something out of young Clara. Let's not disturb her, Mr Rowsley. We might not search without leaving a single trace, but that doesn't mean we can't search, does it? Where would you hide something in this bleak hole? That cupboard? Under the bed?'

There was nothing there except an ornate chamber pot, badly chipped.

The cupboard doubled as a wardrobe, every item carefully

hung or immaculately folded. There was a strong-box, locked, as one might expect, tucked behind a suit. It did not respond to any of the keys Davies produced.

'So he must have hidden it somewhere in here. Drat. Going through a corpse's belongings always feels wrong, even if they're mere rags and rubbish compared with this,' he said at last. He looked at his watch. 'Maybe, if she's finished with Mrs Simpkiss, we could actually talk to your good lady – she might think of somewhere unexpected. And I would like to hear what she says about the Major. If you think she's well enough to talk, of course.'

NINETEEN

'There she is – sleeping like a baby!' Mrs Simpkiss opened the door gently. She had had a truckle bed set up for Clara in her own bed chamber, so, as she put it, anyone wanting to hurt or even scare the child would have to deal with her first. She folded her arms to make her point, looking truly pugnacious. But then her voice dropped to the quietest murmur. 'Thumb in mouth, doll in her arms. Wouldn't think she was nearly twelve, would you?'

I shook my head. It was lovely to see her so calm – but I did wish I could have spoken to her again, to learn more about the man in the dressing room.

She lit the candle although it was not quite dark yet, and we stepped back into the Room itself, where she produced two fine but mismatched glasses and a decanter holding a little port.

'Mr Biddlestone, God rest his soul, always made sure we had a supply,' she said. 'Oh, Mrs Rowsley, who knows where that soul is now? He might have been generous with the Colonel's wine, but he was a strange man in other ways. But it doesn't do so speak ill of the dead.' She lifted her glass in a silent toast to someone, I knew not whom.

Sitting opposite her in a grievously uncomfortable chair, probably Jacobean and far too grand to be hidden away here, even as a cast-off, I matched her gesture. Mr Biddlestone's choice of port at least was immaculate.

'Sometimes,' I said, 'it's speaking the truth, no matter how unpalatable it is, that helps people like Constable Davies discover the killer. And that would apply to both the Gräfin and Mr Biddlestone.' I set my glass down: I rarely drank port, as it always went straight to my head, and I needed to think clearly and remember accurately.

Mrs Simpkiss drank deeply. 'I shall miss this,' she said, adding with a smile that took twenty years off her otherwise grim, set face. 'I shall have to train up Mason, won't I? Fine young man.

Mind you, I don't suppose he'll be here long. He's ambitious. And he worries about his pay, when he hears visiting valets talk about the rates at their places. No, he'll be off. And then where will we be?'

'Billy?'

She looked over the rim of her glass. 'Not ready yet. By any means. We can't get youngsters to come, and if they do then they're off at the next quarter day. I've tried talking to her ladyship, but you know what she's like.' She emptied her glass.

'I've hardly met her,' I said, clutching a vestige of family loyalty to me. But I could not face down her direct stare. 'Yes, I know some ladies make good employers and others do not. Some can't manage the money they have, and some don't have enough money or the sense to ask people like you and me how to make it go further.'

She snorted with laughter. 'And some aren't very nice people either. They'd rather say an unkind thing than a kind one. But I mention no names.'

I didn't need to press her to. I sipped. 'Yes, Mr Biddlestone knew his port, didn't he? But he can't have been liked?'

She dropped her voice, as if he might still overhear. 'He had no end of a temper on him. And when he was cross he sort of loomed. Even over a woman my height! Like this. Well, of course, he tried it on with you.' She stood up, hooking her head and shoulders forward. In other circumstances I might have joked that she looked as if she were doing an impression of one of the man-monkeys Mr Darwin said were our ancestors, but not now. Heavens, could it – no, surely she had nothing to do with his death. Physically she might just have been capable . . . But with her timetable, she would simply not have had a chance to murder anyone outside the house.

'Where I work, the butler and I get on very well, thank goodness. He seems to have a good relationship with the other servants too. Did Biddlestone ever mix with you and the staff or keep himself to himself?'

'Bless you, he kept himself absolutely to himself. But it was strange. He seemed to know everything everyone was doing, family and guests included, I must say. The ladies loved him, would you believe? Always laughing and flirting with him they were. Not that he'd join in any gossip – well, people in our position don't, do we? But he'd be listening. Always listening.'

'Did he have any favourites?'

She pulled a face. 'Favourite victims, yes. That's another reason I couldn't keep staff. Always complaining about first one maid, then another. And I've known footmen take a swing at him. Instant dismissal, of course. But he got a name as a man to be feared, all right. And the villagers don't like the way he . . . You see, Mrs Rowsley, he was in charge of getting minor repairs done. Broken windows or chairs, that sort of thing.'

'There isn't an estate handyman?'

'Not any more. One of her ladyship's economies. But I reckon they didn't actually save any money, because people got so sick of him being a nipcheese and trying to get a job done for two or three pence less – yes, actual pennies! – that they found they were busy elsewhere next time he asked. So a small leak soon became a big one. And,' she continued, 'there were rumours he asked for backhanders, that if there was a big contract, like some re-roofing, he would ask for . . . well, I suppose you might call it a bribe, Mrs Rowsley.'

Might I indeed? 'So was he . . . let us say, did he have a big sock under his bed, as our old butler used to have? Or would that be too obvious?'

She shook her head. 'Have you seen his room? No, obviously young Morgan Davies locked it. Shame. I'd have liked you to see it. Mrs Rowsley, it's even worse than this. Other people's leavings, like that chair you're sitting on.' She found one last sip in the bottom of her glass. 'But the way he was sucking up to the guests he must have made a fortune in tips.'

'Sucking up! It would be hard for anyone to be more insulting to a guest than he was to me!'

'I wonder what happened to the money,' she said, ignoring my comment. She shrugged. 'It's not as if he had anything to spend it on. Or anywhere to hide it.' She peered at the glass as if she might squeeze it to extract one last drop.

She might, if she wished, empty my glass when I had gone. I had seen the same done by more colleagues more times than I could count. 'Did he ever talk about any of the guests – you know the sort of thing, "Old X is a tight-fisted beggar; Y never gives you a halfpenny when a farthing would do"?'

She looked at me sideways. 'You might be a housekeeper, Mrs Rowsley, but you're also a guest.'

'Or put it the other way round: I'm a guest for three or four days, but a housekeeper for three hundred and sixty-one. The guest part of me wants to find a fellow guest's killer; the house-keeper part wants to find a fellow servant's killer.'

'What if they're one and the same?' she asked.

I waited. And waited. My heart was beating very hard. A name. Just a name. A name like Jameson, said a little voice in my head. Her face worked: a desire to help? Fear? Loyalty? Just as she opened her mouth, we heard footsteps outside. And Constable Davies opened the door.

'Mrs Simpkiss, can you see anything different about the room?' Davies asked, gesturing us both into the butler's room to be greeted by one of Matthew's warmest smiles. 'It's a miserable enough place, isn't it? I wonder what her ladyship would say if she had to spend a night here!'

Her face paper-white, Mrs Simpkiss replied. 'Nothing has been changed. Not as far as I can see. But I have to get back to little Clara.' She pushed past him; we heard her running back to the Room.

'She's put her to bed in her own room,' I explained, 'to keep her safe. It meant I couldn't question her, I'm afraid.'

'That's a shame,' he tutted. 'The sooner she's managed to talk about the murder the sooner she can start getting over it. That's my theory, anyway.' He leant closer. 'The word in the village is that she's Mrs Simpkiss' own daughter. But no one seems to know who the father might be. Lots of suggestions, of course.'

'Can you recall the most interesting ones? Though you'd have been just a lad in those days, letting the tongues wag while you got on with other things?' Matthew asked.

'I'll ask my mother, but it's all a long time ago, and there is newer, better gossip these days.'

'About anyone in particular?' I asked, instinctively reaching to straighten the bedclothes. Or to strip the bed entirely. After all, someone had to. But not me, not yet.

He shrugged. 'Just village stuff. Though there's plenty of talk about the cricket match, I can tell you. Is there somewhere in this house where we could sit down and talk privately? Anywhere?'

'There's the sewing room,' I pointed out.

'What about young Turton? And Barrington?' Matthew asked. 'They may well be there.'

'I doubt if Cousin Barrington would be allowed to absent himself from his guests any longer. And would you be worried by Jeremy's presence?'

'To be honest, Mrs Rowsley,' Constable Davies said, 'I'd prefer his room to his company. I have to trust someone, and to be blunt I only trust you and Mr Rowsley because I have to. But the fewer the better. Isn't there a library or some such?'

Matthew looked at me and laughed. 'Harriet's elderly beau may be there. Mr Digby. In his favour he's stone deaf.'

It was clear we were going there. Perhaps I could delay the ordeal, if only for a moment. I held up my hand. 'Indulge me, please. Where would a man like Biddlestone keep his money?'

'Money?' Davies squeaked.

'A lot of tips, apparently, from wealthy guests. There must be a strong-box or – or is there any information about a bank account?'

'There's a strong-box in that cupboard there, ma'am. But we can't find a key, and it's not for want of trying, believe me. And it doesn't look as if it would surrender its secrets – or anything else – to a hammer and chisel.'

Hands on my hips, I surveyed the room, as I had checked so many other rooms for lost items, from ceiling to floor. 'The only place I can think of immediately is the bed.'

'Nothing under the mattress,' Matthew said promptly.

'What about *in* the mattress?'

We left the dirty linen – the sheets had been resewn, sides to middle, to give them extra life and would have been uncomfortable to lie on – in a heap. Nothing untoward there. The pillows? No sign of them ever been tampered with, no matter how darned the slips. The eiderdown was clumped and matted enough to give me hope – but none of us could feel any suspicious hard objects, not even a roll of money. And none of the seams had been tampered with anyway. The mattress turned my stomach.

'My goodness, fancy having to spend your nights on that bag of smelly lumps,' Mr Davies exclaimed. 'Don't they ever air mattresses in this place?'

Matthew's lip curled. 'There's obviously nothing here, so I suggest—'

'*Obviously*, Matthew? You've rolled back the carpet and checked the floorboards?'

The men smirked. 'We have indeed. So— Now what are you staring at? Heaven?'

I might, had we been alone, have stuck my tongue out at him. 'The curtain rail. It's obviously been brought down here from a grander room – can you see how thick it is compared with the flimsy curtains it supports? Would it be worth unscrewing one of those huge finials?'

'Mrs Rowsley, even I might baulk at borrowing a stepladder strong enough to hold me on the Sabbath.'

'The chair?'

'That would fall apart the moment I set foot on it.' He looked sideways. 'Or you, Mr Rowsley.'

Matthew nodded sadly.

'Very well, Constable. I should be light enough to risk it. Then I can perch on that table. But you will have to hold my skirts down while I scramble up. And, of course, catch me if I should fall.'

'Ma'am!'

But I had already moved a wooden chair to that I might climb on the once handsome mahogany table that had incongruously found its way down here. 'I'm still not quite tall enough. Will you pass me the chair up here? Thank you.'

Matthew looked increasingly thunderous, but said nothing, a fact that he was probably grateful for when I unscrewed the ugly finial and produced from inside its hollow grandeur – no, not a key but a bundle of papers. I replaced the empty finial.

'Very well done,' the constable declared. 'But – do you think you might . . . the other end?

It had been easier to get up decently than to get down. Then I had to repeat the process. I shook the second finial. Yes! A key!

But a small one, too tiny for a strong-box. Was there anything else? Possibly. I passed it down. 'Can you find something to prise out whatever is inside? No, I'll stay up here.'

Eventually the constable's pencil did the trick: he flourished a roll of paper, which he tucked safely into his tunic. Only then did they remember where I was perched and come to my rescue. Much as I would have liked to return to terra firma, I had to replace the finial, which proved more awkward than I liked. At long last, holding Matthew's hand and gathering my skirt as decently as I could while the constable, gaze averted, held it down, I made my descent.

'Thank you very much indeed.' The constable peered out of the window. 'It's nearly dark. I must postpone that conversation we planned and be getting back. I don't want to fall in a ditch I can't see and drown, do I?'

I shivered with a sudden fear. 'Surely for your safety's sake you could stay here. We can—' Too late. I clapped my hands over my mouth. 'Forgive me. I forgot that this is not my – shall we call it, my domain?'

Matthew took my hand. 'On the other hand, Davies, what if you persuaded Mrs Simpkiss that you should sleep in the Room to protect her and the child?'

He sniffed. 'It'll have to be on a better mattress than that one, then.' He touched it with his toe. 'Very well. I will talk to Mrs Simpkiss and then we could adjourn to the library.'

'Perhaps we should postpone everything till tomorrow,' I said. 'After all, I seem to recall that my husband is prostrate with a migraine and I am acting as his personal Florence Nightingale.'

TWENTY

'Our hot water will be here any moment,' Harriet declared. 'Quick – under the covers with you. Look a bit more deathly if you can. That's better.' Smiling wickedly she resumed, or more accurately began, sponging my forehead, not with vinegar – I drew the line at that – but with her lavender water, which she assured me would be just as efficacious if my migraine were indeed real. An observer would think she had made a remarkable recovery from the horrible incident in the library. To me she sounded brittle, an instinct reinforced by her unlikely cavorting on the table in Biddlestone's room.

'A certain cure,' I observed, trying to join in her mood, 'would be a little wine mixed with water. But I will add any water myself, thank you. Or even not add any.'

'I'll ask the hot-water footman – though it may well interrupt the poor man's routine. Any particular wine, sir?' she asked, horribly, for a moment, like Biddlestone.

'That white burgundy that came with the fish was drinkable, wasn't it? Or some hock? You choose,' I said grandiloquently.

Once the water and then the wine had appeared – I was tempted by a biblical joke that would have been in particularly bad taste on the Sabbath – I braced myself for a conversation that might upset her greatly.

'My love,' I began, 'I hope I did not betray a confidence when I told Constable Davies about your encounter with Jameson – whose first name, incidentally, I've still not asked about. He will want, I think, to talk to you about it in the morning—'

Her interruption grated: 'I hoped he was going to reveal the contents of the papers in the finial then.'

'I think he might do both. Can you bear it?'

There was a long pause as she looked into the middle distance. At last, with a visible effort, she said, 'If it will stop Jameson – he truly doesn't deserve the honour of his military title, does he?

– behaving like that to others, then so be it. But it won't, will it? Of course it won't. For all they're *called* gentlemen, all too many men behave like animals, rutting animals. Think of that case Mark defended last summer: all those drunken students raping a child, whom they then accused of being a prostitute. Pah!' Springing to her feet, she paced back and forth, ringing her hands. 'Oh, Matthew, how I wish Mark and Dora were here. Or your dear Mama. Or that Mrs Dabbs were Bea. Another woman I love and trust to tell me . . . to believe me when I tell them how I came by my necklace, not to sneer because I can't sing, not to blame me for the rape that took my childhood!' she ended passionately. She emptied her glass in a single draught. Her laugh was rueful. 'I'm so sorry. To hear me anyone would think I was not with the most important person on my world, and that I somehow blamed you. Forgive me. I am . . . overwrought, am I not? Oh, this damned crinoline, this damned corset.'

Wrapping my arms about her, I wept with her – in my case tears of contrition for bringing her here. I had never known her like this. At last, as she quietened, I ventured, 'Did Jameson's behaviour in the library . . . did it make you recall the attack when you were a child?'

She nodded. 'Even the smells. The smell of lust and anger, the smell of animal fear – mine. They still trespass into my dreams, you know. When I am in the arms of the man I love beyond . . . I still get that dream, for all I deny it.'

'I thought you did. My love, forgive me if this sounds crass. We spoke of hypnotism helping with pain, perhaps helping with poor Jeremy's affliction. When we are safe at home, might we discuss if it would help you?' If I hoped she would smile, I was to be disappointed. But there was something even more reassuring, perhaps, as she slowly nodded.

'Yes. Let us research it as Francis would research his Roman remains and make an informed decision. Oh, damnation!'

A peacock was screaming just below our window.

At last we could both laugh, but I admit that the joke wore as thin as our prospects of sleeping. I did the only thing I could think of. I tipped the soapy water from our wash-stand bowl out of the window – to immediate effect.

*   *   *

Neither of us having slept well, we agreed that the best way to escape home was to assist the constable and his still absent cousin – 'Don't forget the pigeon,' Harriet urged – as best we could and solve the hideous crimes. We both prayed with selfish sincerity that no other unnatural deaths would occur to detain us. As for the inquests, I chose not to remind her that one day we would have to return.

Eschewing the doubtful pleasures of late breakfast with our fellow guests, we went straight to the sewing room, bright and cheerful in the early sun, where we were greeted by Mason, who unlocked it with something of a flourish and a readiness to talk. It transpired that Constable Davies had not spent the night guarding Clara; he had gone home to his own bed and the Bible beside it. But both Mrs Simpkiss and Clara had survived, however, not least, in Mason's opinion, because he had found the door to the Room blocked from within.

'I thought I ought to report to Mrs Simpkiss, having no one else to report to,' he added dryly. 'Sir, ma'am, I understand that Colonel Rowsley is under the weather – beg pardon, *indisposed* – this morning, and will join you later. He has days like this sometimes, poor gentleman, but a hot hip-bath has been known to work wonders. I understand that he will leave her ladyship to supervise the guests' breakfast, and present himself for duty at nine, or thereabouts.' Unconsciously, I think, he straightened slightly as he delivered my cousin's words.

'I'm sorry to hear he's unwell. One of his old wounds? Very well, when Constable Davies arrives, perhaps you could bring him straight here, unless, of course, he feels his duties call him elsewhere, so we may talk as we eat. I can't imagine he would like to take breakfast with the guests. Of course, he may well prefer to be with people he knows in the servants' hall,' Harriet said. There might have been the tiniest hint of a question in her suggestion. After all, we knew that the staff did not regard him highly.

Certainly Mason treated it as an invitation to give information. 'Between ourselves, ma'am, he's chapel. A bit stand-offish when it comes to harvest homes and Christmas dances. Regards alcohol as one of the devil's works. So it's awkward for us, serving wine and spirits all the time, not to mention having beer with our meals as part of our pay.'

'What? I thought that practice was long dead!' Harriet rarely squeaked or squawked, but she did now. There was no doubt of her angry disbelief. 'Imagine,' she continued, 'having your board and lodging deducted from your tiny income – especially if you are paid in beer which you might not drink. Lady Croft stopped that practice at least ten years ago. On the advice of his late lordship, I dare say, but stopped it was.'

I winked at Mason. 'I have an idea that Mrs Rowsley – when she was Mrs Faulkner, of course – might have had a part to play too.'

'You couldn't have a word with—' He stopped abruptly. 'Beg pardon for being too familiar, ma'am. I will go and see if the constable has arrived.'

'Just one question, if I may,' Harriet said with something of a rush. 'Dogs! Why are there none in the house?'

He almost flinched at the apparently innocent question. 'I beg you, ma'am, if I tell you, that you'll never mention it in front of the Colonel! Ever!'

'Of course.' She looked as taken aback as I felt.

His voice almost inaudible. 'There was a disagreement about something. And an argument. And by mistake someone shot the Colonel's favourite dog. The one he cared for most. And now he won't have another. Harrison always had a dog with him. Now, out of respect, he leaves it back in his cottage.' He gave punctilious bow and left.

'Dear God,' Harriet breathed. 'So—'

I touched my finger to her lips and nodded towards the wall. 'He fears it has ears, doesn't he? My love, this is not a happy house, is it? Quick, pinpoint the killer and let us run. But not,' I said slowly, 'till I've seen those accounts again. At dawn I knew I had missed something. But I could not remember what, no matter how hard I tossed and turned.'

'So I noticed,' she observed dryly. 'Ah. Constable Davies has left our chart here. Let me look over it again while you start on the accounts. And then we can swap.'

Time and again I forgot that for many years she, not the butler with his ageing eyes, had been responsible for the household accounts. 'Yes, please,' I said humbly. 'Or you could look at the accounts first, if you wouldn't mind.'

'Of course. So long as you find that Jameson could have had the opportunity to kill both men and probably took it.'

For all he was teetotal, Davies looked decidedly the worse for wear when he joined us barely five minutes later.

'Teething,' he said, when I asked if he was all right. 'When one twin stopped howling the other started. Good lungs, both of them. Mason offered to bring me coffee and I said yes. I hope it's all right.'

'Mrs Dabbs provides wonderful breakfasts too. I hope you will join us.'

'You don't eat with the other guests?' He sounded disapproving.

'As you can imagine,' Harriet said smoothly, 'some of them regard us as traitors—' She touched the accounts book and nodded at the statement chart. 'As a consequence, there can be uncomfortable moments.'

He did not look convinced. 'You might overhear something interesting. Or would that be spying?'

'*Tell tale tit, your tongue will split and all the little puppy dogs will have a little bit,*' she chanted. 'Constable Davies, it's bad enough being a jumped-up servant giving herself airs and siding with an eleven-year-old maid who is surely incapable of killing even a chicken. I don't want to add fuel to their fire.'

He almost flinched in the face of her anger.

'I beg your pardon, Constable, I have not been myself since my encounter with Major Jameson yesterday.'

'But last night you were leaping around like a mountain goat, ma'am.' He blushed scarlet, the pimple on his chin almost visibly throbbing. 'But,' he added, surprising me, 'not in front of the others, of course. Beg pardon, ma'am. Tell me, if you wouldn't mind, about that . . . encounter.'

She sat, folding her hands in her lap. 'Have you seen the library? No? Oh, it's the best room in the building. You must find an excuse to see it while you are working here. There are a few good paintings, and some very gracious furniture. And books.'

'Ma'am, I've already found an excuse: the fact you were in danger there. I'd like to see it now, if you please. At least,' he added ruefully, 'as soon as I've had a cup of coffee.'

Mason arrived as if on cue, and withdrew with professional promptness. He had learned to close the door firmly.

'It must be very hard, having to work with so little sleep,' I said.

'It is and it isn't. Most of the time I have, to be honest, a very quiet life. A bit of cattle-rustling, sheep-worrying, setting ricks on fire. I've always dreamt of a bigger crime, like – but I must tell you a bit of routine would have been easier this morning. There!' He drained his cup. 'Shall you lead the way, sir?'

He was silent as we walked through the house, rabbit-eyes wider than ever at the luxury that the owner took for granted. It was only when we entered the library, closing the doors behind us, that he spoke. 'There, I've done something my auntie never managed! She was in service here ten, fifteen years – ended up as chief kitchen maid before she married Uncle Idris. And never once, never once in all those years, did she ever come this side of the green baize door. And she never saw all this!' He sat heavily as he gazed about him but was on his feet in a minute, dusting the leather seat in embarrassment. His notebook at the ready, he said, 'Now, ma'am, could you tell me what happened and where?'

She walked towards a shelf, removing a book, holding the spine towards us: *The History of Tom Jones, a Foundling.* Though she held it out to him, he waved it away as if he was afraid of it. 'Go on,' she said. 'It's over a hundred years old. Many hands have touched it. That's what books are for. If you can hold a wriggling baby without dropping it, you can hold this without fear. And smell it.'

At last he returned it to her. 'You are just an ordinary woman, like, and yet you are so familiar with things as precious as this. When I was taught to read and write, I never knew . . . I thought . . . No, never mind what I thought. You're here looking at this book and Major Jameson comes in.' He wrote in his notebook.

'He was furious to find me there. Not necessarily because I was *here*. He'd have been just as cross to come across me anywhere.'

'Ah! That catch.'

'He believed that it had affected the result of the cricket match.'

He scratched his head. 'If you weren't in the team, the batsman couldn't have been given out, could he?'

'Of course not. But I caused a few minutes' delay—'

'Not as long as if the baby had been hit,' he pointed out, closing his eyes as if imagining the horror.

'He clearly never thought of that. Anyway, while I was trying to recover my dignity, as it were, the heavens opened. And thus the match ended in a tie.'

'All this fits with what I've been told. So why should he be so angry? Did he actually strike you?'

'No. Something in my past – a very long time ago – made me fear he would. Assume he would. Maybe something worse. And his language and demeanour were both threatening. Very . . . frightening. He walked towards me. "What the hell are you doing here?" I attempted a light remark. He was more concerned with attacking me over what he considered my snooping and – of course – the way I had ruined the cricket match.'

'"Attack?" Did he have some sort of weapon?'

'His strength and his hands. And . . .' We understood. What he might have used to rape her. 'Mine were a defensive table, this one, and the paper-knife I dared not use—'

He nodded. 'Might have turned it against you.'

'—and this inkwell, which I would have thrown not at him but through the window.'

'Through the window? Ah! To attract attention.'

'Fortunately Lady Pidgeon came into the room at some point and the Major withdrew. Since I don't know exactly when she entered, and my memory may not be accurate, I can only suggest you speak to her. But you have more important matters in hand, Constable. Two deaths.'

He fingered his giant pimple. 'But a man who is violent in one way might be violent in another. Let me re-read his statement and check that chart of yours. And when I speak to everyone, as I must, I'll watch out for him and this Lady – did I hear her name correct?'

'Lady Pidgeon. With a D.'

He nodded. 'Ah. Tell you what, I sent another sort of pigeon – no D – to my cousin.' We exchanged a smile to acknowledge his gentle quip. 'Told him to get a move on. To be honest, I don't know what I can do if all the ladies and gentlemen just decide to leave. I can tell them not to but I can't hold them back.' He spread his arms, like a man herding sheep without a dog. 'Don't take this the wrong way, ma'am, but I wish he might have committed crimes in other grand rooms like this. It's been an education coming in here.'

'But one of the crimes was committed in a grand room,' Harriet cried. 'Nothing like as grand as this, I admit. You have the key I found there. The Gräfin's bed chamber. Silk wall hangings. A Chinese carpet. Lovely little pictures. And the view! Oh, and you must approach via the house itself, not up through the service corridors, so you see even more wonderful things. And then I can show you where that large key was concealed.'

'What? Now? I mean, I should have looked at it last night, but what with one thing and another, and that other little key I've not given a thought to – don't tell my cousin, will you?'

'Of course not.' But I might have to remind him about it. 'Now's a good time for exploring the house,' I pointed out. 'Most of the guests won't leave their chambers till after nine, possibly later.'

He rolled his eyes heavenward. 'Best of the day is gone by then. Right, you're on. Hang on, I take it it's locked.'

'Mrs Simpkiss will have a door key. And also whatever she took from . . . various pockets.'

His face fell. 'So it'll be the back stairs, then.'

'Collect the key and her finds and meet us in the sewing room. Then we can escort you up the grand staircase.'

'If both of us escort you, it might be a bit too obvious,' Harriet said. 'I will collect the key and go up the servants' stairs and meet you and Matthew there. I might be dressed somewhat differently . . .' And then she stopped dead. Very slowly, she moved from bookcase to bookcase. 'Perhaps Lady Hortensia's guests have turned to literature to console them while they have to stay here.'

Davies joined her. 'Or—? What's wrong, ma'am?'

'Some books are worth more than others. First editions, like those I showed you. And several have gone. You can see where someone has spread out a lot to make it look as if there are no gaps. There. And there.'

'You wouldn't know which?'

She shook her head. 'I think there was one by Richardson there – all the volumes of a long book called *Clarissa*.' She smiled. 'It's not a book one undertakes lightly, believe me. I can understand anyone wanting to read a book by Jane Austen – and look, they've been reshuffled too. Milton . . . Dryden . . . Someone has good but wide-ranging taste and a very great deal of time. Or there may be a perfectly innocent explanation that several people simply want to read a book.'

He looked her straight in the eye and held her gaze. 'Is that an explanation you believe, ma'am?'

'I honestly don't know enough about any of the guests to hazard a guess,' she said. 'If I were bored and without employment, I would certainly have helped myself to a book by any of those authors – maybe not Milton.'

I knew I had to say something that revolted me to utter. 'My love, your love of books is known to several people. What if one of them has removed some from here to make it look as if you have – to put not too fine a point upon it – stolen them?'

'With all due respect, sir, let us cross that bridge if we come to it. Let us do as Mrs Rowsley suggests. Ma'am, how long will it take to make yourself look different – I take it you mean dressing as a maid, again? Because I wouldn't mind spending a few more minutes here before we meet upstairs.'

With a smile, she turned to leave. 'Give me ten minutes. Matthew, it may be that there is some evidence Mr Davies should see in the picture gallery. If you want to see really grand things, Constable, you will see them there.'

TWENTY-ONE

E ven as I struggled with the buttons on the uniform I had worn the previous day, I wished I could have seen the young man's face as he looked on the wonders of the gallery. Would it be like the one I loved to see when maids or footmen mastered their letters, found their first delight in reading a whole book?

At least I could watch his response to the Gräfin's bed chamber, as concealing the key in my pocket, along with the papers Mrs Simpkiss had removed for safekeeping, I headed upstairs. I was anxious: though my escapade was probably widely known amongst the staff by now I would prefer not to run into anyone. There. I was safe. Now all I had to do was escape from the Stygian gloom of the brown and green painted back stairs into the bright sun lighting up the guest corridor.

As I unlocked the Gräfin's door, I heard footsteps in the corridor. Surely only one person's. I was ready to panic, to run back to the service stairs for cover – but then, as I cowered in the doorframe recess, I heard Matthew's voice. It wasn't, however, much comfort. It was raised in anger. As was another: Major Jameson's.

A third, soft and with a Welsh accent, came with surprising authority. 'Gentlemen, gentlemen: this is a house of mourning, is it not? Pray, moderate your language. And it may be that folk are still asleep, so please lower your voices.'

Major Jameson fired off a salvo of invective. He was not, it seemed, a man to take orders from one of the lower orders. I could only assume that his language was that of the barracks – though would a man of his rank not be in the more august company of officers?

'That is quite enough, Major. Now, the Colonel has instructed Mr Rowsley here to act as my deputy and to obey my instructions. I am sure that the two of us could see you safely installed in the village lock-up, if that is your desire. No? Best be quietly on your way then, sir.'

Apparently as calm as if he dealt with noisy military men every day, not just with poachers and labourers, Constable Davies stepped into the room and looked round with a mouth as wide open as his eyes. 'And only one old woman sleeps here? Lord!' But then he was easing that tight tunic collar and mopping his brow. 'Lord, ma'am! My old granny would call that Major a nasty piece of knitting. But much as I'd like to I can't arrest him for that.'

'You handled the situation very well, Constable,' I said.

'He did. Far better than me. If I'd got my hands on him I'd have thrown him out of the window,' Matthew muttered, earning a sideways glance from Davies.

'All this and we've not even had breakfast,' I said lightly. 'Constable, might I ask you a question? No, nothing you mustn't tell us. Can you tell me what the Major's Christian name is? It's just that I've never, ever heard it used.'

'Really?'

'It's something to do with the strange etiquette that passes as normality in people like this,' Matthew said. 'My papa is an archdeacon whose bishop's wife apparently calls her spouse "My Lord" and "Bishop", never using his first name even among close friends. So – Major Jameson?'

'Major Algernon Dalrymple Wycombe Jameson.' He seemed to relish each syllable – and who could blame him? He ended with an ironic smile.

'Indeed,' I said. 'Thank you. What a shame none of his initials matches the one on the love letter I found. Now, Mrs Simpkiss sent you this,' I added, passing the young man an envelope.

He fingered it for a while. Did I hope he would open it so we could share the contents? In the event, he buttoned it firmly into a tunic pocket.

It was the work of moments to show him where I had found the key, but he began, as thoroughly as Mrs Simpkiss or I could have done, to search clothes, underclothes, her reticule – and every nook. It fell to me to replace everything as best I could.

'All this comfort and luxury,' he said, 'and then this!' He snapped his fingers. 'Truly in the midst of life there is death. But there is no evidence of her actual life, is there? The things she found precious? Just so many clothes and shoes. Is that what it all comes down to in the end? But I'm rambling, aren't I?'

'On the contrary,' I said. 'In many ways her death has been like taking a cup of water from a bucket.'

'It makes a bit of a splash then everything settles down as normal?'

'Exactly. Our investigations apart, the Gräfin's death seems to have touched no one on a deep level – no one is *missing* her, lamenting the passing of a friend, being reminded of her at strange moments. My excuse – if excuse is needed – is that my acquaintance with her was no more than that. But our fellow guests and our hostess especially must have known her for years. They must have known her as a person, known what she held precious.'

He regarded me steadily.

I added, 'I dare say she found her jewellery precious, and that's somewhere within this house.'

'With luck,' said Matthew. 'But not necessarily. The person who killed it might have had an accomplice to get it away. And – how had I forgotten this? – when we looked at her body on the bed there her stockings and skirt hem were wet. Yes, and Barrington ordered a search for her shoes, which were nowhere in the whole house, according to the servants searching for them.'

'The sooner my cousin gets here the better – and every last detective in Scotland Yard, too.'

'What would it mean for your career if you solved it before they arrived?' I asked.

His face softened. 'Maybe a promotion. Maybe a move from a tiny damp house in a village no one's ever heard of to a bigger dry one in a flourishing town.'

Everything, in other words. Matthew and I had better get busy. When better to start than over breakfast in the sewing room?

I pushed the plate of scones towards him. Surely he could not resist reaching for one, especially as pots of conserve and a dish of golden butter were marshalled beside them.

'I know you have been – well, I couldn't have got this far, not nearly this far, without your help, yours and Mr Rowsley's. And I dare say all these papers, and those from that curtain pole – they'd make more sense to you, probably.' He writhed. 'The thing is, see, the papers might not help in this case at all. Or they might. I don't know. And the person involved . . . he might . . . or she might, not wishing to give anything away, see.'

I could have pointed out that Matthew and I knew a great deal about people who might not have anything to do with the case. 'Of course you must exercise your discretion. But remember we are here if you feel you need to discuss anything. Or you might prefer to wait till your cousin arrives and see what his advice is.'

I could feel rather than hear Matthew's comment: 'Or you could consult a pigeon.' I did not dare catch his eye.

'He's such a stickler . . . What are those, ma'am?' he pointed.

'Some of Mrs Dabbs' special pastries. I believe she got the recipe from a foreign guest. Very unusual but – oh, try one.' I waited till his mouth was full. 'Of course, if you think your cousin would object to our interference, we could simply withdraw. Though where we should sit and where we would eat . . .'

Matthew was swift to grasp my strategy. 'The servants' hall, of course. I just wish we could go home, to be honest, Davies. God knows there's work we should be doing there. The trustees – ah! Let me explain about our roles. They're rather different from those of the average agent and housekeeper, since Lord Croft is too unwell to perform any of the functions associated with his rank. Although we are answerable to a board of trustees, effectively Harriet runs the house and I the entire family estate.'

'So why does everyone treat you so badly? You're as important as lawyers or doctors – and probably do less harm than either.' He got to his feet, rather spoiling the effect by chasing crumbs from his uniform. Licking a fingertip, he dabbed up the biggest morsels and conveyed them to his mouth.

'When you go home tonight, make sure you ask Mrs Dabbs if you can take some of these: they'd be such a treat for your family.' I added, with some irony, 'I'm sure the guests won't miss them.' I poured us all more coffee; Matthew and I also helped ourselves to scones and some strawberry conserve that was almost as good as Bea's.

'What's the most useful thing we can do before we decamp?' Matthew asked.

'Decamp? No, Mr Rowsley, I'm afraid you can't leave here. None of the guests can. If you went, and I can see you have responsibilities, they'd all be off.'

'I only meant from this room, Davies!' Matthew laughed heartily, if duplicitously. 'If you have nothing else in mind, I thought Harriet might go over the accounts that so puzzled me last night. And she has asked me to double-check her chart . . .'

The pretty clock chimed eight-thirty, as if in approval. Ten minutes later the silence was interrupted by Mason. He spoke discreetly to Davies but clearly intended us to hear the news that the village doctor had arrived on horseback, a farm cart accompanying him to carry away the corpses. Was that the best the family could do for a godmother and a senior member of staff? It was clear that Davies, whose eyes were more like a rabbit's than ever, shared my unease: 'Shouldn't there be a guard of honour or something?' he asked.

'Of course there should,' I said, 'but not for another few minutes yet. The servants will still be at breakfast.' I clapped my hand over my mouth again. 'Constable Davies, forgive me. I've done it again, imagining I have authority when I have none. This should be a decision for the Colonel and Mrs Simpkiss, shouldn't it, though perhaps you should give more weight to one than to the other! Could Mason perhaps convey a note to him? And consult Mrs Simpkiss in person?' I added with a smile.

Mason waited while Davies wrote his note, bowed and left us.

There was an uneasy silence as we all pretended to work.

Mason returned. 'Beg pardon, ma'am, but Dr Highworth is waiting. Both parties stated a preference for a servants' guard of honour but as you said they're in the middle of breakfast.'

'Constable Davies, do you think we should invite him to take coffee here until everyone is ready?

'He drinks only tea,' Mason said in that discreet way experienced butlers seem to share. 'If I might recommend a pot of his favourite Darjeeling? No milk and no sugar, I must tell you.'

My mind's eye saw a wizened old man in a monkish robe. I thought it best not to share the vision. 'Thank you, Mason. And would the good doctor eat Mrs Dabbs' wonderful Continental breakfast fancies?'

'Brown bread only, ma'am. And honey, not jam or marmalade. Shall I bring those, ma'am?'

'Yes please. And also more coffee for the more self-indulgent of us!'

Dr Highworth filled the doorway. He was a good six feet tall, his shoulders as broad as Matthew's. He looked askance at us, me in particular, but the constable explained what we had been doing, and at last he offered a slightly grudging hand first to Matthew and then to me. At last, he sat surprisingly carefully, as if, like Cousin Barrington, he suffered from back ache. His handsome face was deeply lined, as if he took on his patients' pain as well as his own. Yet it was not that of an old man: I put him at about the same age as me, in his forties.

Constable Davies added, 'Mr Rowsley was with the Colonel when Mr Harrison took them to find Mr Biddlestone's corpse, Doctor. Ah!' The door opened to admit Jeremy Turton, who stopped abruptly when he saw the visitor. 'Ah, Mr Turton. Dr Highworth, this gentleman has drawn pictures of Mr Biddlestone's body where they found it. Would they be any use to you?'

'Not as much as the actual corpse. The sooner I take it off your hands the better. And that old woman, too, while I'm here.'

I bridled on the Gräfin's behalf. 'Her ladyship was the first to die, you will recall. By strangulation, as opposed to a blow to the head and possibly drowning.'

It might have been the table that spoke for all the reaction he gave.

'So I've got to sit and twiddle my thumbs till the servants have finished their porridge.' He looked ostentatiously at his watch and crossed his arms in irritation, then drumming his fingers on them.

'I think you will find that Gräfin Weiser and Mr Biddlestone can wait a few minutes longer,' Matthew observed, coldly polite.

Davies froze. He was after all dependent on the doctor's good graces for the treatment of all his children's ailments – and

Highworth might not be as benevolent as our good doctor friend at home who forgot to present bills to the poorest families and accepted payment in kind from others.

Jeremy had not yet spoken. I could not even offer him coffee as there was no spare cup. Fortunately Mason, bringing tea and brown bread, could remedy that, but Jeremy remained as resolutely silent as the doctor, who looked with increasing frequency at his watch, or, by way of variation, at the pretty clock.

At last Matthew, presumably unable to bear it any longer, asked, 'Dr Highworth, do you do a full post-mortem examination or just look at the more obvious injuries?'

'The latter. Why do you ask? Oh, are you one of these people who believe a hospital surgeon should cut the dead into pieces in the name of "scientific enquiry"? Let me tell you, sir, I do not. Let the interment be as swift and dignified as possible, say I. And I may add that Father Howells agrees.'

Davies coughed. 'As soon as possible after the inquest, Dr Highworth. Inquests, I might have to say.'

Dear God! We have to come back here for them. Why hadn't I realised? It took me all my self-control not to cry out loud. Thank goodness the arrival of Mason with a laden tray gave me a moment to regain my composure.

Matthew and I were the only guests to bid the Gräfin goodbye, standing alongside Mrs Simpkiss and Mason and the other servants, who naturally arranged themselves in order of their status, men on one side of the steps, women on the other. Cousin Barrington and Lady Hortensia stood at the top, perhaps on the last out, first in principle. But their ways parted as soon as they were in the house, Cousin Barrington waiting to fall into step with Matthew as we walked back to the sewing room.

Constable Davies more or less accompanied me. At last he took a deep breath. 'I'm not sure I should have left Mr Turton on his own in there. But it would have looked very rude to turn him out. And that stammer of his fair turns my stomach.'

'If you could bear to, sound him out about Major Jameson, who apparently bullied him cruelly.'

'You're determined to make him the killer, aren't you, ma'am?' He gave a rueful laugh.

'One of the killers,' I responded with a smile. 'Both the Gräfin and Biddlestone were disliked, but I still can't see why a guest should murder the butler or a servant should kill the Gräfin. Unless her ladyship caught a servant stealing her jewels, of course. But if it was a servant, what did he or she do with them? What could they do? They were clearly too expensive to be given to a sweetheart as fairings.'

'And presumably the jewel box was big and heavy? I suppose you never had an occasion to see it? Have to be big if that key you found fitted it.' He stopped, shifting from one foot to the other as if he was a village lad caught scrumping. 'Ma'am, I still don't know whether I should show you those papers, any of them. Yes, I need a second opinion – third with Mr Rowsley, of course – but . . .'

'How long do you think it will be before your cousin arrives? If it is likely to be today, then waiting won't hurt, surely. If he's delayed, Matthew and I can swear on your family Bible to say nothing to anyone.'

'Ma'am, you've got the Colonel and his bad back, the doctor and his bad back – do you want me to have a bad back too? No, I'm sure they'll have a Bible here, and I'm sure Colonel Rowsley can find the proper oath for special constables. Even for you, a lady . . . no, I'm sure he'll find a way. But I worry about Mr Turton, I do indeed. All the stick he has to take for that stutter – it might result in violence, in my opinion. He might easily have turned on a tormentor, see.' Davies retired to stare out of the window, stroking his chin as if to make sure the huge pimple had really burst and started to subside.

I thought back to the afternoon tea in the pavilion. 'Except that his main tormentor, possibly his only tormentor, was Major Jameson. Most people simply avoid the poor boy.'

He had the grace to blush.

TWENTY-TWO

Possibly like Constable Davies, I had a sudden longing to be outdoors. After all, that was where I did so much of my work. Could I commandeer a horse? Perhaps one for Harriet too – she was now only nervously managing to ride side-saddle, so it would have to be a very gentle animal.

But a ride out for pleasure might encourage all the other guests to demand the same privilege, so unless I could persuade Davies, and even, if he put in an appearance, my cousin, that it was a vital errand, not a pleasure jaunt, I would have to remain in the house.

'You all right there, Mr Rowsley?'

I jumped. 'Yes, indeed. I was just wondering, Davies,' I extemporized, 'if I have the germ of an idea. You said that the state of the bridge to the village was common knowledge. I was just wondering if the thief might have tried to stow the missing jewel case behind a loose stone.' As I spoke, the trivial excuse became almost a conviction. 'And what if that was what took Biddlestone there? It's not the natural habitat for a butler.'

'Was he the thief?' Davies asked, catching on quickly. 'Or trying to catch the thief? Or meeting the thief? But whatever the answer, it's worth looking at the bridge.'

'Shall I ride out and check? We could all ride – I'll send word to the stables. Davies, you must come: you alone have the absolute right to question people about anything we find. And you, Turton? Harriet, would you like to come too?'

She shook her head firmly. 'But you should go, Jeremy. You and your sketch-pad in case you need to record anything of interest. I still have the accounts to check, after all.'

'If you are sure, ma'am? No, it's not safe, is it? What if our friend the Major got wind of the fact that you are alone and undefended? He might want to finish what he started yesterday. Unless—' He strode to the door with a smile on his face. 'Unless you lock yourself in.' He tried to turn the key, and failed. Repeatedly. He withdrew it, staring in disbelief. In a well-ordered household, surely every lock would be well lubricated. He even opened the door to try the key from the corridor side. The result was the same.

'Has the door been locked all this time? Ever since the Colonel chose it as his headquarters, as I'm sure he'd say?'

'Yes,' I said. 'I've locked it myself, and unlocked it every morning. Either me or the Colonel, that is. Though of course in most households like this even rooms with priceless paintings are left unlocked. Guests don't bother. Why should they? They know that penalties for even the smallest theft are so severe even the poorest servant could not risk stealing so much as a handkerchief. How on earth has the key been changed this morning? And when?'

Mine were not the only eyes turning in Jeremy's direction. He blushed scarlet, and then went so white I feared he would faint.

'The privy. Only five minutes. I thought I'd closed the door but it was open when I came back so I thought I'd made a mistake.'

Davies was almost pulling the words out of him, but could not speed up the agonizing delivery. 'Was anything different when you returned?'

'Nothing. Just as I'd left it. Even a pencil I was sharpening.'

'Are you absolutely sure? Even your sketch-book is untouched?'

He flicked through his pad. 'Just as I left it.'

The accounts ledger and the big chart seemed to be in order too.

Davies seemed to grow an inch taller and three inches broader. 'Mason!'

It was Billy who, after a few minutes' delay, answered the summons. 'My apologies, sirs and ma'am. Mr Mason has been called away. The Colonel needed his assistance.'

'So no one has been on duty in this corridor since?'

Biting his lip, Billy shook his head. 'It was only for a few minutes, Morgan. I mean Constable Davies. I was just on my way here – in fact, I was just outside the door – when her ladyship told me to carry her sewing box to her private sitting room.'

'And you came straight back?'

'Pretty well. I – er – I think Mr Turton saw me as he came back from the privy.'

Jeremy nodded.

'I understand. Now, before you return to your post, I want you to find another key for this door. If you can't, the moment the roads are clear you send for a locksmith. On my orders. I think someone has deliberately swapped the keys to leave the room vulnerable.' Davies sounded far older than his years. Not for the first time I wished he could be given a greater role in the police force – or elsewhere.

It took only a few minutes for Billy to return, flourishing a key. 'It's the one Mr Biddlestone used, Mrs Simpkiss says. Shall I try it?'

'Perfect. Thank you, Billy. No, I'll keep the one that doesn't work, thank you very much.' He waited till the door was shut. 'All the same, ma'am, I'd really like you to accompany us as we look at the bridge. It'll do you good to get a bit of fresh air, and I'd welcome an extra pair of eyes.'

She shook her head. 'My eyes will be better employed going through these accounts. If I went, I would simply be a liability. See, Matthew isn't arguing! If Billy stays outside to guard me, and I lock the door, I shall be perfectly safe.'

Davies frowned, as if doubting Billy's prowess in a crisis.

'Safer than on a horse, at any rate,' she conceded. 'I'm sure Cousin Barrington will soon be down, too.'

I should never have suggested the jaunt in the first place – but now it seemed quite essential to the case. I could not be happy.

Neither, it seemed, could Davies. 'Have you an inkwell to hand, ma'am?'

She flourished a hideous vase. 'But I have another idea! Why not suggest that Roddy and Charles practise their bowling within earshot? They'd love that!'

I despatched a bemused Billy with the message. Their reply was prompt and enthusiastic: they'd present themselves outside the window the moment they'd despatched the last of their boiled eggs.

Davies sighed in acquiescence, but as he ushered us from the room, he muttered, 'If only my cousin would come soon.'

* * *

The presence of the boys reassured me; undoubtedly they would kill anyone hurting Harriet – except that was, if I thought about it, less encouraging.

'Just one thing, Rowsley,' Webbe said, 'we never did have our tête-à-tête with Jameson. He'd just disappeared. Should we try again?'

'I think I may know where he was. No, don't do anything for now except practise and keep your ears open.'

'How have you been able to get backwards and forwards with the bridge in this state?' I asked Davies, as Turton got to work.

'There's the ford, if you're very careful. And there's a stone bridge, old as the hills and just as solid, if you're prepared for a two-mile walk. I just picked my way across what's left of this bridge, though now I see it from this side I'm not so sure I should come back this way.'

'Borrow the horse. I'm sure Barrington would be happy to help. Stable it at the village inn, if you've got one, at his expense.' He looked awkward, embarrassed so I didn't pursue the notion. I could raise it myself later with Barrington. 'Now, where do we start? You'll have seen it being rebuilt, of course, and you knew that it was a poor job.'

'Look – all that rubble. Rubbish, really. Nothing with any weight. A bridge like this has to withstand all weathers. Proper dressed stone they should have used too, for the walls proper, not these old bricks. From the house, they'll be – left over from when some of the modernization was done. Modern bricks wouldn't have been as good as these old stone blocks – look, you can see some boy's carved initials there, by that rough heart: J A and E M, 1679. Stood ever since then, those blocks. And look at that rubbishy stuff. Couldn't even get the mortar right. Should have used lime mortar, see.'

'It would have been very easy to prise out a brick or two if you wanted to, wouldn't it?'

'Wouldn't even have needed a hammer and chisel – just a strong blade,' he said, demonstrating with a pen knife on a block of several bricks. 'There. And what,' he continued, 'do you think someone might have wanted to leave there? That jewellery box?

And if they did, did he – or she, since you say the Gräfin had a wet skirt – come back and get it or might it still be there?'

I stared at him in total disbelief. And then I remembered that he had not seen the skirt for himself. 'I can see that the thief might well be a woman, but not the Gräfin – it was only the hem of her skirt that was wet, not the whole of it.'

'But the rain stopped, didn't it, after the deluge? So she could have made her way out and back again. And don't forget her shoes or boots or whatever have never been found. Could she have hidden them somewhere in the house herself? Maybe she even gave them to a servant – the Colonel and his lady are not known for their generosity . . . I'm sorry, you're his cousin, aren't you?'

'Cousins we might be, but I suspect from what I've heard that the servants aren't well paid. So whoever has the shoes might be very tempted to keep them and tell no one . . . And maybe even if another servant knew, they would keep quiet. Oh, dear. But as for the Gräfin gallivanting about the countryside, I'm not convinced. Ladies don't in general, do they?'

'But,' Turton said startling us both, 'the Gräfin was no ordinary lady. People think,' he said with his usual difficulties, 'that because I'm mostly silent I can't hear. So they are indiscreet. She didn't just play whist for pleasure. She made money. A lot. And people were afraid of her. Hated her. Your wife was taken in, I'd say.'

'Deliberately?' Davies asked.

Turton nodded. 'More people could be the Gräfin's killer than you imagine.'

'I should check that chart again. I might need your help,' Davies added humbly. 'Thank you. Now, before we go, I'd really like us to do one more check round here. The water's sinking fast. We should be able to see things we missed even ten minutes ago. Now, exactly where did you find Mr Biddlestone? Ah.' He stared at the spot. 'A very funny place indeed for a butler to be taking the air. And a funny place for somewhere to agree to meet him. Or plan to find him. If only – we need some help here.'

His wish was granted almost immediately. Turton pointed. His sharp eyes had picked out a hammer, some twenty paces from where Biddlestone's body had lain.

Retrieving it from the stream with some difficulty, Davies weighed it in his hand. 'Strange, to be talking about one murder and find the weapon possibly used in the other. Anything else, gentlemen? No matter how big or small.' He spread his arms almost hopelessly. 'Yes, hopeless as searching for the famous needle in a haystack. I might ask the villagers to search here – but people might be tempted . . . It's a hard time of year for us, waiting for the crops to grow after that late snow.'

'My cousin might offer a reward?'

'For what?' Turton managed.

'And how much? You don't want people to "find" something just to get some money,' Davies pointed out.

Chastened, I nodded. 'It needs proper consideration, doesn't it? And I would say that you are the one to advise my cousin. Gentlemen, as you know I left Harriet behind when we set out. For all that business of finding the right key and her locking herself in, I would much rather return to her if—'

Turton grabbed my arm, pointing. 'What's that there?'

TWENTY-THREE

With a smile, I watched the young gentlemen, for all the world as happy and carefree as the now Lord Halesowen was when he and I spent those wonderful hours working on his batting and his bowling. At very least they meant that I had to catch and throw as well as any boy. Would anyone know if I slipped out and joined them for half an hour? They would help me scramble through the window if I asked, for all I was old enough to be their mother.

But I had said I would look at the accounts that had defeated Matthew, so look I must. I got so desperate I actually pushed back the pages as far as the spine to see if some had been cut out. I was forced, however to reach just two conclusions – that the book-keeping was incredibly lax and that an exorbitant sum had disappeared about the time that the bridge had allegedly been repaired.

Sighing, I turned back to the chart, double- and triple-checking each entry against the next. Constable Davies was right: there were many half-truths – and two half-truths never added up to a whole one. I was stumped.

Hearing the laughter outside, it occurred to me that the young cricketers had actually posed the question I should be trying to answer now: who benefited from the Gräfin's death? The reactions of both Lady Pidgeon and Cousin Barrington when I mentioned her suggested that her ability at cards might mean she fleeced her opponents. I'd seen an IOU. What else had I found and passed straight to Constable Davies? And why had he, amenable in so many ways, so far refused to share it? Dared I hope he'd left it somewhere in this room? Dared I search for it? And of course if I found it, dared I read it?

Fortunately for my conscience, Cousin Barrington, rattling the doorknob with some irritation, demanded to know what in Hades was going on. Swiftly I admitted him, apologizing profusely.

'And where are the men? At the bridge? What are they doing there? God bless my soul, they've not found another body?'

'Not to my knowledge. It's such a lovely morning, between ourselves I suspect they needed an excuse for a breath of fresh air. So they left me holding the fort, and I'm a bit jumpy after yesterday and . . . I thought I'd feel safer if I locked the fort gate, as it were.' Though I had opened the window so my calls for help, if any, would be heard.

'Yesterday? What about yesterday?'

I needed his sympathy, so I played a card I rarely used, I despised it so much. I would be the helpless little lady. Maybe I would even need my own vinaigrette. 'It's nothing. Not really. I dare say I was just being silly.' I dabbed my eyes. 'It was just that something reminded me of something that scared me half to death when I was a little girl. About the same age as young Clara.'

'But you're a grown woman now,' he said. 'Time you snapped out of it. Maybe some coffee will help you pull yourself together.' Then he sat down, indicating that I was to do the same. His voice, his tone, changed completely. 'Tell me – do things come back to you? Sounds?'

'And smells. Certain smells.' My shudder was genuine.

'Bad thing, memory, sometimes. Just when you think you've put the lid on something, out it pops. Horrible. Ah, thank you, Mason. Just what we needed, coffee. And those biscuits look good.'

'Some of Mrs Dabbs' finest, sir. Might I ask if the hot bath did the trick, sir?'

'You may and it did. Thank you, Mason.' He smiled but the nod was a definite dismissal. He turned to me. 'Things I don't care to talk about either in case the genie pops out of the bottle again.'

'Of course. May I change the subject – change it quite violently?'

He nodded.

'This may strike you as being very trivial. But who keeps the house and estate accounts?'

He bridled. 'And what business of yours might that be?'

'Just that . . . the poor and expensive work on the bridge has been mentioned by a number of people. Davies says you were robbed and I don't like to hear such imputations. The accounts ledger was here, and—'

'You just thought you'd have a look, did you? I don't believe I gave permission!'

'You didn't. But I know you agreed that Matthew could and I know he was puzzled by them – although he is responsible for all his lordship's estates. So I was simply wondering whom he should speak to when he returns.' I hoped my lie could be excused – but preferably not exposed.

'How on earth does he think a broken bridge is connected to two murders, for heaven's sake?'

'It was something someone said . . . There's always talk, isn't there?'

'Since you mention it, there's talk about you. Always poking round in the library . . . valuable books missing.' His demeanour was quite changed again. 'That sort of thing, ma'am.'

'Really?' I hoped my terror did not show. It would be all too easy for someone to secrete them in our bed chamber, even in our cases. 'I wonder where the rumours might emanate from,' I continued, as if the idea was entirely academic.

'Well, you know about books.'

'I should hope so!' Now I was on safe ground, and I could speak with assurance. 'The late Lord Croft, who was like a father to me, taught me all he knew, and I now have the legal duty to guard and cherish all the priceless books in the House until places are found for the most valuable in libraries open to scholars. Then they can be on loan, no more. In fact, some experts from the British Museum and the Bodleian Library are coming up next month to discuss the matter with my fellow trustees and me. I have to say, now I have your ear, that in my professional judgement no one should ever be allowed to smoke in your library. Ever.'

'You'll be saying next we need a librarian,' he grumbled – at least this time he was not furious with me.

'I don't need to! You said the same thing only yesterday,' I said, allowing a dimple to show.

He sagged in the chair. 'So I did. This is for your ears only, Harriet. We had one but we had to let him go. Things amiss

. . .' He waved his hand in the direction of the ledger. 'Damned finances, you know. Whole estate is . . . worrying me. I'm a military man – don't understand these things. But I do understand this – if people are saying that about the bridge, what else might they be saying about how other things are run? Matthew's the man, isn't he? He could come and put things right here.'

'You'd have to speak to him. But he is as loyal to his lordship and his properties as I am. Oh, you cannot know how we long to take a Continental tour, but there is no point in the year when one or the other of us is not deluged with work. I look at the wonderful paintings in your gallery here, and yearn to return to Florence, to Rome! Even,' I added ruefully, 'to London.'

'Not in the summer. The great stink! Wait till that Bazalgette chappie sorts it all out! Meanwhile,' he said, no longer jovial, 'people are also saying you stole that jet necklace. Might even have killed the Gräfin for it.'

I could hardly bear it. I was on my feet. 'Do these "people" want to see a copy of dear Lady Croft's Will? Cousin, she left far more than this – she left a king's ransom! – for my use until his lordship marries. And now no more than a tiny piece of it is hanging round my neck like a veritable albatross!'

He didn't know how to deal with my anguished fury. 'Shall I call my wife? Get you some smelling salts?'

I gripped the back of a chair. 'Thank you, no. But I might pour us more coffee.'

'Here,' he said gruffly. 'I'd best pour it, hadn't I? Don't want it spilt everywhere.'

'Thank you.'

'"A king's ransom". Why should she leave it to you?'

'Because she knows that I will always run the house as if she were still with us, expecting visitors. That I treat poor Lord Croft, even at his worst, with respect and ensure my colleagues do. That should he ever recover enough for marriage to be a possibility he will be able to hand his bride the jewels I have in my keeping as clean and bright as they should be, holding nothing back. She trusted me, and in her own way was fond of me, perhaps. That is why I wear that wonderful jet – to remember her.' I took a deep breath. 'Forgive me. I do not like to speak of my life at all, let alone in such a way. And it takes us away from what we should be doing.'

'You really are a friend of Halesowen's?'

'I am honoured he should consider me in those terms. But our paths have obviously diverged widely.' There was a shout from the boys still diligently playing. I smiled – but now perhaps more at the memory of that long-gone golden summer than at the boys' fun.

'If anyone is to be trusted in this life, I suppose the friend of a judge as distinguished as Halesowen should be,' he said with a rather endearing naivety. 'So I can trust you not – hell and damnation!' he snarled, as Lord Webbe's face appeared at the window.

'Mrs Rowsley – I keep getting this wrong. Can you spare just five minutes to help me get it right?' he asked.

'Better make that fifty,' his friend suggested. 'He's a slow learner!'

I was cursing under my breath at least as freely as Cousin Barrington. Why not five minutes later? I might never get that chance again.

'Can you lend her to us, Colonel?'

'Nice bit of sun. Good fresh air. I'll come myself.' He turned to me. 'Do you want me to lock up while you run and get your bonnet, my dear?'

Emphatically I did not. I wanted to lock up myself. But I could find some excuse to double back, I told myself as I did indeed run upstairs. Outside our bed chamber door, however, I hesitated. What if I did really find precious books secreted amongst our belongings?

All seemed well. None of the places where I would have concealed them were occupied by anything other than shoes and clothes. So I ran down the stairs again, my heart alight at the thought of the sun and the boys. And yes, Cousin Barrington had remembered to lock the door.

TWENTY-FOUR

Mason was dealing with our soaked and muddy garments as if it was an everyday request, absolutely not even hinting that he would love to know how we had got into such a mess. He undertook to find replacement clothes for Davies until his uniform trousers could be worn again. The tunic might be damp, but Davies would not be separated from it.

Clean and dry, I ran down to the sewing room to find it locked. Billy very discreetly believed that Harriet and the Colonel might be outside with Lord Webbe and Mr Forsyth. Asking him to tell the Constable and Turton where we were, I went into the garden. I was greeted by the sound of Harriet's laughter – the first time I had heard it in public since we had arrived here. Even Barrington, perched on a shooting stick, looked if not happy then at least contented.

Glancing at me, Harriet passed the ball quietly to Webbe. 'I think I have work to do – unless you want to bowl just one ball for the pleasure of it?' she asked me.

'I'd love to. And I believe there is time for you to, as well.'

Strangely Barrington would not accept her refusal. I bowled as I usually did, troubling but not bowling either young man. She, as calm as if she were reaching to pick a flower, flighted the ball slowly and gently. Webbe looked to hoick it over the rooftop. It bowled him. Forsyth, who could barely stop giggling, was more circumspect – but his shot sent the ball ballooning into Barrington's hands. He did not have to move an inch. With an appraising nod he threw it back to Harriet.

'I know from Matthew's face that there is news, but I have to see if I can work out what you're doing.' Staggering to his feet, he commandeered Forsyth's bat.

How would she react? Would she risk irritating him by bowling him out? Or would she be circumspect, and let him off her tantalizing hook?

I caught him out.

'No, no! She has to do it three times, like at the match!' the boys insisted.

She obliged, though it took four more balls to do it. Or perhaps she was being tactful.

To my delight Barrington was still applauding her as he led the way back to the sewing room, where he insisted on regaling Turton, spruce in a summer suit, and Davies, dressed in a footman's trousers four inches too short in the leg for him, with the story. He even laughed when he realized that Davies had needed to borrow carpet slippers.

'Dear me!' Barrington chuckled. 'What a morning, eh, Cousin Harriet? All that fuss and palaver earlier and then you take me right back to my boyhood! I think we deserve a cup of coffee after all that exertion, don't you? Then we can give proper attention to what these gentlemen have to tell us.' He rang. Billy came and went.

Fuss and palaver? What had been going on? Harriet personified silent female docility as she took her seat opposite him, something that clearly signified something had been going on – and, I suspected, more than just a display of clever bowling. Were his words a euphemism for sharp words between them?

The silence grew. At last the coffee appeared. Hands loosely clasped in her lap, Harriet let Billy serve everyone. She was making a point, wasn't she?

At last, Barrington said expansively, 'Now, Constable, I can see that you and the gentlemen have been engaged in something. Can you tell us what?'

'Sir, we went to the bridge. The water had dropped allowing us to see things we could not have seen before. Amongst them was this.' He produced the hammer. 'We have no means of knowing if this was the weapon that struck Mr Biddlestone – it's just as likely to have been used to knock out some of the brickwork – but it seemed to us that Dr Highworth might have an opinion.'

'Good man. Well spotted. But obviously you all got wet. To what end?'

'We found other things, sir,' Davies said doubtfully, frowning slightly at the awkwardness of the question. 'Very sharp eyes, Mr Turton has.'

Turton didn't argue. Silently he unwrapped his handkerchief to reveal the treasure that we suspected might have come from a rich woman's neck.

Barrington peered at it, but shook his head. 'What do you make of it, Cousin Harriet?'

'I don't recognize it: I only saw one of her outfits, and those gorgeous emeralds would not have matched it. But there is someone who might identify it. If she can bear to look at it, that is. Young Clara, who, you'll recall, acted as her dresser while she was here.'

'Still working with Mrs Simpkins, is she? I'll get someone to fetch her here now!' He reached for the bell.

Harriet shook her head. 'With respect, Cousin, I think she'd be scared out of her wits; she's not used to lovely rooms like this, and she's terrified of men at the moment. Might Constable Davies go down to the servants' hall? He could watch from a distance while Mrs Simpkiss and I ask her about it?'

Davies nodded enthusiastically, Barrington much less so. 'I need to give that some thought.' He sipped the rest of his coffee.

Meanwhile I dug in my own pocket. 'It's not working after its immersion but this is a very fine gentleman's watch. Not the sort a fashionable lady or a butler would sport.'

'God bless my soul! You found that in the stream?'

'Eyes like a sparrowhawk's, Mr Turton's. I reckon we might find more things as the waters drop. There were a few odds and ends of wood that might have come from a jewellery box if the flood smashed it against rocks and stones. Assuming it was the flood, and not a human hand. Now, sir, we did wonder if we – if you – might offer a reward for any villagers bringing me any other treasures. Once word gets out there's rich pickings there, you can bet your life folk'll be tempted. And a reward might help them . . . to be a bit more honest, might I say?'

'As to how much,' I added, 'I think we should take Constable Davies' advice – he will know best what would be attractive enough to people to stop them selling finds to pedlars and so on. And I think Harriet's idea is a good one. Clara's a shy little thing at best. Even just being asked will be terrifying enough for her.' I spoke as sincerely as I could: I would dearly have loved to be present when she was questioned.

'Hm. Now, this reward business: what are you expecting to be found, Davies?'

'Who knows? That watch was a surprise. So anything and nothing, I think it's fair to say.'

Knocking discreetly, Mason opened the door a crack. 'Beg pardon, Colonel, but her ladyship craves a word in her private sitting room.'

'Better see what she wants. I'll return as soon as I can. And remember, all of you, be prepared. Lock the door if you're alone. Lock it if you're the last to leave.'

'What was all that about?' I asked the moment the door closed.

'I had to explain why you . . . why I . . . felt I needed protection. He was in a really strange mood this morning. One moment he was accusing me of stealing books from the library, next he was hoping to poach you to run the estate. And then the cricket. Was he always as changeable as this?'

'I know he's my cousin but we've never been close. You probably know him better than I do, Turton. And you, from a different perspective, Davies?'

Davies shifted in his borrowed slippers. 'I hardly like to say – I mean, it's not my place, is it?'

'Strong man with weaknesses, as you can see when that bastard Jameson manipulates him,' Turton said. 'And the pain makes him tetchy. Very changeable. Can't blame him for that when his back's bad. But when he's well he's a decent man. Very decent.'

Davies nodded agreement.

'Perhaps something else is troubling him,' Harriet mused, as gently as when she was preparing to bowl. 'Did the papers I retrieved last night throw any light on anything, Constable Davies?'

It must have been hard to be dignified when you were wearing someone else's trousers and slippers, but Davies did his best. 'Ma'am, I really think they ought to be confidential. For the time being at least. Dear me, I wish the Colonel had given permission for me – for you, ma'am! – to speak to Clara.' He looked at his watch and then at the clock. 'Time is going on, and as sure as eggs are eggs some of the guests are going to leave, whatever I say or do.'

'He didn't say no, did he?' Turton said.

'He certainly didn't say yes,' Davies snapped. 'All the same, I've a good mind to—'

Loud voices in the corridor interrupted him. The door burst open.

'There you all are!'

'Good morning, Jameson,' I said, stepping forward and blocking his way. 'How may I help? Or, since you've gone to the trouble of coming to the Colonel's headquarters, can I assume you have come to help us? That you have information that will help Constable Davies solve a particularly difficult case?'

He snorted. 'What, are you Verges to his Dogberry?'

Harriet's eyebrows shot up at the allusion; I must ask her why later. Meanwhile behind me, there was movement – with luck Davies covering up our morning's finds. And sitting down, of course, to hide his chaotic clothing. In fact, he sounded and looked quite magisterial as he said, 'Good morning – Major Jameson, isn't it? I was hoping to speak to you today.'

'Why, might I ask?'

'The reason I wish to speak to everyone: two terrible deaths have occurred and it is my duty to find who is responsible.'

'You! And this motley crew. Including her! My God, are we supposed to speak to servants and yokels?'

'I believe a gentleman is supposed to be polite to whoever he speaks. And to obey the laws of the land, which include assisting the police,' I said firmly, hoping my voice drowned the very slight click as the door handle turned.

'I am not speaking in front of that—' He jabbed a finger in Harriet's direction.

From behind him came an outraged intake of breath at the epithet he used. But Barrington was letting me deal with this.

'Nor will you have to, especially if you persist in your insolence. You will apologize now.'

He mumbled something.

'In fact, you will have to wait anyway. My wife and Constable Davies are just about to interview another witness. If you agree a time with the constable, I am sure he can arrange for the Colonel to be present.'

Davies reacted wonderfully. 'Two, shall we say, Major? If that suits the Colonel, that is. Oh, sir!' He half-rose as Barrington stepped forward.

'It does indeed,' Barrington declared, seating himself stiffly. 'My study. No. Two-thirty is better for me. Two-thirty. Prompt. And now, if you will excuse us?' He did not stand. He simply watched and waited.

Red to the ears, Major Jameson withdrew.

'Insolent puppy!' Barrington nodded grimly. 'You did very well there, Davies. And you, too, Matthew. Harriet, my dear, I did not believe my ears. A decent officer using language like that! God bless my soul! How dared he! Is that how he behaved in the library yesterday? And yet you can smile?'

'Dear Cousin, I am actually amused – admittedly in a very dark way. When Lady Pidgeon and I were leaving the library yesterday, I hoped – aloud – that the village constable would not be a Dogberry. And the wretched Major quoted me! Constable Davies, I apologize to you.'

'This Dogberry would be a yokel, I take it,' he supplied, staring at some point over her head.

'Countryman you may be, Constable, but yokel you are not. We all respect you and are proud to know you – and,' she continued, smiling broadly, equal to equal, 'you had the sense not to stand up wearing the wrong trousers!'

To Davies' blushes, Turton and I applauded. So did Barrington. This was a man who had appeared so completely under Jameson's thumb that he had been prepared deliberately to lose a cricket match. What had changed?

I took advantage of the generally benign atmosphere. 'Barrington, do you think now would be a good time for Harriet to talk to Clara? And for Davies to eavesdrop?'

He nodded. 'Excellent idea. And when you come back, we'll have a bit of lunch here to celebrate.'

TWENTY-FIVE

B illy might have been inclined to snigger at Constable Davies' borrowed trousers, but he stopped abruptly when I asked, 'And when, Billy, will the Constable's uniform trousers be dry enough to wear? Heavens, get a laundrymaid to press them until they are. That's what you would do for the Colonel, is it not? Off you go: we can find our way from here. I hope!' I added quietly to Davies, making him laugh for the first time since the yokel incident. He might not have understood the Shakespearian allusion, but he certainly recognized and resented the offensive noun. 'Where do you think is the best place for me to talk to Clara? And for you to hide, of course.'

'I'll ask Mrs Simpkiss. Ma'am, those papers. I don't mind you and your husband knowing all this private stuff, but we'd have to shake off Mr Turton. And he's sticking in that room like a wasp after jam.'

'Have you any reason to doubt him? He seems to have done very well to spot things in the water today.'

'Not really.' He gnawed his lip. 'Like I said, I don't have to lug the family Bible here, but both the Colonel and I have sworn our oaths to God and the Queen. And any Bible would do. But I'd like you made official, like. If you get my meaning.' As always, as his confidence slipped, so his ease with language ebbed too.

'Of course I get it. My advice would be to talk to the Colonel alone and tell him straight what you'd like. You have right on your side, Constable. Remember, Matthew and I only want to help, and if our stepping back helps, that's what we'll do – after I've spoken to Clara, perhaps. Shall I take that necklace? Lead on!'

At least the Constable was smiling broadly when I emerged from my short encounter with Clara. He tucked the necklace back into a tunic pocket.

'Fancy her being able to confirm it was the Gräfin's and no

one else's by the difficult catch! Clever little girl. But still very nervous, I'd say.'

'And near to tears when I hinted I'd like to know more about the man in the room. I wish Mrs Simpkiss would try to get more out of her, but—' I shrugged. 'Who does village gossip say is her father?'

'Oh, one of the servants, ma'am,' he said repressively, walking in silence until we were away from other ears. 'Or her ladyship's father,' he continued as if in the same breath.

I stopped dead. 'Constable Davies, forgive me if . . . Now, the rumour is that Mrs Simpkiss kept her job when she was pregnant? And continued to work here? You see, I know of a very few married housekeepers who managed to combine motherhood and their job – but of no unmarried mothers at all. To a woman, they were sacked – or if they were pregnant by a so-called gentleman, rather than a servant, they were despatched to an estate in a far corner of the country where they lived under a different name.'

He frowned. 'Well, I wasn't here myself then, of course. I could ask my auntie. Now you come to mention it, it does seem strange, a place as respectable as this run by a fallen woman.'

'Respectable?' I snorted. 'Gambling debts? Two murders? Respectable indeed, Constable!' I managed not to scream at his assumption that an illicit pregnancy must be the woman's fault. 'I should have thought a *respectable* woman like Mrs Simpkiss would have felt very uncomfortable with some of the gentry's goings on.'

'Ah. Yes. So I wonder how that rumour sprang up. It must have some basis. Except to my mind Clara doesn't look much like Mrs Simpkiss, does she? I mean, a big strapping woman, and no beauty, if I tell the truth, is mother of a tiny little mite like that who promises to be – well, not pretty, in a head-turning way, but . . .' He scratched his head. 'The sort of girl who looks . . . well, my wife is a case in point. Hill-farming stock but looks like a lady. Lovely straight nose . . . Mind you, there was talk of the lord of the manor somewhere in her family's past, if you get my meaning.'

'I do indeed,' I said grimly, fighting to keep a surely unwarrantable suspicion at bay. 'Tell me, how well do you know Mrs Dabbs?'

'Mrs Dabbs? Why?'

I raised my eyebrows. 'Gossip, Mr Davies. Gossip.'

'I suppose you couldn't—?'

'I would find it very hard: after all, Mrs Simpkiss and I – we've become fellow-conspirators, in a way.'

He touched the side of his nose. 'My job it is. Yes, Billy?'

'Your trousers await in the Room, sir,' he declared in sepulchral tones, earning a cuff round the ears.

I doubted if the Constable would ever be at ease in his company, but Barrington did his best to make him relax, readily agreeing that it was reasonable of the young man to worry about who might have access to sensitive information. He despatched a footman to bring a Bible, promising to look up the appropriate oath for us both. 'Yes, why not Cousin Harriet too? After all, Her Majesty is a lady and has ladies waiting on her. Cousin Harriet's waiting on her in a different way, that's all.'

No one argued

Almost immediately, Billy brought in luncheon, leaving it on the table before being dismissed. We would serve ourselves. What Mrs Dabbs probably called a light repast was in fact probably a miniature version of what the other guests would be enjoying as they speculated about what us outsiders were up to, with even a miniature galantine as centrepiece among an array of cold meats and salads.

Davies watched us very carefully before accepting any of the delights on offer and especially before picking up his cutlery. Perhaps he did not truly relax until we had reached the dessert course: certainly he did not join in the conversation, though we all made an effort to include him as an equal. Nor did he touch any wine.

At last, over tea and coffee, he took a risk – an entirely justified one – in asking quite without preamble, 'Sir, who was responsible for repairing that bridge of yours? I'd really like you to see why it's in the state it's in. They used the wrong in-fill and actually replaced decent stone with poor bricks and even worse poor mortar. It was as if they wanted it to fall down. Well, if not actually fall down then at least be somewhere they could pull out a few bricks and hide something.' In the face of a deepening silence, he continued, 'And I'm thinking the thing they wanted to hide – maybe one of the things – was the Gräfin's jewel box. You see, young Clara was quite clear that it was her necklace. But not on much else, to be fair. She might have been struck dumb when Mrs Rowsley asked her about the man she saw on the night of the murder.'

'Frightened, eh?'

'Very, I would say, Cousin. Almost too frightened to breathe. Still is.'

'Does that suggest the man is still alive? What do you think, Matthew?'

'It would have been . . . poetic justice . . . if she had screamed at the thought of Biddlestone. I wish no one dead, but since he is dead anyway . . .'

'I fear I agree,' I said. 'I had reason to dislike him, and if we could have dusted our hands of him . . . But we can't, can we? We can't simply assume that a dislikeable man is our killer.' Or I would be pointing at Jameson with a quivering accusatory finger. And it seemed I was not the only one.

'On the other hand, ma'am, you can't rule out a man just because he is nasty and unpleasant and you think it's obvious he's evil too. Begging your pardon, Colonel, but having seen Major Jameson in action, as it were, I really think he could be our man. One of our men.'

'He was very rude to you, very. I know that. But his bark is worse than his bite.'

'Mr Turton might think different,' Davies said stubbornly. 'I've heard how he tormented you, sir.'

Jeremy shrugged. 'People do. Can imagine turning on him and breaking his jaw. But he's bigger and stronger than me. My jaw would be the one broken.' He grinned in response to the sympathetic smiles and struggled on as we shared his agony of embarrassment. 'But he is strong enough to have strangled the Gräfin. And like me tall enough to have hit Biddlestone. He may have had a motive we don't know about. Davies is right. Some people get bad reputations because they're bad people.'

'Look here,' Cousin Barrington spluttered, going as red in the face as the Major himself, 'you're talking about an officer and a gentleman! A guest under my roof!'

'Of course, sir,' Davies said, with far more aplomb than I could have imagined he could summon, 'which is why I think that you and I should not just quietly speak to him together, but actually accuse him and see how he reacts.'

It was wonderful to watch this supposed bumpkin manipulate an erstwhile leader of men – though I did wish, as I am sure the others did, that we might have witnessed the interview.

But he was speaking again. 'I believe, Colonel, that one of the young gentlemen staying here is studying the law at university. Do you suppose he might take notes for us? So we can concentrate on what is going on? Doesn't one of them know a very important judge?'

'Charles Webbe,' Matthew murmured. 'What a good idea, Constable. Meanwhile, would this be a good moment for all of us here to swear an appropriate oath of secrecy and loyalty to the Queen as a temporary officer of the law?'

'Webbe too, I dare say. I can deal with that if he agrees. Meanwhile, here is the Bible, and I want you to put your hand on it and repeat what I say.'

We swore our oaths. Barrington and Davies left us – but Davies dodged back. In silence, he put a small bundle of papers on the table, catching my eye in the process. Some people might have imagined that he winked.

I dealt the papers out as if they were playing cards. 'If we share the work – making notes, perhaps – it will be much quicker. Matthew. Jeremy.' Sitting down, I picked up my pencil.

The men did the same. I had found nothing at all relevant in the first four I examined, though Matthew was already jotting. Suddenly Jeremy was on his feet. 'Might be an outsider but these are families I mix with. At least my people do. Don't mind hearing what you two think I ought to know. But other stuff. No. Not spying. Going for a walk.' He picked up his sketchbook and headed for the door.

'Please – don't go! Harriet and I can deal with this.'

'Davies thinks there's incriminating material here, doesn't he?' It came out with slow, painful anger. 'I don't mind catching a murderer. But I don't want to have to identify a mere gambler or a debtor. No!' He threw the hideous vase at the wall. 'I resign!'

TWENTY-SIX

Harriet ran to the door.

'Where are you going?'

'Surely one of us should go after him?'

'Is his conscience sensitive – or guilty?' I asked, with much less sympathy. 'Davies has always had reservations about him, hasn't he?'

'If he's guilty, I fear what he might do. To someone else or to himself.' I pointed to the shards.

'You're right. Of course you're right. I'll go – I can run faster. Lock yourself in, remember.' I paused long enough to kiss her. 'What did I get us into, my love?'

What indeed?

Billy stopped me as I stepped into the corridor.

'I'm sorry, Billy, I can't speak now. Have you seen Mr Turton?'

'Yes, sir. Has he had a shock? Looked as if he'd seen a ghost, he did.'

'Which way did he go?'

'Out into the garden, sir. As a matter of fact,' he called after me as I set off, 'I followed him to make sure he was all right. But then I saw him talking to Harrison, and so I came back inside. Lot of common sense, Harrison.'

'You really are worried, aren't you?'

'I just like to keep my eye on things, sir. And my ears pricked. And because I'm a footman, people often forget I'm there. I see and hear things I can't talk about out here.'

'Would you care to step inside and talk in private? As I'm sure you know, Davies and the Colonel are in the Colonel's study.'

'With Lord Webbe, I understand.' He gave an interesting smile. 'Meanwhile, if you tell me to bring tea, sir, I will be happy to oblige. Mr Turton is in good hands, you know.' He bowed and set off at the regulation stately pace.

Harriet responded cautiously to my knock. 'Who is it?'

'Only me.' I slipped in quickly, taking the key from her shaking hand to lock up behind me. 'Harrison has his eye on Turton,' I said, 'and Billy is bringing us tea and, I suspect, information. Have those scraps of paper given you any idea what might have made Turton behave like that?'

'Probably these. According to Constable Davies' own notes here, they were what Mrs Simpkiss found in the Gräfin's pockets. IOUs. Most are signed with initials only.' She passed them over. 'Look at the sums involved. And make sure your eyebrows don't disappear into your hair for ever.'

Obviously I was not one of the house party set, but I could not imagine that losses of up to fifty guineas were normal at a social gathering. Heavens, there was even an IOU for a hundred. As for the mostly scrawled initials, I thought I might make out the odd letter – but even borrowing Harriet's reading glasses did not make up for the appalling handwriting that prevailed. But Billy would be with us soon; I gathered up everything both innocent and incriminating. Harriet took it calmly from me, popping it into her reticule as I admitted him.

He did not attempt to pour the tea.

'What is worrying you, Billy?' Harriet asked gently.

He stared at the carpet. 'It's one thing to want to say something. It's another to open your mouth and get the words out. Sir, ma'am – they're planning to get rid of you.'

'Who? And how? And why?'

'Who? Some of the guests, ma'am. How? By making out you're stealing things – you especially, ma'am, because someone, don't know who, snitched about seeing you dressed as a maid. Why – because they've got something to hide and they know you're asking questions, well, both of you, of course. And if people ask questions they usually get answers. Sorry.'

Her voice was remarkably calm. 'What am I supposed to have stolen?' She already feared being accused of robbing the library, of course.

'I don't know. But one of the servants is going to be told to say they saw you take it. Just saying, ma'am. And you know that these ever so nice genteel people can be right buggers if they want. Begging your pardon,' he added, clapping his hand over his mouth.

'So what would your advice be, Billy?'

'It's not my place to tell you what to do, is it, ma'am?'

'What would you do?'

'I'd scarper. Then maybe they'd forget all about it. And your reputation would remain intact,' he said, as deliberately and expressionlessly as if he was repeating a Sunday school lesson.

'Or they might send the police after me and certainly write to all their friends.' She gave a deep sigh. 'So I'm damned if I do and damned if I don't. Oh, dear.' She averted her face, pressing a handkerchief to her eyes.

'Thank you, Billy,' I said. 'And yes, some tea for my poor wife, please, and for me before you go.' I pressed a coin into his hand. As he left, I locked the door behind him.

We both drank the now lukewarm tea in silence. She mouthed something, pointing to the window. Bemused, I followed. At last it dawned on me she suspected he might be eavesdropping, and she wanted to make it harder. 'I think he's acting under orders, don't you? Even been bribed?' she breathed. 'And I really thought he was on my side.'

'I think he probably is,' I replied equally quietly. 'But venal. Or simply afraid of losing his job. And you yourself suspected someone is hoping to plant stolen books in our room, so there may be an element of truth. And he might even be sincere, don't forget that.'

'Of course. Except I really did not credit him with the line about my reputation. I have been too confiding, too trusting, I fear.' She thumped a clenched fist into the palm of her hand.

'Or he has orders from someone with power that overcomes his loyalty to you. That would be my theory. Ah! It sounds as if they are back. I wonder how they'll take the news that Turton has had a crisis of conscience?'

'Perhaps we should wait until we have Constable Davies alone? Unless you really think he has been gone so long we should check on him?'

The decision was made for us. Barrington, returning to the sewing room with a grim face, noticed his absence and asked where he was.

'He went for a walk,' I said, with enough truth to salve my conscience.

'Why in Hades would he want to do that? Did he take a gun?'

'To shoot rabbits, presumably?' I asked quickly, seeing Harriet's face pale.

'Of course I mean rabbits! Or pigeons. What else would I mean? Oh. Oh, I see. Well, did he?'

'No, not as far as I know. But Green, the footman on duty, would know more. Apparently Turton was last seen with your head gardener, Mr Harrison.'

'Why on earth would he want to talk to a gardener?'

'They got on well when they had to deal with Biddlestone's body,' I said, not quite in reply.

'But a guest – he's from a good family, a Church family your father probably knows – and a servant?' My cousin shook his head in disbelief.

Now was not the time to observe that Christ made friends with a wide swathe of people who weren't from good families.

'Maybe they like talking about cricket, sir? Same team, after all.' Davies might have spoken without a flicker of emotion, but I sensed an undercurrent. And he earned a sharp look from Barrington.

'Got to keep an eye on the foot-soldiers,' Barrington declared, looking with clear disapproval at each of us in turn. 'I suppose you had your reasons for not going after him, though I can't say I'm impressed. I'll do it myself. I could do with a breath of fresh air. Telling you about Jameson will just have to wait.' Glowering at each of us in turn, he stumped out.

Davies broke a guilty silence. 'Nothing personal, I should think. He's got the devil on his back at the moment, hasn't he? But why didn't you go? I'd have thought you'd be charging after him.'

'This is an apology as much as an explanation,' I said. 'But Billy said he was in safe hands – and from the dealings I've had with him, I'd say Harrison is a decent man. And then Billy wanted to speak to us in private.'

'About me in particular,' Harriet said. 'He gave me some information and advice.'

He listened in silence to her account. Then he could contain himself no longer: 'Billy – or Green as they will insist on calling him – suggested you did a runner?'

'Yes. He used the words "your reputation can remain intact", which didn't seem to me to be what he would say himself. What with that and the books already missing from the library, we suspected he was acting on someone's orders. I thought he was a good lad, too, Constable . . . Look,' she said, her voice more positive, 'Constable, I do feel we're sufficiently acquainted to use each other's Christian names, if you have no objection.'

'I'm happy to be called Morgan, ma'am. And I know you implied I might use yours but I bet there'd be hell to pay if I was heard doing it. Thank you all the same,' he added with a grin. 'And the same applies to you, sir. For what it's worth, I think young Mr Turton put you in a difficult situation, and young Billy just made it worse. And you're right, sir: Caleb Harrison is a good man, and wouldn't have let him do anything stupid.'

'Assuming Billy told us the truth,' I said grimly, 'what should we do?' I looked helplessly from one to another.

'Wait for the Colonel, I'd say. Now, did you recognize the names on any of the IOUs?'

'We failed there too, I'm afraid.'

'So did I.'

'No. But Mr Turton could read enough to refuse to look at any more. That's when he bolted.'

His eyes widened. 'You think he saw his own initials there?'

Harriet lifted her hands as if she were pushing away the notion. 'Surely not! Surely not! What he said was that he didn't like random spying on people who are after all friends of his family,' she added. 'He sees himself as an outsider because of his stutter, but he's still one of them at heart – isn't he your cousin's godson?'

'I'm not sure: heavens, Barrington didn't seem sure himself. Probably. Or why would he be here?' I asked, adding, 'The poor lad had such amazing self-control when it came to finding Biddlestone's body, and to spotting the Gräfin's necklace – I would never have imagined that this task would be too much for him. I really am sorry, and so I will tell him.'

'You couldn't work out any names at all? What a shame – some of those people had a powerful motive for doing her harm, if not actually killing her. What about the notes hidden in the ends of . . . what did you call them? Finials, that's it. What did you make of them?'

'We haven't even got to those.' Harriet gripped her forehead in irritation – her chignon was too tight for her to tear her hair. 'But,' she added quickly, 'I shall die of curiosity if you don't give us some hint of how Major Jameson behaved!'

Davies grimaced. 'Shall we invite Billy to bring us some more tea first? And perhaps have a short conversation with him?'

'I shall lose my place here if I tell you,' Billy said simply, and probably with perfect truth. 'Yes, I was wrong to do it, ma'am, but no, I couldn't not. That's the truth, Morgan.'

'Constable Davies when I'm on duty. And were you telling the truth about Mr Turton?'

'Why shouldn't I be?'

'That's not an answer, and you know it. If he's done himself a mischief and comes back here on a farm gate, it'll be at your door, my lad. Orders from above or not.'

'I did follow him because he did look upset, like. And I did see him go into the garden and I did know Harrison was in the garden.'

'But not that the two of them were even talking to each other? Dear me, Billy, I expected better of you than that.'

'Well, I had to do what I was told and speak to Mrs Rowsley, didn't I?'

'Cheeky young whelp! Get out of my sight before I box your ears for cheek. Now!' Davies turned to us and sighed. 'Giving me lip at a time like this. You wouldn't credit it, would you?'

TWENTY-SEVEN

'I've not told you about our interview with the Major yet,' Morgan Davies pointed out as I poured the tea Billy had left and passed him a cup. 'Thank you. And I know you'd want to know all about that, ma'am, seeing you and he don't exactly see eye to eye.'

'I was worrying more about Jeremy, to be honest. How could we have failed him so?'

'I'm not sure anyone has failed him yet. If I go scampering round the countryside in search of him, the Colonel will think I don't trust him to do it. And I am here to do a job. Between ourselves, this is all beyond my rank. But my cousin's ignored my messages. Scotland Yard will only come if someone sends for them – and that someone must be your cousin, Matthew. Sir.' The men exchanged a grin. 'But threats of violence I know about – even if it's usually poachers promising to get their own back on gamekeepers. And your Major Jameson is like a gentleman poacher. He knows he's done wrong to behave as he did to you – Lady Pidgeon complained to your cousin about it, so he can't deny it. But instead of repenting and changing his ways, I'd say he's going to want revenge.' He put down his cup. 'What I'd like to do is send him packing, for all our sakes, nasty bullying man that he's turned out to be. But since I can see he's strong enough to have killed the Gräfin and even a tall man like Biddlestone, I have to treat him as a suspect and keep him here. Your cousin and I are agreed on that.'

'Is Barrington still – to put it bluntly – under his thumb?' Matthew asked.

'There's something going on there, isn't there? All that talk about the match – my wife tells me it's still not died down.'

'If you want it from the horse's mouth, talk to Harrison. He believes the game was, for want of a better word, fixed. It was only a combination of Harriet's heroism and divine intervention that whoever tried to do it was thwarted.'

'I wasn't heroic,' I said. 'I had the instinct to do something and the skills to achieve it. My theory is this. Jameson was short of money. Most people would have bet on the gentlemen's team to win. He bet on the village team, probably heavily, and did everything he could to undermine Barrington's captaincy and the players' talents and endeavours.'

'But why purloin the village team's best player?' Matthew asked.

'And then not let him play properly?' I added. 'I can't explain either of those.'

Morgan shook his head. 'But the rest of your theory is making sense. Presumably the tie meant the bet was void. So – still short of money – he decided to find a way out of his situation. Possibly he signed one of those IOUs. He goes to reason with the Gräfin and, when she refuses to help him, he kills her, steals the jewels and hides them – or, better still, gets Biddlestone to hide them.'

'In the unsafe bridge,' Matthew concluded. 'I can't think of a better explanation. But we need, as Mr Gradgrind would say, Harriet, Facts.'

Davies stared. 'Mr –?'

'An acquaintance of ours,' I said quickly.

Davies nodded 'And then, just to finish your theory, he and Biddlestone fall out, he attacks Biddlestone and comes back here, clutching what he can of the jewels. But we have no facts, convenient or otherwise. If only we could ask young Clara who she saw. Better still, make all the men in the house walk in front of her and watch her reaction. But if she could see them, they would see her, and that could put her in danger.'

'Jeremy could help! His sketches!' I cried. Then I added sombrely, 'If he comes back, of course, and if he's prepared to help any more. Big ifs. Meanwhile, Morgan, I can see only one way to deal with the IOUs. You and Cousin Barrington have to present them to each guest in turn and ask which is theirs.'

'It's a big risk, ma'am.'

'Especially as I suspect Barrington has IOUs of his own to worry about,' Matthew said. 'Letting go important staff like the steward and the librarian, not having enough servants in general, incompetent building work – there must be financial problems aplenty here, if only we could trace them in the accounts.'

'And of course it is hard to pin down Barrington on anything. The team sheet for the match that we asked for. The list of guests and their rooms. Both of these would have made our lives much easier.' I clenched my fists in frustration. 'Morgan, the rumours about Clara's parenthood. You were going to talk to your aunt, weren't you? Did you have time?'

'Time!' he snorted. 'At least I managed to ask my wife. But all this is many years ago, of course. At one point Lady Hortensia's father let this house out, and moved his family and staff, all of them, to London or somewhere in the south. Lock, stock and barrel. The villagers here actually preferred the new family – they took on servants from the village, see, and paid them well. One of Bronwen's cousins became their nursemaid and was happy to move with them when they went to Devon. So no one bothered to ask too many questions. And then they came back, all the same as before. As for Clara, no one seems to know much about her at all, except she came from a workhouse somewhere. Not the local one. She's been here about nine months. No one quite knows where these rumours about her birth came from. Or when.'

I nodded. 'I'm a workhouse brat myself. You always wonder who your parents were – and believe me other people wonder too, often aloud to your face. So if one of us – and it won't be me, Morgan – ever asks Mrs Simpkiss about Clara, let it not be in front of the child herself. Meanwhile, I made my own list of the rooms that are occupied and by whom.' I removed it from my reticule and laid it before him. 'Heavens, Morgan, Matthew and I are tiptoeing about trying not to tread on people's feelings. Two people – I know that they might have been monsters in their way – didn't have their feelings considered one bit when they were killed. Let's just speed this up.' I tried to control my voice, which was clearly showing my frustration, my exasperation. 'Morgan, before I forget again – that big key. The one I found in the Gräfin's bed chamber. Have you managed to identify it yet? Because if not it dawns on me it's quite like the one we have at home for the house safe. Actually we need two – the butler has one, and I have the other. And no, before you ask, I have no idea why this key should have been in the Gräfin's room. I'm sorry.'

He looked at me with some concern. 'You sound quite upset, like, Mrs Rowsley.'

I wanted to scream aloud. *Of course I'm upset. I've got a job at home that I do very much better than I muddle along doing this. I hate it here. I hate being hated. I hate upsetting a nice young man and not running after him when I should have done.* I said, 'I am just so aware of the passage of time, Morgan, and a feeling that I'm walking up a staircase that keeps taking me back down. I'm sorry. But the tension that is obviously affecting everyone is affecting me too, though I have no family loyalties to worry me.' I glanced at Matthew.

Morgan nodded slowly. 'And it's not as if you can go home and shut your front door on it all, is it? So we'd best do what we can as quickly as possible. Now, if that key is the one for the safe, is it fair to say there's probably a spare somewhere in the house?'

'Mrs Simpkiss might have one?' Matthew suggested.

'Why don't I ask her?' Davies said. 'And I can collect the other one from the police office if needs be. Borrowing that horse was an excellent idea, Mr Rowsley. It will make life much easier. Meanwhile, since everyone else is enjoying a nice bit of early summer sun, why don't you take a stroll too? You might even come across Mr Turton.'

Before we found the young man, we encountered our hostess, standing beside her horse and clearly in a temper. The beast was not doing what it was supposed to be doing, and she was slashing at it with her crop. Because of her grip on the bridle, it could not avoid the blows raining down on it.

'Stupid animal!' she said over her shoulder.

I inched closer. 'It's a beautiful creature, isn't it?' I remarked mildly.

'And damned stupid. Here, come and hold it,' she told Harriet. 'Cousin, throw me up.'

It was easier for us both to obey. Easier for the horse too.

We watched her out of sight. 'Are you thinking what I'm thinking?' I asked quietly.

'I might be. In a riding habit and with that crop she looks rather different from the be-crinolined lady you dislike so much.

Taller. Less – less lady-like, I suppose. And to grip, to hit as hard as that, she must be very strong as well as cruel.' As one we nodded. 'Strong and cruel enough to throttle a friend? To stun a man and leave him to drown?'

'No one would ever tell us if they did think she could have done it.'

Still speculating aloud Matthew and I walked at a spanking pace along the paths designed to give ladies and gentlemen an elegant place to stroll. To one side were trees and shrubs, now overgrown to form almost a hedge. A lawn, actually pretty much a meadow, was on the other side, rolling down from the house. Everything was draining quickly, with unofficial streamlets across the path, which was otherwise quite dry. I could imagine a mass exodus of guests taking place despite Morgan Davies' best efforts.

'Our hostess apart, this is a very good way of saving our sanity. You were so fierce with young Davies there you nearly had him hiding under the table. If our position is awkward, imagine how hard his job is.'

'I know, and I will apologize when we get back. But none of us has proper experience of what to do in this strange situation and I fear we are doing things in the wrong order and getting them wrong. Despite all our activities at Thorncroft, we are rank amateurs; he is young and inexperienced. I can't fault his intelligence – it shines through, doesn't it? But he – everyone – let people like your cousin get away with things. Why? Because he is a gentleman, of course. But in the wider scheme of things he doesn't succeed. Is he thwarted by the servants? By his wife? By the pain he is clearly in? For a leader of men, he is certainly not leading now. Why on earth will he not send for Scotland Yard?'

'Perhaps the telegraph office is too far. Perhaps the roads are too bad. Or perhaps the trains are not yet running.'

'Or perhaps he does not want the investigation to go any further because it would be embarrassing for him and his guests. Perhaps he thinks if there is mass departure he can't control, he can "lose" the evidence of his guests' debts and somehow convince everyone that Biddlestone killed the Gräfin and then drowned himself.'

'Not when the doctor will have seen the bruise on the back of your so-called suicide's head. And not while Turton has his sketches.' He gripped my arm. 'Harriet, what's that? Fluttering in the mud over there?'

'A scrap of paper?'

'Rather more than a scrap, I'd say.'

I followed as he ran over, cursing as my elegant hat threatened to fly free of the equally elegant hat-pin that was supposed to hold it in place. Matthew was right. He retrieved, crumpled and wet, Jeremy's sketch pad.

'Dear God – what's he done?' I cried. 'I should have—'

'He may not have done anything. I can't believe someone intending to harm himself would go out armed with this.' He lifted the pad. 'He was certainly alive not long ago. Look: here's Harrison, both gardening and oiling his bat. All rural calm – apart from that tightness about the jaw. Then here's Cousin Barrington haranguing Harrison – you can even see that shrug. Then Lady Hortensia arrives in the garden – that hat of hers would really suit you, my love – presumably before going riding. Riding unaccompanied too. Why should she risk her reputation to do that? No groom. No guest.'

'Perhaps she just needed to escape from the house for a while. Or perhaps she was meeting someone . . .'

'Ah, but who?

'Let us see if Turton has done any more sketches. Has he caught them in a moment of tenderness? Oh dear. Anything but! There's Mr Harrison at a discreet distance.' He flicked over the page. 'Dear me, look what he's done with her refined aristocratic features!'

'Yes, and he's made her stand arms akimbo, like a fishwife arguing with a cowed customer.'

Next she was brandishing a finger under Barrington's nose, pointing to something off the page with the other hand. Soon we found the young cricketers at play. Major Jameson was glowering furiously at them. Then Billy, the footman, who appeared on his hands and knees gathering up his wig. Then there was a jagged line where a page, no, several pages, had been torn out.

'Turton? Turton! Are you all right?' Again Matthew was running, this time along the hedgerow.

Once more I could only trail behind him, doing my best with my billowing skirt and the wretched hat. At last I pulled it off altogether, sticking the pin in the thickest part of my skirt, which I could now hitch up with both hands.

Matthew stopped and turned back. 'He's here. He's alive. But you need to get to Dr Highworth fast.'

'You go. You can run much faster. I'll stay with him.'

'No. Far too dangerous.'

'I will scream if I need to. Any blood? I might need your shirt to bandage him? Thank you. Just go.'

TWENTY-EIGHT

'Mr Turton is in the hedgerow on the walk approaching the big gazebo,' I told the first outdoor lad I saw. 'Take the fastest horse in the stable and tell Dr Highworth the young man could well die. And tell them to saddle a horse for me.'

He blenched; I probably did myself at saying aloud what I feared.

I couldn't fault his obedience. He was into the stables and on a horse in moments. As he clattered off, I ran indoors, calling for towels and sheets and blankets and a team of footmen to carry them. At home at Thorncroft there would have been an instant and efficient response; here it seemed I had to ask for each item from a bemused maid. At last Mason appeared, and took control. I could dash back into the bright sun again, to be greeted by an alert stable lad who threw me swiftly into the saddle. 'We'll need a gate to carry him on, too,' I shouted over my shoulder.

At Thorncroft the trustees had set a whole wing set aside to nurse Lord Croft. Gradually it had become a well-run hospital for villagers and estate workers too, and always ready to deal with emergencies. Our excellent village doctor was a man to whom I would trust my life; I could only hope that Highworth, who had not endeared himself to me, would be half as good and would know where his patient could be safely treated – certainly, in my view, not the house. There was still no sign of him as I galloped back along the quiet walks – and then I recalled his bad back. Pray God it did not require him to drive a sedate dog-cart.

Harriet had propped her sunshade over Jeremy's head to protect him from the increasingly warm sun. Pads and bandages made with her petticoat and my shirt covered his wounds – I realized for the first time that I had stripped it off and not replaced it. But she was not there. What could have separated

her from a young man she was so protective, so fond of? I was
torn in two: should I stay with him, talking to him and trying
to bring him back to consciousness, or go in search of the
person who mattered most to me on earth?

A scream. A loud scream! But it wasn't her voice. Surely it
was a man's? Abandoning Turton, I ran towards the thicket from
which the sound seemed to be coming – to find Harriet, still
tearing at a cloth that blindfolded her, stumbling towards me. As
I unbound her she pulled something from her mouth – pieces of
paper?

'Who did this? Has he hurt you?'

'Someone – a man – I don't know. And I am unhurt, I think.
A bit of a headache and my dignity apart. How's Jeremy?' She
clutched my hands in fear.

'Alive. Highworth should be on his way by now. But you –
what happened?'

'Someone came up behind me. Hit me on the back of my
head, but not – I don't think it was very hard, because I'm still
just about able to think.' She ran her fingers over her thick
chignon. 'He tied this over my face. Dragged me off.'

'Good God – did he . . . did he . . .?'

'Whatever he intended, he did not manage it. I remembered
my hat-pin.' She smiled, almost impishly. 'The one you bought
me in Venice. And I stuck it quite deep into him. That's when
he let me go. Matthew, what if I killed him?'

'What if you did? It would save me the job.'

Shouts from the path told us Mason and his team were on the
way. Some farm lads were staggering in the rear, carrying
the gate I had asked for. We could make the young man as
comfortable as we could – but we still awaited the doctor. I
sent two of the youths to see if there was any sign of the monster
who had attacked Harriet – 'No, don't touch anything he may
have left, and don't touch him either!' I told them, more out
of duty than a hope the assailant would survive intact.

'Can we give chase, like, if we see him? Run fast, we do.'

'I'm sure you do. But just follow him – see where he goes,
but don't try to stop him.'

The farm lads dumped the gate, rolling up their sleeves as if
they intended to lift the still unconscious Turton. I joined them.

Shaking though she was, Harriet stopped us. 'Dr Page would insist he was kept still until a physician had examined him. I am sure Dr Highworth would want the same. I do believe Jeremy's pulse is stronger, less tumultuous. Maybe – dare I risk using my vinaigrette to see if that helps him? And maybe someone could fetch some water?'

Mason proffered a flask. 'I have brandy, ma'am, if you think that would help?'

She took it, doing no more than moisten the boy's lips. 'Thank you. But some cold water to treat the bruises? The colder the better.'

'Ice? The ice-house is just beyond the gazebo.' Off he ran.

As he did so, up ran one the lads I had sent to see if there was any sign of Harriet's attacker. There wasn't – Harriet might have hurt him but not, it seemed, fatally.

The boy was a scrawny child with the biggest knees I'd seen working their way through breeches that had surely been worn by many thin legs before his. Tugging his forelock he said, 'Please, your honour, you can see where someone's been, your honour. And there is stuff caught in tree branches and some paper. We thought it best, begging your pardon, if we left it where you could see it, there being not a breath of wind to blow it away. Albert is standing guard, just in case anyone comes back to tidy up, like. I could show it you if you want, sir.'

'It sounds like a good idea, but it's Constable Davies who needs to see it. He's the one in charge, after all.' And as if on cue he came riding up. It was more than a canter than a gallop, and he didn't manage a heroic leap from the horse; in fact it was the cautious approach I had come to expect from him. But at least there was now someone with genuine legal authority among us.

'Dr Highworth is following me, Mr Rowsley,' he said. 'Damn whoever let that bridge fall down – it means everyone has to go the long way round.'

'Of course. How could I have forgotten that?'

'He's in his gig – it's got a little trailer attached, which he uses to carry any patient who can't walk. He keeps a spare bed chamber for patients – his wife is already preparing a bed – who need help and can afford it, of course.'

'What Mr Turton can't pay, I will.' At least I could now see the gig, which was coming at a very decorous pace. 'Davies, this lad has found evidence you may want to look at before you move it. But it's evidence of a man who attacked Harriet, and not necessarily the criminal who beat Mr Turton like this.'

An anxious glance at Harriet told him that Turton was in more immediate need. He knelt beside him, looking at each bruise as if he was a doctor. 'Poor gentleman,' he said at last, getting to his feet to peer at Harriet's face. 'And you, ma'am – you were attacked too?'

'I retaliated,' she said. 'With my hat-pin. He screamed as if I had hurt him badly. I couldn't get it out – and it was quite a favourite item.'

Ignoring the sudden tremor in her voice, he said, 'Excellent. That should make him easier to track down and bring to justice. Right, young Morris, take me to Albert, and make it snappy.'

Dr Highworth's examination of his patient was as frustratingly slow as his journey here. But no one wished to rush him. He was as thorough as Ellis Page would have been, which was praise indeed.

'It is my belief that no bones are broken, but that he is suffering from a deep concussion possibly brought about by a fall when he was kicked and beaten. There may of course be internal bleeding, which would be regrettable: you did well, Mrs Rowsley, not to have him moved. Ah! Do I smell brandy?'

'I moistened his lips with some – no more. And here is Mason bringing ice. For those poor bruises.'

'Excellent. There is a widespread belief, which I do not share, that steak is a remedy for black eyes like this. My own preference is for ice. But not straight on to the skin, if you please. Wrapped in fabric.' He looked about him expectantly. 'Ah. You extemporized, I see. I have proper bandages in my bag, if someone would be good enough to pass it to me.'

At last, a slow procession round through the estate, the young men walking alongside the trailer which they could lift off the road and carry when it had to cover rough ground. The gate stayed where it was.

Davies called and beckoned us, Harriet bustling along as if

she had simply spent a serene day in the garden. 'Look what these clever lads have found. Eagle-eyed, that's what they are.'

I slipped them appropriate coins. 'Well done. Now, what can you see, lads?'

'There's a bit of material on that bush, see,' said the one with knobbly knees. 'And he's left a footprint in the mud. Left boot. Right boot over there, we think. But we didn't want to go trampling all over the place, see. That right, Albert?'

Puce with embarrassment, the boy nodded.

To my amazement, Davies dug in one of his tunic pockets, producing a tiny ruler, hinged in the middle – ivory? Bone? 'My father was apprenticed to a carpenter,' he said. 'Matthew, could you write down the measurements if I call them out? We could really do,' he reflected, 'with young Mr Turton at this point, couldn't we? To sketch the footprints.'

'I'll do my best,' Harriet said. 'But I'm not in the same league as Jeremy. Just leave that ruler where I can see the markings, if you please. Oh, botheration – I find my hand is shaking.' It was. But she battled on anyway and by the time she had finished her normal demeanour was almost restored. 'Do you suppose that he will throw away his shoes? Or perhaps he doesn't even know he's left prints. Now, can one of you safely reach that piece of material?'

Albert almost literally swung from tree to tree – at least supporting himself by clinging on to one handhold while he reached for another branch.

'Excellent – it looks like a piece of rather good gentleman's suiting, doesn't it?'

'Would it be possible to repair a tear like that?' Davies asked.

'It depends where it is. I think it would show wherever it was, actually, especially if someone unused to darning tried it. Even an expert to be fair. It would be hard, would it not, to explain away the damage. But I would truly prefer not to go through gentlemen's wardrobes myself, not now you are here to do it. Oh, dear me!' She turned to Albert. 'I'm sorry. I forgot you were hanging on by your fingertips. Can you try to reach the piece of paper? Thank you.'

What would someone looking at us from afar have thought? On this perfect day, with the bushes alive with birds, with plants ready to flower, and the sky the clearest blue, why were all these solemn faces looking at such tiny and probably insignificant scraps as if they were as precious as Holy Writ? And why should the trim and hatless woman, surrounded by urchins and tall men, be straightening out a disgusting mess she had retrieved from her pocket?

'How dare he?' she cried. 'Look what he gagged me with – one of Jeremy's sketches. What's on the other piece of paper, Constable?'

'Nothing special, ma'am. Any more than the sketch on your gag. I can't see any reason why he should choose to destroy those, can you?'

I peered over her shoulder. The gag showed young Lord Webbe bowling; the other was a nice study of a bat. Entirely innocent, as far as I could see.

'I suppose he could have just grabbed a couple of pages at random,' Davies said doubtfully. 'But somehow I don't think he did.'

'Both to do with cricket,' she said. 'But . . .' She shrugged, almost helplessly.

'If you've got a man capable of killing one or two people and attacking two more, I'd say there's a corner of his mind where this makes sense. Ma'am, did you notice anything at all about him? Smell, touch, anything on his hands? I'm sorry if this seems impertinent, especially at the moment when you've had a double shock, like, and I'm sorry if it upsets you, but I really want you to think.'

'There is something – it's lurking. But the more I try to recall the further away it drifts. Does that make sense?'

'Something to do with the bang on your head, I should expect,' I said, rather too bracingly.

Davies watched her, eyes narrowed, head slightly on one side. Whenever Harriet did the same, she reminded me of a robin eyeing a morsel. Now he reminded me of a blackbird – less, perhaps, when he took off his heavy hat and mopped his brow with its red furrow where it had pressed into his flesh. 'Sometimes when you are really thinking about something else a memory will come to you. And in this case it could be important. And it may not be very nice when it does.'

TWENTY-NINE

'We have never yet left the bounds of this estate,' I said. 'I agree I should perhaps let Dr Highworth inspect this lump, but I will go to him. I am what your cousin would call walking wounded, after all. And I would not for anything take him away from Jeremy's side. A ride on a quiet pony should do me no harm – think of Fanny Price, who relied on it as a means of taking the air.' That should be a clincher, surely.

It appeared it was. We set off sedately, with a groom and Morgan Davies as escorts: it had become an expedition, which rather thwarted my desire to see the village and the surrounding hills as an antidote to the last few days of what felt like the incarceration.

'Those are Welsh hills over there, ma'am. But I'm afraid they're the grandest thing round here.'

I could not argue. The houses braced themselves against their local hills, clinging to the narrow little streets. The church was clearly very old, Norman, perhaps; the chapel where the Davies family worshipped was still a new scar rather than an inspiring building. The few people around – I had hoped to see women working their gardens in the warmth of the sun – showed all the signs I recognized from the Thorncroft area of a low income and poor food. Lord Croft, on the advice of his trustees, was having built on his land a new village intended to provide work and reduce poverty as well as providing decent houses. Sadly I suspected that our hosts did not have, or perhaps could not afford, a similar social conscience. Worse, every person the Colonel had to let go meant one person less to buy in the village shop or the market. The effect would be even worse when vacancies for servants were left unfilled. No wonder the young men of the area were seeking work in the new and still dangerous industries. And no wonder Morgan wanted a promotion that would see him in better accommodation. His wife had tried to improve the police house with bright flowers and an assortment of vegetables which nonetheless appeared to be struggling in what seemed very stony soil – at least it had been spared by the floods that had washed away much of the road surface.

The rectory, which stood on rising ground a little away from the heart of the village, was a very pleasant gentleman's residence, but Dr Highworth's was even better, a Regency house with all the elegance that that period could command.

Even as Matthew and I waited for him in his spacious drawing room – the Welsh hills seemed even closer from here – I could feel myself relaxing. For a few moments I could submit to someone else's care and not feel bound to poke and pry into others' lives. Mrs Highworth was quick to join us, offering refreshment and pleasant conversation.

'The young man is already recovering his wits – I believe it may be possible for you to speak to him for a very few minutes, Mr Rowsley.'

'Thank you. Are those your sons?' He nodded at portraits of attractive-looking children.

'They are. Both at school now, up in Shrewsbury. No, Owain. Put it down. Basket!'

An elderly spaniel slunk off to a corner, eyeing us reproachfully.

'Good boy. Now you, Mrs Rowsley, are quite our heroine – helping to rescue the villagers in that terrible storm. See – we have lost two of our finest trees! As to the cricket, you can imagine that opinions are somewhat divided, but I remember my mama playing when she was young. Times have changed, have they not? Ah!' she greeted her husband, who sadly looked no less saturnine in her company, 'Mrs Rowsley has come to consult you.'

'Mrs Rowsley has been *brought* to consult you, Dr Highworth,' I corrected her with a gentle smile. 'I fear I am wasting your time, but as you know, troubles have beset the house and I am one of the victims – in a very minor way.'

'You have a lot to thank your hair for,' the doctor said, as he took his seat again behind his desk. 'I do not think you were hit with the intent that stunned Biddlestone, but your chignon absorbed some of the force.'

'Not with a hammer, presumably?' I tucked in place some of the locks of hair that he had disarranged.

'As it happens, I do not believe he was struck with a hammer either. The shape of the wound is too irregular. Look.' He sat again, and drew a hammer. 'See, a rounded flat surface. What hit Biddlestone had a more random outline – a common stone, I would say.' He drew again. 'And I would blame a stone for your injury – or more accurately, a stone wielded by a miscreant who wanted to stun, rather than kill you. The skin is not broken, but as the bruise comes out you may be in some discomfort. Did you lose consciousness for long?'

'I came to when I was being dragged to that straggle of bushes. By then I was already gagged and blindfolded. Thank goodness for my hat-pin.' I mimed the jab into my assailant's person.

He smiled. 'Thank goodness indeed.' It took him an obvious effort to stand. I looked rather than spoke my sympathy. 'Indeed. A hunting injury. I could wish that science might one day discover pain relief that is not addictive.'

'Unlike the Colonel's laudanum?'

He blinked at my question, which I should have put more circumspectly. 'Ah, Mrs Rowsley, you know I can't tell you that.'

'Of course. I'm sorry. I just wondered if a drug like that might cause his strange mood swings.'

He smiled opaquely. 'All I will say is I wish we had better medical knowledge.'

'And yet you were adamant that you would not be conducting a post-mortem examination of the bodies – I would have thought that a man of science would be keen to delve further.'

He blinked. I was almost sure I had gone too far. But, with a faint sigh, he said, 'No matter how interested a man may be in science, he needs to keep his patients happy. If only one of them got wind of such an investigation you can imagine how many patients I would have left round here. I am fortunate to have independent means, Mrs Rowsley – but I would not wish to lose all my fees.'

'So – simply by *looking* at the bodies! – what did you discover?' I allowed my dimples to show.

'Among other things that Morgan Davies had dabbed them

with reddle! I can understand why he did it, but it has proved a damned nuisance.'

'So I can imagine!' We shared a laugh. 'But I hope you will forgive him: he is doing his very best to deal with a situation he wouldn't have been trained for. He hoped that anyone trying to search the dead people's clothes – even their bodies! – would be clearly identifiable. Heavens, we need some clarity, do we not?'

'And some protection, given the state of your head. You must be tempted simply to go home.'

'Get thee behind me, Satan! If we left, how could poor Constable Davies hope to control the other guests' movements? He needs to keep us all in one place until he has discovered and arrested the killer, does he not? Who may of course be the person who attacked Jeremy Turton so fiercely – and took aim at my head. I have to admit, Doctor, that I hope my hat-pin did sufficient damage to drive the recipient to seek medical assistance.'

To my surprise he frowned. 'It is no small matter for a female to stand as a witness in a court of law, Mrs Rowsley.'

'It is no small matter for a female to be murdered in her bed, Doctor. And if my standing up in court helps convict the Gräfin's killer I will do it.'

'But you will have noticed all the rumours flying around about her – more accusations than rumours, in fact. As if she somehow deserved to die. Surely you would not wish to expose yourself and of course your husband to that.'

It was hard to remain outwardly calm when I was inwardly furious. 'I have been exposed to rumours here already – I have even been accused of the theft of a necklace left to me by my former employer – by people who know nothing of me. So I stand by what I have said. And will appear on the witness stand, as I am sure Mr Turton will. Is it possible for me to speak to him before I return to Clunston Park?'

'I will ask if he wishes to see you.' He stood. Our conversation was over.

Naturally Matthew accompanied me to the bed chamber which served as a sick-room. Jeremy's smile was welcoming, with luck reassuring the doctor, who stood beside him, that I was not his assailant.

'You and Rowsley saved my life,' he said through bruised, split lips. I hoped his beautiful teeth had survived.

'And your sketch pad. Do you know who hit you, Jeremy?'

'Hit me from behind first,' he said, fingering what was probably a lump in the same position as my lump. 'When I came to myself I hurt all over. Bruises.'

'But his bones appear to be intact,' Dr Highworth said. 'I believe he is safer here than at the Park, however – there is certainly mischief afoot there. My gates and all windows are locked at night to ensure the medicines I require for my patients' treatment do not get into the wrong hands. My gardeners and indoor staff are more than handy with pistols or fists. But now, Rowsley, I believe you and your good lady might wish to return and discover the miscreant.'

Which was an effective a way as any of dismissing us from Jeremy's presence. But not until I had kissed him chastely on the forehead and wished him well. 'When you can remember anything useful send for the Constable or for us.'

'You. My stammer scares Davies.'

'Your sketches inspire me, Jeremy – did you know that whoever attacked me used one of them to gag me? Believe me, it has had the opposite effect. And when all is done and dusted, come and stay with us and sketch our Roman remains!'

Matthew and I were impressed that in all the confusion of the afternoon Constable Davies had remembered to retrieve the key I had found from the police house safe. Mrs Simpkiss had already confirmed it looked very like the one Biddlestone had used, though she could not, it seemed, be certain.

'I don't suppose we might be present at the grand opening?' I asked, looking from one to the other.

'Oh, ma'am. I'd love to say yes, but how can I? In any case, Dr Highworth tells me you had a bad blow on the head and should by rights be in bed.'

'And if I were to tell you that after this afternoon I would not feel safe in my bed chamber?'

'I would not argue. In fact, I want you to spend the night elsewhere, if you don't object and provided we can find alternative accommodation suited to your status.' He frowned. 'You made a list of which rooms were occupied and who by. I don't suppose you recall any vacant ones?'

'Mrs Simpkiss would know.'

He shook his head firmly. 'The fewer people who know of your removal the better. That includes the footmen and acting butler too. And no one at all should know that I will be occupying your present one. I know there's the matter of bed linen and your clothes, but we can surely spirit them out by way of the back stairs.'

'Let me talk to Clara and see if she can help.'

'A child!'

'Even a scared child like Clara might enjoy a little adventure, which involves no more than removing sheets from the store from which I got her released. Or even less than that. She may know if any rooms are already ready for unexpected guests. Her late ladyship always liked me to keep at least one aired and the bed made up. I'll talk to her while you and Mrs Simpkiss open the safe.' I added wistfully, 'But I should like to see in that safe – as would Matthew.'

He looked horribly shifty. 'I would indeed. But not until I know that you are safe.'

'I can't imagine that I would not be safe with both of you to protect me.' But I was beginning to whine, and I could feel embarrassing tears welling up. 'Let us find Clara, then.'

'Clara, this is a beautiful room! But you say no one ever uses it – how strange!' I added to myself. It was better to turn my attention to that than resent being excluded downstairs.

She blushed as if she herself had received the compliment. Or because she knew that Matthew and I originally had been stowed in a vastly inferior one. This was at the corner of the house, a few yards from the picture gallery, and had glorious views from windows on two sides. It took her several journeys using the rush basket that had once held my clothes while I was in a maidservant's uniform to spirit everything down the service stairs. She also promised to deal with the hot water and slops herself.

'Remember,' I said, 'that water must be left outside our original room and not taken inside. Officially I am lying down after a fall this afternoon. Whereas you know I am avoiding that noisy peacock!'

I cursed as I opened *North and South* in a profoundly unlady-like way, that I could not see the grand reveal.

THIRTY

To my surprise and embarrassment, Davies suggested I might like to be present when the safe was opened. To my even greater surprise, another police officer was already leaning against the safe when I arrived.

'My elusive Cousin, Sergeant Reece. I brought him in the back way, with a bit of help from Mrs Simpkiss,' Davies said. 'And this, Geraint, is Colonel Rowsley's cousin, Mr Matthew Rowsley. He's become my right-hand man, and surely will become yours. He's been sworn in as Special Constable. As has his wife,' he added uneasily.

Reece, a man in his late thirties, shook my hand firmly. If I had any expectations at all, he met few of them. Five or six or seven inches shorter than Davies, he was stocky, confident and appeared more than happy to take charge. His accent was different – it would have been hard to place his origin. I reserved judgement.

'Surely my wife should be here, Sergeant Reece – she has worked so hard to bring all this about.' I pointed to the still-locked safe, which the three of us were staring at as if it might produce a magic image of its contents. 'Furthermore, although thanks to your cousin we have moved to a different room, I do not think she should be left unprotected.'

Sergeant Reece nodded sagely. But his eyes twinkled as he said, 'As it happens, Mr Rowsley, I happen to agree with that. What I ought to do is send you up to defend her. On the other hand, that might involve you in criminal violence, perhaps worse, if you have to fend people off. So I shall tell my superiors that it was in the interests of witness safety, not to mention Law and Order, that I ordered her to be escorted down here.' He smiled and nodded at Davies.

'Right you are, Geraint! *Sergeant!*' He saluted impeccably and headed out.

Now Reece was opening his notebook. 'Is there anything you

and Morgan might have missed when you were telling me what you've done so far?'

'Ah. One thing. When my wife consulted Dr Highworth about the bruising on her head, she was able to deduce that my cousin, the Colonel, takes laudanum for his various afflictions.'

'I like the way you put that, sir. And what do you deduce from the information?'

'I wondered if it might account for his inconsistent behaviour. For the way he forgets to do things he has undertaken to do. I also wonder if his need for the drug might put him at the mercy of other people who know his need.'

He looked at me shrewdly. 'Are you hinting at blackmail, Mr Rowsley? In connection with the strange cricket match my cousin has told me about?'

'I wish he could have been there. Yes, everyone involved believed that Major Jameson was pulling Barrington's strings. And there is plenty of evidence that Jameson is a truly unpleasant individual. I would love him to be punished for something, and blackmail is as good as anything – because to be truthful I do not know why he should want – need! – to kill either victim.'

'Who might *need* to kill Gräfin Weiser? That's a strong word, but I suspect you chose it with care. Someone might *need* to kill her if they owed her money at cards? So let us double-check all the papers your wife and Mrs Simpkiss retrieved. Otherwise I shall have to put the Colonel on oath to identify all the signatures – believe me I will, if I need to. Here.' He passed me a magnifying glass and donned a pair of spectacles. 'One name before they come down! A challenge! Look, could that be GD?'

'It could. Or OD? But it could be CD – a man whose first name might Clarence; certainly his surname is Digby. He's a civil servant. Was. Heavens, where did a civil servant find two hundred guineas to lose in the first place?'

'Where indeed?' he asked grimly.

'If it is indeed Mr Digby, I am astonished and appalled in equal measure. He's the last person . . . He spoke up against the incarceration of the maid someone told us had killed the Gräfin. He stands for Empire and Justice and . . . Physically he is a big man, tragically stricken with deafness, who infuriates Harriet by smoking cigars in the library. But it's not just the chance of fire that worries her: some valuable books have been removed, as I'm sure Morgan has told you. We fear there's some plot to allege that she has stolen them. One of the servants has already suggested she – er – scarper.'

'Someone thinks she knows too much. And so it's not so much *cherchez la femme* as *cherchez les livres!*'

I gaped. I realized too late how rude I was being. Fortunately the sergeant looked amused.

'Ah, I may be Morgan's cousin but I had huge advantages he was denied. Huge. My other uncle was the Dean of Worcester Cathedral, close friends with the Bishop. He intended me for great things. Benignly, the Bishop paid for me to be educated at the same school as his sons – until there was a major theological falling out between the two men and it came to pass that I had to earn my living. And I can't complain, Rowsley: I become the inspector in Worcester next month. Yes, I'm sure strings were pulled. Why else should I be moved from the Herefordshire Constabulary? But God moves in mysterious ways: perhaps this is the Almighty's way of making up for the destruction of my dreams of university.'

'What a waste!' I began.

'I thought it was. Now I see things differently. People like you and I, we are going to become more important, you know, than these idle folk. You run an estate; your wife runs a house big enough, I gather, to swamp this – you deserve to stand alongside me as the equals of those who never work, our so-called superiors. If I had my way I would do away with all these expensive schools – why should some boys have better education than others? Look at Morgan – and don't tell me that without all my advantages he deserves to do as well as I! Every boy deserves the same chance.'

'Why stop at boys? Do not girls deserve such chances?' came a familiar voice.

'Mrs Rowsley! It's a pleasure to meet you, ma'am. Geraint Reece at your service.' He kissed Harriet's hand, clearly disconcerting but not displeasing her. Davies gawped. 'I would educate everyone in the same schools,' Reece continued smoothly, 'and at the same universities, taking the same degrees in whatever subject they choose. But don't tell my uncle that, Rowsley! First, thank you both for all you have done. And now I ask you to do some more. We believe we may have deciphered more initials. Can you help with just a few?'

'I have already done my best,' she said.

'One more push. Do you think – here – might this be an R?'

'I wondered that myself,' she said doubtfully. 'But the guest list showed no Rs. Sergeant Reece, one lady who has been truly gracious to me has been Lady Pidgeon—'

'With a D,' Davies added.

'—And I fear that that may be a P with a slight blot on it. She saved my life once, almost literally, but she was very evasive on the subject of cards and gambling. Her poor husband walks and stands and drinks but . . .' She shook her head sadly. Straightening her shoulders, she checked her watch. 'Sergeant, you may need not just the key in Constable Davies' possession but also Mrs Simpkiss' key – and she is likely to be otherwise engaged very soon. Surely these papers can wait.'

'Indeed, let us summon Mrs Simpkiss and her key and whisper, "Open sesame!"'

The great skirts of the two women, Mrs Simpkiss perhaps over-awed by Reece, concealed whatever it was that had made them gasp in unison.

Unsurprisingly Harriet moved first, presenting Morgan with a fine gold casket, about twice the size of a house brick, though infinitely more beautiful. 'Do you think that little key we found would fit this?'

Davies presented the key with more of a fumble than a flourish, but waited in silence while she opened her find.

'My God! Sorry, Lord,' he interrupted himself. 'Have you ever seen so many guineas?' he asked rhetorically. 'Especially in such a pretty box.' Making an almost visible effort, he asked gravely, 'Does that strike you as something a butler would own? Mrs Simpkiss, you knew him better than anyone, I should imagine. What do you think?

She shook her head, not sure perhaps to whom she should address her answer. She settled for Reece. 'If you asked me who owned that, I'd say the Gräfin. But since when did guests start stowing things in the house-plate safe? How could she do that without my knowing? Oh, of course – it must have been inside her jewel box, which I do recall being locked in here. No, I don't know why. All my staff are as honest as the day is long! And the footmen,' she added in what sounded like a rather defensive afterthought.

Reece was more interested in an obvious fact. 'There's no sign of a jewel box now. Nor of any gaps where it might have been.' As the women stepped aside, he peered in every corner. 'Just silver-gilt tableware. Ah. Look, this elegant epergne must be a Matthew Boulton piece. Now, if that were solid, no one could lift it, so my guess is that it's hollow. Yes.' He lifted it down and, having carefully removed the centrepiece, tipped it on its side. 'Would the jewel box have fitted in that, Mrs Simpkiss?'

'Easily, for all it was big. Not there now though, is it?'

'We think someone put it in the bridge that got washed away,' Davies said.

'Why on earth would someone put . . . Ah. I see what you mean, young Morgan. Tip it a bit further, can you, Sergeant, because I think I can see – oh, my laws.' She pulled out a fistful of paper notes and several strings of jewellery. Clasping her hands over her mouth and raising almost terrified eyes to Reece's, she asked, 'How did these get in here?'

'You didn't put them there?' He took the edge off the question with a charming smile. 'No, of course you didn't. I imagine this butler of yours asked you to help open the safe, and when you'd obliged sent you on your way.'

'He often did. It was easier not to argue. Do you think Mr Biddlestone stole all this, sir?'

'Or was he storing it for the person who did? I wish I knew.'

Mrs Simpkiss sniffed. 'What else is in there?'

He tipped up another silver-gilt piece. Out fell a pair of shoes, stinking and showing signs of mould.

'Mr Biddlestone's work again, I presume,' I said. 'Why on earth should he have put them there when Barrington had explicitly said he wanted them?'

'For no good purpose, I suspect. But I don't pretend to know the answer now.'

'To think I worked alongside him every single day!' Mrs Simpkiss wailed. 'If only I'd – I don't know what . . .'

'The man was a vile bully,' Harriet said, putting her arm round her. 'You couldn't have done anything.'

'Let's lock it up again, shall we? Then you needn't worry about it any more. Thank you. No, you keep your key – unless doing so makes you uneasy. I shall certainly keep this one.'

Reece's smile clearly set her all a-flutter; she made a red-cheeked and deep-curtsied exit.

'Mrs Simpkiss asked the right question, didn't she? Did you recognize any of the jewellery, Mrs Rowsley?'

'No. In fact, I'd speculate that it was all lost before the cricket weekend, when cards were very much on offer. The Gräfin wasn't invited to stay for it, according to Cousin Barrington – but just didn't move out. Lady Hortensia is the person to ask.'

'Of course. Now, back to our initials. So far we have Lady or Lord Pidgeon and Mr Clarence Digby. The cigar-smoking reader – ma'am, are you unwell?'

She had gone pale. 'Unfortunately Mr Digby . . . my behaviour . . . Mr Digby got the impression when I asked him to show me the gardens – in fact I was simply trying to remove him and his cigar from the library. He thought that teaching me how to play croquet should involve his holding the club – the mallet! – for me – his arms being round my waist.'

What was the matter with her? Harriet, whose calm was sometimes worrying, was gibbering incoherently. With a concerned look at me, Davies slipped from the room.

Reece said gently, 'But you eluded his grasp. Yes, I've heard about that incident. Please don't give it another thought.'

Though effectively he had closed the conversation she pressed on. 'My memory could be deceiving me – I believe, I *suspect* that I smelt the same smoke on the clothing of my assailant this afternoon. Thank you,' she added as Davies passed her a glass of water. 'I am talking nonsense. That bang on the head! Forgive me. What happens next? Please – the sooner all this is resolved the better.'

'Might we all sit down somewhere? Somewhere no one can see us? Not even a servant?'

'There's no such thing as privacy in a country house, Sergeant,' Harriet said with a faint smile. 'Does anyone apart from Mrs Simpkiss know you're here?'

'No. And I would prefer for the time being to keep it that way.'

'In that case I could not recommend the sewing room that the Colonel refers to as our headquarters. The best I can suggest is the Room, provided Mrs Simpkiss does not object and can also get us in there without being seen.'

'I will speak to her,' Reece said quietly.

Within moments, Mrs Simpkiss, curtsying deeply, ushered us in before withdrawing and closing the door. I looked at the place, paradoxically made all the gloomier by the sunlight outside. None of the chairs matched any other, of course. The most handsome was surely Jacobean. With an extravagant gesture, Reece offered it to Harriet. Unwontedly demure, she declined, settling for a battered oak one of indeterminate age. When pressed, I accepted it – soon to realise why my dear innocent-seeming wife had not.

'This is what we need to achieve,' Reece said. 'An arrest. I want everyone in the house to believe that Mrs Rowsley has been forced by an unpleasant incident in the garden to rest in her bed chamber – not this new one you mentioned, ma'am. She believes she might recognize her attacker. Rowsley, I suspect that you could no more leave her unattended in the face of danger than fly, but you must drift around drinking your sherry looking increasingly anxious. No, I'm sure sitting down to dinner is not necessary: your appetite might well be affected by your distress. With luck before this point, the attacker will sneak out and head upstairs to finish the job. He will be greeted by none other than Morgan and myself. If he leaves it till later, that might complicate things a little, but not irretrievably.'

'Wait! Harriet must not be on her own, even if no one knows her location. That blow on her head, and – well, her motto is "just in case".' We exchanged a smile.

'In that case either Morgan or I might play a chaste game of cribbage in her new location until you can leave your fellow guests and come and guard her yourself. In fact I hope the assailant does leave the visit till after dinner, or even when he thinks you might be asleep and both my cousin and I are there to apprehend him. So far so good? Morgan?'

'Refreshment of some sort, sir?'

'Of course. Good point. I've no idea how to organize that yet but I will. For all parties.'

'At some point, are the guests going to be examined for injury?' Harriet asked. 'I must have drawn blood at very least.'

'Of course they should! But I fear I have no legal power to require a man to strip to his smalls. Only if we arrested him and detained him might it be possible – unless you stabbed him in a highly visible area, ma'am.'

'You might look for a torn jacket: Davies has threads the assailant left behind when he made his escape.'

'Excellent. Much easier.' He looked at the ugly clock. 'Rowsley, you need to go and change this instant. Don't forget to look haggard. Mrs Rowsley, is there anything else you need? That cribbage board and some cards? I will ask Mrs Simpkiss. Morgan!' They went out together.

Left alone, Harriet and I clung to each other. 'My love, you will take care?' we said in concert.

THIRTY-ONE

Though he came into the elegant room armed with cards and a cribbage board, Sergeant Reece did not mean to play cards yet. He placed the game on the bed, alongside his notebook and pencil. Sniffing the stale air, he looked around him. 'Why is such a lovely room completely unused?'

'It's not even aired,' I agreed, opening a second window. 'When I was searching the room, I wondered, but Mrs Simpkiss had no idea, Sergeant.'

'Now, that service door was very useful a moment ago but it is the most vulnerable part of the room. Forgive me if I move the washstand a foot or two. There.' Then he took one of the lovely Regency chairs to where it would stop the main door opening. He sat, leaning back. 'I prowl sometimes, you see, and this is my way of reminding myself to stay well away from the windows. *Just in case*,' he added with something of a twinkle, 'though I truly can't imagine our miscreant scanning the building for signs of life. Nonetheless, you might prefer to sit at that desk for the same reason.' As orders went, it was polite enough. 'Allow me to bring over a chair for you; it looks more comfortable than that stool. Ah, that must be your book. An interesting author, Mrs Gaskell.'

'Indeed. Thank you.' What a strange man he was: he strove for effect – but not quite a dandyish affectation. Clearly with an impressive and well-trained mind, he had strange political views for a man bound by oath to maintain the laws of the land. I had an idea that if we played any game it would be verbal chess. Perhaps I should make an opening gambit myself. 'Heavens, the number of times I have cursed the intricacy of furniture like this – all these pierced galleries collect dust and must be dealt with inch by inch. A housemaid's horror. And I always wanted to look inside, to see what was hidden by all the lovely wood.'

'Please feel free to peer in that one. In fact, let us both do just that. But first I must read and re-read all these statements.' He gathered his pencil and pad and sat with a shoulder firmly against the door. 'I wonder which will prove the greater work of fiction, your book or these . . .' He looked at his watch. 'Matthew must be joining the others about now. How long before dinner is served?'

Matthew? After so short an acquaintance? But there was something about his eager egalitarianism I liked. 'Sometimes unconscionably long. Up to an hour. Poor Mrs Dabbs must be driven wild. I hope Matthew managed his studs. Unless I'm there they can end up in the most inaccessible crevices.' The thought brought an embarrassing lump to my throat.

The evening sun bathed the room in ruddy gold. Whoever had chosen the curtains and hangings had done their job well, as they glowed quite sumptuously. As the desk caught the rays, the mahogany caught fire. I found myself setting aside Mrs Gaskell to surrender myself to a moment of pure enjoyment.

But, with a look at the clock, which showed half an hour had passed, the Sergeant had set down the last of the papers. 'What a ramshackle lot! And what a shame that so few of the names match the initials on the IOUs. They would no doubt be those of the previous weekend's guest. Never mind: all the fewer for me to interview if our plan for this evening doesn't work. What's the biggest puzzle for you?'

Caught off-guard, I blurted, 'Why Cousin Barrington married Lady Hortensia in the first place and why he continues to put up with her. And I suspect the answer is the one that is at the bottom of your investigation. Money. But why did he endure Biddlestone and why Jameson? Perhaps not even your plan will uncover that . . .'

'Is the child his?'

'I beg your pardon?' I could not believe my ears.

He spread his hands. 'He needs an heir, despite the injuries that everyone speaks of but no one defines. Perhaps one of those men obliged and now has him under his thumb.'

The idea! And that he could expound such a theory in the midst of all this beauty was doubly, triply shocking. 'Sergeant, that is an appalling notion! Pray, do not repeat it to Matthew.'

Family honour might force him to release his terrifying inner violence. Please God, no.

'Would it shock you to know that Morgan mentioned it to me, so he's probably already mentioned it to Matthew? Village gossip, big-house gossip, can sometimes be based on fact, as I'm sure you know. There is also a theory that one of the servants is actually her ladyship's daughter.'

'Or Mrs Simpkiss's,' I said as dryly as I could. 'But Matthew told me,' I found myself saying, 'of a very strange conversation he had with Lady Hortensia. He asked her if the storm had upset her son. And she said something about it – he! – being as brave as you'd expect a soldier's son to be. At the age of six months, for goodness' sake! Barrington himself doesn't want a military career for the little chap. But not all marriages entail love at any point, particularly with land, money and titles involved.' I froze. 'What's that noise?'

'I fancy that our betters have decided to postpone dinner and enjoy further refreshment on the terrace. But I might be seen if I tried to peer out. Don't lose heart. It will be easier for both Matthew and our miscreant to slip away.' He looked with some irritation at his watch. Suddenly on his feet, he swathed himself in the elegant curtain and peeped out. 'Everyone is drinking champagne!'

'Which will make it hard for poor Mrs Dabbs and her team to serve them their dinner without it being spoilt.'

He turned back to me. 'But it gives us longer to look inside the desk. My uncle had one very like it which delighted me when I was a child: as a treat he sometimes let me look inside. All those drawers and mirrors. I was always convinced that there must be hidden compartments. But I was never allowed to look.'

'Look, the whole interior is spotlit by the sun.'

'As if that is an omen? I think it might be. It is so beautiful. Like a microcosm of this room, in its attention to detail, if not the actual detail itself.'

We took it in turn to open the exquisite drawers, exclaiming at interiors as perfect as the exteriors. There were tiny cupboards too, opening with minuscule handles, and lined with bevelled mirrors.

He stepped back, arms akimbo. 'I can't understand this – this level of perfection – in what is after all an object designed to be used by one person only.'

'At least it provided work for people,' I said flatly. 'I just hope they were properly paid. Oh, the tiniest flaw! That little chip on that mirror.' I touched it lightly – and the mirror moved, to reveal another cupboard. It was empty. I believe we both sighed with disappointment. But then we tried every mirrored cupboard and touched every tiny flaw.

'My God!' Reece breathed, removing a bundle of papers tied with pink legal tape and sealed with wax. He grinned impishly. 'What do you think, Harriet? Time for an adventure?'

Harriet? Adventure? It was like being young again, in those wonderful heady days of cricket and laughter with the boy who became the distinguished judge Lord Halesowen. But would that boy, now in his forties, approve of this idea?

'Much as I should like to be part of the adventure, Geraint,' I said, picking up his name challenge, 'I suspect all I should do is keep cavey. You're leading a murder investigation, after all. I'm just an incidental victim.'

'Actually, you're now a witness, to testify in court if necessary that I am not unlawfully retaining any part of this document.' For the first time he sounded as I supposed a police officer ought, serious, authoritative.

I watched in silence as he read each sheet, jotting in his notepad as he did so. And I saw enough to make me cover my mouth with my hand lest I gasp out loud.

THIRTY-TWO

was being avoided. There was no doubt of that. And I was almost glad of it, because it meant that I was beginning to learn what it had been like for Harriet. But there was Lady Pidgeon, raising a glass and smiling in my direction. 'Such a good idea, to encourage us all out here on the terrace, don't you think? Except it does so make one wonder when one will ever eat.'

'Indeed. The sun is really so pleasant, isn't it?'

'Are you quite well, Mr Rowsley? You look quite . . . *distrait* . . . shall we say?'

My sigh was genuine enough. 'I am actually very worried about Harriet. I had to leave her for a few moments when we were walking through the park earlier and came back to find her unconscious on the grass.'

'She had fainted? Not the type at all I'd have thought.'

'No. She doesn't faint. She was actually knocked out.'

'A poacher, perhaps?' Her notion of when and where poachers operated was clearly different from mine.

'Perhaps. So poor Constable Davies now has another crime to solve. And she is lying in bed in a darkened room with a terrible headache.'

'Yet you are here?'

'For a few minutes only. She said that all my fussing with pillows and lavender drops only made things worse.'

Her ladyship snorted with laughter. 'I can imagine. But the village doctor? That miserable-looking man – more like an under-taker than a doctor!'

'He advises rest and liquids, so in a very few minutes I shall go and make sure she sips a little more water.'

'Good man. Did you hear that, Horatia?' She leant into someone else's conversation. 'Poor Mrs Rowsley has been attacked!'

I could have sworn that the lady she was talking to – the one whose child Harriet had saved, as it happens – muttered something about upstart busybodies getting their comeuppance. 'Did she see who did it?' she asked more politely, as she realized I was present.

'She would certainly recognize the assailant again,' I said clearly.

As always, conversations rose and fell – but quite inadvertently I chose the perfect moment to make the announcement. I prayed that my bait would be taken. I was ready to follow anyone sliding away.

But then I was foiled. Mason had actually brought out a miniature gong. 'Dinner is served.'

It was time to approach Lady Hortensia, repeating what I had told Lady Pidgeon and saying I must go and see how Harriet was.

She was far from interested in her guest, more concerned, I suspected, in the table plans I had just torn up. Maddeningly, as I left I stumbled, colliding with a massive flower arrangement in an urn almost as large as that epergne. Dare I pull it down on top of me in the hope it might conceal something? On the whole I thought not. It was something Reece might want to think about. I left to the sound of a cultured voice: 'Dashed bad form to be drunk when your wife is on her death bed.'

I spoke to Mason telling him that I doubted if Harriet would be able to eat, but I myself would welcome a tray of refreshments when he had time. Perhaps he might leave it outside, so she was not disturbed. He at least sounded genuinely concerned, promising to send for Dr Highworth immediately if I told him that there was a change for the worse.

I had drunk enough to necessitate a visit to the privy, so it was a few minutes before I ran upstairs to our original bed chamber, which is where any stray onlooker would expect to see me. Someone was ahead of me, reaching the landing and heading along the corridor leading to our room. Who? The sun lit his silhouette, so I could not identify him. I ran as swiftly and as silently as I could. Should I shout? No, that would ruin Reece's plot.

He stopped by our door. A maid approached, one I hadn't met – taller by a head than Clara. Screaming, he charged at her.

I ran.

He had her by the throat. 'Give me my money back. I warn you! Give me my money back. Should have done a better job before. Thought I had. You bitch.'

Davies and I tore his hands away. Viciously strong, they suddenly went limp. He slipped, unresisting. A dreadful rattle came from his throat and he slumped to the floor.

Lord Pidgeon was dead.

'So the poor old gentleman thought he was attacking the Gräfin again?' asked Reece, whom I had summoned from his hiding place myself. He surveyed the landing, corridors and stairs all alive with chattering guests.

'If he thought anything at all. If he was capable of thought, in fact,' Davies said. 'He was like one possessed.'

Reece nodded. 'Get that doctor here. Now. It's too late for the old man but the maid will need attention. And the widow. Now!' he snapped at the goggling staff and guests. 'Yes, you!' He turned to me. 'Which is your hostess? Someone must see the poor widow back to her room and sit with her. For goodness' sake – Sir?'

My cousin had arrived.

'Colonel Rowsley. Sergeant Reece.' There was no time for a more formal introduction. 'Barrington, where is Lady Hortensia?'

'Damned if I know.'

I looked for Harriet. Reece had put his hand on her arm, asking her something with some urgency. She shook her head, pointing downward.

'Ladies and gentlemen, might I ask for silence?' Reece raised his voice. 'Lord Pidgeon will be conveyed to a temporary resting place downstairs, where he will lie until Dr Highworth can attend. I suggest that we make his departure as dignified as possible. Major Jameson, will you supervise the staff in their solemn duty, please? Yes, Mason – as before, please.'

Why put Jameson in charge of anything? But I did notice Davies slipping off in the other direction – towards the Major's bed chamber – as all eyes watched the sheeted corpse being carried down the stairs, presumably to the cellar. Why not in a spare bed chamber? Harriet, for some reason ignoring the despair of Lady Pidgeon, scooped up the still gasping maid and guided

her to the care of Mrs Simpkiss. That was why Pidgeon would
not lie in state. He was a killer. As for his wife, as soon as Harriet
knew the maid was safe, she looked for her. But whether Lady
Pidgeon wanted her company or not, the other ladies at last
surrounding her ensured she would not get it.

'Ladies and gentlemen, this is a time for sober reflection, not
idle chatter,' Reece said, his voice as sonorous as if he were
mimicking his ecclesiastical uncle's. 'So I ask you all to retire
to your rooms. I must tell you that I have obtained a search
warrant for these premises, and it may be that Constable Davies
or I will need to inspect your property. I am sure we can rely
on your cooperation as we do so. Please do not embarrass the
servants by asking them to replace or dispose of anything you
might not wish to be seen.' One or two people dropped their
eyes under his penetrating gaze. He continued, 'It may be that
some of you will wish to speak to me on the matter. In any case,
none of you may leave the house till I give permission. None of
you. Colonel, might Constable Davies and I continue to use the
sewing room? Thank you. Should anyone need me I will be there
till late tonight and from very early on tomorrow morning.
Good night.'

As a hubbub rose, he dropped his voice to a discreet conversa-
tional level again and inched closer to my cousin. 'Colonel, there
are things you may wish to discuss with me in private, are
there not? Some documents have come to hand, you understand.'

'What the devil?' For a moment I feared he would strike the
Sergeant.

'Calmly, please, sir. Thank you. I had the forethought to equip
myself with a search warrant, remember. Would you care to talk
to me now or leave it till tomorrow?'

'I'm sure there will be plenty of time tomorrow,' Barrington
said, almost, but not quite, as if he was discussing a meeting
with Harrison to talk about greenfly. 'For the time being, I will
set an example to our guests and retire.'

'Why on earth leave something as sensitive as that in the house?'
I asked Reece, setting down my single malt. The sewing room
seemed strange without young Turton, now in Mrs Highworth's

care as her husband dealt with the problems of this house. I raised a silent toast to him.

'Where else would you want to leave it? What if fire had broken out at his lawyer's? Or a clerk had gossiped? Had it not been for the extraordinary chance that your room was not safe, had it not been for the love of fine furniture Harriet and I share then the desk would still be closed.'

Harriet, sipping some of the champagne that Mason had suggested as a substitute for the whisky, said, 'I suppose you would need some documentation about the baby. Just in case,' she added with more than a hint of self-mockery. 'Does it need to be known?'

'It may be mentioned in court. The child is innocent. Barrington is almost a victim – though not entirely. Many men would have brought the marriage to an end, of course, so I suppose it is to his credit he was prepared to raise another man's child as his own. And by being complaisant he was able to stay as the lord of the manor, as it were. But he had reckoned without the blood father being such a deeply unpleasant man with a love of gambling. Heavens, this place must have been like a casino when the Gräfin was in business!'

'Little Clara said that the Gräfin's husband ran one – the child pronounced it "cashino", which sounds unnervingly accurate. So I gather the Gräfin was a card-sharper, who relieved her fellow guests of huge amounts of cash and then mocked them, humiliated them, when they couldn't pay. And there I had assumed she was being kind to me.'

'Only at the start, Harriet,' Davies said, sipping his water.

'And do I deduce that Jameson was also in debt to her?'

'He need not have been, of course. He could just have been bled dry by the man who discovered that he and Lady Hortensia were lovers – the completely unlovable Biddlestone. That was why he could never be corrected or dismissed. Like many butlers, he knew too much. And we saw the extent of his wealth.' Reece smiled dourly. 'You may have noticed that while Jameson supervised the removal of Pidgeon's body, Morgan was busy doing something quite different.'

'Searching his room?' Harriet asked.

'Exactly. And finding a torn jacket and a bloodstained shirt. Well done, Harriet: we'll keep an eye open for your hat-pin.'

'And if they don't find it I promise to take her to Venice to buy a replacement. My apologies – I interrupted.'

He nodded. 'Mrs Simpkiss took it upon herself to cast an intelligent eye over her ladyship's sitting room while everyone was at dinner. She pushed a helpful note under this door.' He flourished it. 'Did you ever venture in there yourself, Harriet, when you were a maid?'

'Would you have done, in my place?'

'I might not have been able to resist. However, I honour your reservations. It's a pity, because you would have been able to corroborate that the room is always kept completely tidy. Today, however, its chilly perfection was marred by some books tucked behind and under cushions. So I fear we may not be able to exclude her from that unpleasant plot to accuse you of theft. I am very glad you declined to help her and her friends any more. Even Lady Pidgeon could have given you a much stronger warning against mixing with the Gräfin. I suspect you will find it in you to forgive her. Personally, I would find it hard. Incidentally I cannot believe that Lady Hortensia was unaware of the situation given the state of the estate finances.'

'It was she who had the librarian dismissed,' Harriet said.

The room was almost in darkness now, but no one called for candles, and Mason would know – with that strange instinct of people who always served others – not to disturb us till he was summoned.

'I can see that people wanted Biddlestone dead,' Harriet admitted. 'But which man wanted it so much that he did the deed? And, more to the point, how? The Colonel spotted only one set of tracks leading to that bridge, did he not?'

'He drew attention to one set of tracks. He might even have matched his stride to Biddlestone's. No, not with his limp! Perhaps he used waders. Equally, Jameson might have done the same. I think we shall know more tomorrow when we can question him in the presence of his lawyer. But now we need our beds. I think, Matthew and Harriet, you deserve the sumptuous room that you were denied when you arrived, and Morgan and I will occupy yours. After all, another desperate man might still seek revenge, and we will try to deny him that. We will even stand guard as your water is delivered and make sure your barricades are secure. And we will escort you down in the morning. Be kind to your cousin if he appears tomorrow, Matthew. And be understanding if he does not.' He peered through the gloom. 'Let us call for our chambersticks!'

'Dashed rabbits making a terrible mess of the home farm vege-table garden, I hear,' Barrington declared in something like his usual tones as sunlight flooded the sewing room. He'd been waiting for us when the officers, true to their word, had escorted us down. Somehow they managed to merge into the background.

Barrington touched a weapon on his desk. 'Thought I'd take advantage of this lovely weather and pot a few for Mrs Dibbs or whatever her name is. Got to be careful – damned gun favouring the right. Now, I may be away for a while so if you two want to head for home now this new policeman here has sorted everything out I'm sure you can. Damned good bowlers – yes, the pair of you. Never seen anything like it, Cousin Harriet.'

'But you worked me out quickly enough,' she said, putting her hand on his sleeve for a moment.

'Well, well – could do with someone like you to teach my son, couldn't I? Ah, Reith – hope you slept?' The sergeant stepped forward, bowing, as if he had just entered the room. 'I was just telling my cousin and his wife I fancy getting a rabbit or two for the pot before everyone gathers for breakfast. Poor old Pidgeon. Who'd have thought it? Always drunk as a lord, of course. Brain quite addled, I should think. Rowsley, old chap – I mentioned to your clever little wife that the estate could do with a bit of a steadying hand. I know you can't leave your present post, but maybe you could spend a couple of days now and then? Appoint a decent man? Yes?'

'Of course.'

We shook hands solemnly.

'That cousin of yours did his best, Reith. Wasted in this hamlet. See if you can give him a bit of a leg up in the world, eh? And get him to put this in his children's money box. Four children in that doll's house, imagine it . . .'

Reece said slowly, 'Colonel, I'm sure those rabbits can wait till you've had your gun repaired. Can you tell us what happened? Or shall I speculate? Wearing waders, you went to see how the floods were affecting your land. You came across Biddlestone, who was probably insolent. You argued. What happened next?'

'I pushed him,' I made out. 'He slipped. Hit his head. Out cold on his back. On his back. I should have waited – seen the man was all right. But I couldn't bear to. He must have rolled over.'

'Unless someone else came along and decided it was more convenient to help him die,' Reece said quietly and firmly. 'There is no evidence at all as yet to show conclusively who killed Biddlestone.' He took a deep breath and continued, a different note in his voice, 'Sir, what about your son? Will Jameson admit the attempted murder of Mr Turton and the attempted abduction of Harriet? Will he confess to the murder of the infernal butler? I doubt it, though I will do my best to make him. I'm sure the prosecution will try to break him down in court. I think he will make unpleasant counter-allegations, reveal unpleasant truths, about this household. I'm sure any jury will find him guilty of the first two crimes, but not necessarily the third. Whatever the verdict, what is said in court will make rumours swirl. Life will not be pleasant. It will not be easy for you to decide what to do with your wife. Divorce? Those papers might be quoted in court – again, not pleasant. All speculation, I know. But I do absolutely know one thing. In the nursery is a child who needs someone to love and look up to. A father.'

There was a very long silence for the pretty clock to tick away.

At last Barrington cleared his throat. 'She can keep this damned place. Hers, come to think of it. But I suppose a wing each . . . As for the lad . . .' He shook his head, as if the last thing he wanted to think about was the unfortunate child.

It was Morgan Davies' turn to step forward. Barrington jumped.

'A lad needs a proper father, Colonel. A good man.'

'Make sure he grows up a decent man,' Barrington mused, clearly thinking of the alternative. 'Someone'll need to teach him his cricket, won't they? No cheating, that sort of thing . . .'

Gently, unobtrusively, Reece took the gun.

THIRTY-THREE

'So apart from the dratted Major who might get his come-uppance, everyone gets away with it!' Bea cried at last. 'Gets off scot-free!'

Bea had taken one look at us as we returned to Thorncroft and taken charge, her main decision being to have our bags taken to our own home rather than our room in the House. 'A bit of peace and quiet is what you need, by the look of you. And, before anything else, a nice cup of tea. There's a table set on the terrace already – a little suntrap, and out of this wind. I'll bring the tray myself. Off you go!'

We didn't argue.

'There,' she said a few minutes later. She sat down, pouring tea and passing it to us. 'Now tell me everything.'

It felt good, cathartic almost, to obey. When I flagged, Matthew took over.

'You had to do what? Good Lord! And she said – heavens above!' Kind, loving interjections punctuated our story – which we edited carefully as we went along.

Slices of her light-as-air sponge cake revived us further. A robin bounced round, hoping for crumbs. Two blackbirds had a tiff.

'So you've got this lady who knows her husband's half-crazed and does nothing about it? Heavens, I can see she'd want to be loyal but even so . . . And then that stuck-up woman who wouldn't dance at your wedding.'

'Her pregnancy—' I ventured.

'Hmph: she might be called a lady but what sort of lady foists a love-child on her lawful husband? And what sort of man accepts it because he doesn't want her to spread the word he's impotent? What sort of people are they? And what is the Law going to do? What the Law always does, if you ask me. Favour the rich and titled.'

'I think Sergeant Reece is more concerned with justice than

the letter of the law,' I said. 'At least I hope that was behind his reasoning. If the Colonel were convicted of murder, the child would be left in the hands of his mother. She was not only generally unpleasant but actually very violent when she was angry. You should have seen her beating a horse; we believe she shot her husband's dog. What sort of a mess would she make of her child's life?'

'She spoke of him as she might have spoken of an item, not a baby,' Matthew added. 'No, not a fit person to be a mother. Whether Barrington will make a decent father, who knows? But at least he knows right from wrong.'

'Beg pardon, Matthew, and I know he's your cousin, but are you sure of that? When I met him at your wedding he didn't look as if he'd have had the strength to push over a flowerpot, let alone a grown man. And why didn't he tell someone straightaway what he had done? It sounds as if that butler was a truly nasty piece of knitting and deserved to die, but the Colonel should have owned up earlier, if you ask me.'

'You're right. He should have done. He certainly felt enough guilt to try to kill himself. But what good would that have done? The estate and the village would have collapsed. The child, who would have been brought up by vile people, will now be cared for by a good nanny whom my mama will help Barrington find. My parents will play a bigger part in his life, as, I dare say, will my other cousin and his wife. At the very least I will help him find someone to put his estate in order – someone who will work with the villagers, rather than ignore their needs.'

'He will get good support from our opposite numbers there,' I added. 'They are good loyal women who have done their best, just as you and I always do. But Mrs Dabbs' sponge is nothing like as good as this.'

She smiled, but her face clouded again. 'I can't help but feel ordinary women like us would not have gone unpunished, whatever the consequences to everyone else.'

'Oh, Lady Hortensia's got life imprisonment, never fear! Firstly she'll be banished to one wing of what is technically her own house. And who would visit? Her friends don't have a kind bone in their bodies, as Harriet knows from experience. I suspect Barrington will eventually let her go into exile on the Continent

– like her disreputable god-mama, perhaps. She's just the sort of woman to run a gambling hell. What was it little Clara called it, Harriet?'

'A cashino.'

'A what?' Bea threw her head back and laughed. '"Out of the mouths of babes and sucklings!"'

We laughed with her. 'I hope Clara'll get over the horror of the murder – if anyone can help her, Mrs Simpkiss can,' I said. 'She loves her like a daughter. There's a good young butler there who sees her as his young sister – I think he will stay to help everyone weather the storm. Bea, we did our best but we couldn't make everything right. We'll find out more when we go back for the inquests. Meanwhile, it's so good, so very good, to be back at home with our friends.'